P9-DNH-725

My Life in Black and White

My Life in Black and White

by

NATASHA FRIEND

Viking

An Imprint of Penguin Group (USA) Inc.

Viking
Published by Penguin Group
Penguin Group (USA) Inc., 345 Hudson Street, New York, New York 10014, U.S.A.
Penguin Group (Canada), 90 Eglinton Avenue East, Suite 700, Toronto, Ontario, Canada M4P 2Y3
(a division of Pearson Penguin Canada Inc.)
Penguin Books Ltd, 80 Strand, London WC2R 0RL, England
Penguin Ireland, 25 St Stephen's Green, Dublin 2, Ireland (a division of Penguin Books Ltd)
Penguin Group (Australia), 250 Camberwell Road, Camberwell, Victoria 3124, Australia
(a division of Pearson Australia Group Pty Ltd)
Penguin Books India Pvt Ltd, 11 Community Centre, Panchsheel Park, New Delhi—110 017, India
Penguin Group (NZ), 67 Apollo Drive, Rosedale, Auckland 0632, New Zealand
(a division of Pearson New Zealand Ltd.)
Penguin Books (South Africa) (Pty) Ltd, 24 Sturdee Avenue, Rosebank, Johannesburg 2196, South Africa

Penguin Books Ltd, Registered Offices: 80 Strand, London WC2R 0RL, England

First published in 2012 by Viking, a member of Penguin Group (USA) Inc.

1 3 5 7 9 10 8 6 4 2

LIBRARY OF CONGRESS CATALOGING-IN-PUBLICATION DATA
Friend, Natasha, date–
My life in black and white / by Natasha Friend.
p. cm.
Summary: When beautiful high school student Lexi is involved in an automobile accident that leaves her disfigured, she must learn who she really is beyond a pretty face, and she must also learn to forgive.
ISBN 978-0-670-01303-6 (hardcover) / ISBN 978-0-670-78494-3 (paperback)
[1. Self-acceptance—Fiction. 2. Beauty, Personal—Fiction. 3. Peer pressure—Fiction.
4. Friendship—Fiction. 5. Dating (Social customs)—Fiction. 6. Boxing—Fiction.] I. Title.
PZ7.F91535My 2012 [Fic]— dc23 2011021436

Printed in USA Set in Dante Book design by Nancy Brennan

For my mom and dad,

who knew me when I was fifteen

and loved me anyway.

My Life in Black and White

Prologue

HERE IS A picture. I am three years old, and I am perched on a stool in front of a dressing table, sweeping blush over my cheeks with a feathery wand. In the background, my mother hovers. Her hair is a waterfall of gold, her waist the circumference of a cantaloupe. She is wearing a sheath dress, pearls, and crocodile pumps with sensible heels. The image is so clear I can actually smell her Shalimar perfume. I can hear her voice—smooth, with the hint of a Carolina accent. "You," she says, "are my beautiful girl."

Ha!

It is unavoidable. Wherever you go in my house, there I am. Hanging in the alcove over the stairs, propped on the mantel, stuck to the refrigerator door with alphabet magnets. After what happened, you would think that someone would tear down every photo in the universe so I wouldn't have to look at myself. But no one has.

This used to bother me. I used to skulk around my house, staring at all the shiny, happy Alexas and imagining the ways I could destroy her. Knock her off the wall and watch the glass shatter. Hole-punch her face. Microwave her into oblivion.

In the end, though, I didn't remove a single photo. I left that girl exactly where she was, suspended.

Poised in time.

Waiting to become me.

Two Things

WHEN I WAS in fourth grade, my best friend, Taylor LeFevre, and I would ask each other these crazy questions: "Would you rather be burned alive or frozen to death?" "Would you rather be deaf or blind?" "Would you rather have a genius IQ and a butt the size of Texas or be model thin and dumb as a box of rocks?" While other girls were skipping rope and scaling the monkey bars, we were pondering worst-case scenarios. Like, what if tomorrow you got leukemia like Jenny Albee's brother? Would you take the chemo that makes you bald or hold on to your hair so you'd look good at your own funeral? "Hair," Taylor said at the time. "Definitely hair." A tragic choice, but classic Tay. She had the best hair in fourth grade, the bi-level cut—short on one side, long on the other—which my mother would not allow me to get. She also had the best clothes—Juicy Couture hoodies in every color and jeans with a rip in the thigh—which my mother would not allow me to buy. Taylor's mother, Bree, let Taylor wear whatever she wanted, unlike mine, who insisted on "classic lines" and "quality fabrics" whenever we went shopping.

But at least I had one thing going for me that Taylor didn't. The one thing that drew her to me on my first day of kindergarten, my first week in Connecticut, when she marched over to the dress-up corner where I was trying on shoes and poked me in the arm. "Hey," she said in her low, gravelly voice. "You're pretty."

"I know," I told her. Because by the age of five, I had already heard it a million times. Not just from my parents, either. From total strangers. Every morning, I would sit at the kitchen counter while my mother brushed out my long, butter-colored hair until it shone. I stood patiently while she fussed over the pleats in my smocked dresses. It didn't matter where she took me that day—the park or the mall or the grocery store—someone would always comment. "What an enchanting little girl. Look at that skin. Those eyelashes."

"You can play with me," Taylor said, holding out her hand, as if there were a direct connection between my appearance and her willingness to be my friend. Which, of course, there was. But so what? I, too, was awed. Taylor was the only girl in kindergarten wearing earrings. Real ones. Tiny glass orbs that shimmered like disco balls. I thought of my own ears—bare and boring, because my mother didn't believe in piercing. She wore earrings herself, but they were the clip-on variety. I shared this information with Taylor as the two of us tied aprons around our waists, preparing to flip plastic burgers in the kid-sized kitchen.

"Clip-ons?" Taylor raised a doubtful eyebrow. "That's what grandmas wear. Real pierces are better."

She was right, of course. Real pierces were better. Everything, I would learn, was better in Taylor's world.

Two weeks later, she invited me over for a playdate. I

walked into the LeFevres' foyer, gaping like a fish at the splendor before me. It was nothing like our old condo in Charlottesville, or the Connecticut cape we'd just moved into. This was a McMansion—the type of dwelling my mother considered tacky—but I loved it, anyway. I loved the sky-high ceilings and the chandeliers. I loved the sleek, leather couches and Taylor's canopy bed and the kidney-shaped pool in the backyard. I remember thinking to myself that *this* was a house, *this* was living.

My mother had other opinions. "There's a difference between a house and a home, Alexa," she said the first time she picked me up at Taylor's. Then, "Money can't buy happiness, you know." She seemed to believe what she spouted. There wasn't a speck of jealousy on her face when she saw the size of the rock on Taylor's mom's finger or the apple-red Porsche in the driveway. The car, as well as the forty-two-foot schooner docked at the Millbridge Yacht Club, belonged to Taylor's dad, a TV sportscaster who worked in Manhattan. "*Your* daddy is a public servant," my mother loved to remind me. "A public defender."

"I know, Mama," I said every time.

"He *helps* people for a living, Alexa."

"I know."

But all this was beside the point to my elementary-school self: me being pretty, Taylor being rich, whatever our parents thought of each other. From the second we met, Tay and I were best friends, and that was all that mattered. We wore matching bracelets. We spoke in code. We loved the same things (Hannah Montana, peppermint-stick ice cream, the color green—*kelly* green, not hunter or lime). We joined Girl Scouts together. We slept at each other's houses. We talked on the phone ad nauseam. We were, in a word, inseparable.

There was one other girl we played with, Heidi Engle. She was Taylor's oldest friend because Mrs. Engle and Mrs. LeFevre had been childhood BFFs. "We have no choice," Taylor told me once. "We're forced to play together." But the truth was that Heidi worshipped Taylor. She had to be ticked when I came along and she got demoted to third wheel. Oh, she hid it well enough. Heidi was nice to my face, but I could tell from the minute I met her that she secretly wished my dad would get fired and we would move back to Virginia.

I remember in seventh grade, when Heidi and our new friend Kendall were planning their joint thirteenth birthday party, which would take place in Kendall's basement rec room and would consist mostly of Cool Ranch Doritos and spin the bottle. I said something like, "I'll eat, but I'm not kissing anyone."

"Oh, great," Heidi said, throwing both hands in the air. "We might as well not even *have* a party." She glared at me, then shared her theory that none of the boys would come to the party if there weren't at least a *chance* of making out with me. She called my reluctance to play spin the bottle "downright selfish" and said if I were really their friend I would "suck it up."

I turned to Taylor for support. She shrugged one pale, freckled shoulder. "Heids does have a point, Lex. Even if she's being obnoxious about it. Loyalty to the girls."

Kendall, and her best friend, Rae, nodded in agreement.

"Fine," I said, not wanting to be a party pooper.

The whole thing was a disaster. First off, the boys were jerks. By definition, seventh-grade boys are thoughtless and immature. Playing kissing games with them just proves the point. There's nothing romantic about it, even if you're the one they all want to kiss. *Especially* if you're the one they all want to kiss. I spent half the party in a closet getting felt up and the other half in the bathroom bawling because Heidi called me a slut and Taylor did nothing to defend me.

Later, when I recapped the story for my sister, Ruthie, she had no sympathy for my plight. Not a drop.

"You know, Lex," she said, frowning up at me from whichever tomb-sized book she was reading at the time, "you need different friends. Those girls are wenches."

For about a nanosecond, I believed Ruthie. I trusted my straight-A, honor-student big sister, who was smarter than I would ever be. But then I considered her *X-Files* sweatshirt. And the mustache of zits across her upper lip. And the trombone case propped against the edge of her desk. And I knew that she was jealous, pure and simple. Jealous of everything I had that she didn't. Like Taylor. And Kendall and Rae, who, because they'd gone to the other elementary school, we had only started hanging out with the summer before junior high when their moms began playing tennis with Taylor's mom. The four of us—Kendall and Rae, me and Taylor—were the only girls in seventh grade who ever got invited to ninth-grade parties. Which was more than I could say for my sister.

I felt bad for Ruthie, whose friends were not remotely cool. I'm sorry, but it's a fact. You cannot play the accordion (Sasha) or wear a purple cape to school (Beatrice) and expect to be invited anywhere. But it wasn't my fault Ruthie turned out the way she did. If my sister wanted someone to blame, it should be our dad, who gave her his beak nose and woolly eyebrows. He also stuck her with the name Ruth, after some great aunt we never met. (Incidentally, I was supposed to be named Harriet after his cousin, but I was born by C-section and came out so perfect my mother made him change his mind. She named me Alexa after the actress on the cover of that month's *Redbook*, which she happened to be reading when her water broke.)

Anyway, I told Ruthie she was wrong. My friends weren't wenches; they were just upset at the party—understandably—because the boys were being tools. First, Jason Saccovitch called Heidi a porker. Then, Kyle Humboldt said Taylor was so flat you could bounce a quarter off her chest.

"Whatever," Ruthie said, shrugging. She wasn't convinced, but I knew I was right. I thought about the look on Taylor's face when Kyle made his crack, and how Kendall dumped a whole liter of Coke on his head for payback. Which is what friends do for each other. Which Ruthie wouldn't understand. Sasha and Beatrice never even *talked* to a boy, let alone dumped Coke on him.

That's when it hit me: *I* was the bad friend for not defending Taylor to Kyle. If I had told Kyle off instead of just standing there, Taylor would have told Heidi off for calling me a slut. Quid pro quo, as my dad would say.

So the next morning, I apologized to Tay. And she apologized to me. We cried, we hugged, and our friendship resumed stronger than ever. The two of us coasted through the rest of seventh grade. Then eighth. Then—with the exception of one tiny hiccup of a fight when Ryan Dano and I started going out—we rocked our last year of junior high together. The irony is, when the town first rezoned the schools, making ninth grade part of the junior high instead of the high school, we were mad. But ninth was the best. We ran that place. Taylor and Lexi, the Dynamic Duo. Cocaptains of the field hockey team; rulers of the center table in the caf; chairs of the yearbook committee, ensuring plenty of photo representation for us and our inner circle. The day after graduation, Taylor's mom, who was mad at Taylor's dad and needed to punish him, threw a lobster bake for our whole class. Tay wore a cherry-red halter dress with a slit up one leg, and silver, strappy sandals. It was her best outfit ever.

Over the summer, I practically lived at the LeFevres'. My parents needed to do the college-tour thing with Ruthie, and Taylor's parents said I was welcome anytime. Which turned out great because Tay's dad was always working and her mom was always shopping, so we had the house to ourselves.

Most days Taylor and I would hang out by the pool in her backyard, drinking Crystal Light and working on our tans. Sometimes Heidi, Kendall, and Rae would join us. On July Fourth, Taylor's brother, Jarrod, invited a bunch of his varsity football buddies over. I wasn't a big fan of Jarrod—who was loud and hairy and always stripping off his shirt in front of me like I was supposed to be impressed—but Taylor adored him. She also had a massive crush on one of Jarrod's friends, Rob. And on that particular afternoon, Taylor happened to notice Rob noticing *me* in my bathing suit, and she got all weird about it. I told her not to worry: A) I was in love with Ryan; and B) I wasn't the least bit attracted to Rob.

I remember the look on Taylor's face—the slight flush of her freckled cheeks and the furrow between her pale, almost nonexistent eyebrows. "I can't compete with you, Lexi."

"Who said we were competing?"

She shrugged, then eyed my plain, blue Speedo tank suit—the only thing my mother would let me buy. *It's a classic, Alexa. It will never go out of style.*

"*You're* the one in the two-piece," I said to Taylor, "from Barney's, no less." Which, while true, missed the point. The point was that Taylor still had the same body she'd had since kindergarten: tiddlywink chest; slender hips; knobby knees. No coral-colored Brazilian string bikini in the world was going to change that. Just as no amount of mother-approved Lycra was going hide my boobs. They were here to stay.

"You look great," I told Taylor.

"Whatever," she muttered.

"You *do*. And you know what else? One of these days, Rob is going to notice how hot you are and he's going to rip that bikini off with his teeth."

This time, Taylor smiled. Having Jarrod for a brother, she knew all about high school boys and their pervy ways. One time when Jarrod was at football practice, Tay and I snuck into his room and browsed his computer history. There were pictures of things I'd never seen in my life—not even in *The Joy of Sex*, which my parents kept hidden under their mattress. I was glad that my gorgeous but well-mannered boyfriend wasn't into that stuff. For the six months we'd been dating, Ryan was perfectly content with my clothes-on hookup policy. Why wouldn't he be? We were in love. Madly and deeply.

Okay, I know how stupid that sounds now. But at the time, I honestly believed I had it all. Looks, friendship, true love. I honestly believed I led a charmed existence.

And then, halfway through the summer, Taylor's brother, Jarrod, had a party, and in a single night two things happened that would change the course of my life forever:

My best friend betrayed me.

And my face went through a windshield.

It's Not What You Think

MY LIFE IS OVER.

It's the kind of pronouncement teenage girls make every day. They say it after such traumatic events as, say, farting out loud in gym class, or discovering they've gained three pounds at Christmas and can't fit in their winter formal dress. *Oh my God, you guys! My life is over!* Then they bawl to their girlfriends, eat a bunch of Oreos, and move on.

But this was different. I wasn't saying the words for effect; I meant them. Because when you're fifteen years old and you're lying in a hospital bed listening to things like "multiple facial fractures" and "reconstructive surgery," there is only one coherent thought in your mind: *my life is over.*

"You're lucky to be alive," said the nurse who was checking my blood pressure the morning after the accident.

No, I thought, trying to shake my head but it hurt too much to move, *I'm not.*

I couldn't expect some stranger in Mickey Mouse scrubs to understand. But the truth was, what happened to my face wasn't even the worst part. The worst part—the reason I was in the hospital at all—was Taylor.

It should have been a perfect night. The first Saturday in

August, and Mr. and Mrs. LeFevre were both away for the weekend (him, golf tournament; her, spa), leaving Taylor's brother, Jarrod, in charge. Which, of course, meant throwing a midsummer blowout. Tay and I were thrilled, because what better way to kick off our high school career than to party with a bunch of seniors? I may not have liked Jarrod, but his status as varsity football captain, and my status as his sister's best friend, had their advantages. Taylor even suggested I invite Ryan, who, although he hadn't tried out yet, was hoping to make varsity instead of JV and could only benefit from meeting Jarrod.

"You're the best," I said to Taylor when we were up in her bedroom getting ready.

"I try," she said.

I felt a wave of love for my best friend. Not only was she looking out for me, she was looking out for my boyfriend, too. Taylor was the kind of person you could count on. The kind of friend who would loan you her best vintage tee—the new one that she hadn't even worn yet. Who assured you that the blue mascara you put on wasn't bogus; it made your eyes pop.

As the two of us walked out into the hall, she grabbed my hand. "How do I look?"

I studied her kelly-green halter and matching miniskirt. "Awesome," I said. Then I asked if she was sure I should wear the jeans. Wouldn't I be too hot? It was August, after all. What about the shorts I had on earlier?

Taylor shrugged. "The jeans look good." She hiked up the waistband of her skirt another inch.

"Okay . . ." I said. "Thanks."

Then the two of us headed downstairs to the kitchen, where Jarrod and a dozen of his football buddies were already standing around a keg, red plastic cups in hand.

"Well, well, well," one of them said. He smirked at us from under his baseball cap. "What have we here?"

Another punched Jarrod's arm. "Where are your manners, LeFevre? The ladies are thirsty."

Jarrod filled two cups: one for Taylor, one for me. I shook my head and smiled, a gracious refusal, but Taylor gave me her puppy-dog look. *Please?* her eyes said. *Pleeeeaaaase?*

So I took the beer. I knew before long she wouldn't care if I drank or not. She'd be too busy flirting to notice.

"Bottoms up." Jarrod's friend Rob hoisted his cup in the air.

Taylor giggled. "Bottoms up."

As she raised her beer and threw back her head, I thought about how long she'd been crushing on Rob, and how badly she wanted him to notice her—not just as Jarrod's little sister, but really notice her. Maybe tonight would be the night.

Taylor drank with the speed and ferocity of one of those hot dog–eating champions, who can down fifty wieners in ten seconds. When she finished, Rob whistled, long and low.

Of course, that was the point.

I waited for Tay's next move, which was to smile winningly at Rob, flip her hair over one shoulder, and hold out her cup. "Beer me."

But Rob wasn't looking at Taylor anymore. He was looking at me. Looking and smiling. Looking, smiling, and leaning in so close his lips grazed my earlobe. "Your turn," he said.

I pulled away fast, like I'd been burned. Because that is

what you do. When your best friend's crush flirts with you, there is only one acceptable response: *Disengage.* As in, *Do Not—Under Any Circumstances—Flirt Back.*

"I'm a sipper, not a chugger," I mumbled. Which was exactly the right thing to say because I sounded like an idiot, making Taylor seem cooler by comparison.

Rob laughed.

Of course, that ruined everything. Now he thought I was funny.

Taylor shot me a look—the briefest flash of annoyance—before she turned away. "Beer me," she repeated, this time holding out her cup to Jarrod, who filled it. I didn't expect her to drink it; the most Tay ever had in her life was one beer. But here she was, chugging again. And it must have made her feel better because as soon as she finished she grabbed my hand. "Let's dance!"

So I followed Taylor into the living room and helped her roll back the rug like we'd done a thousand times before—to play sock hockey, or to practice for lip-synch contests, or just to crack each other up with our dance moves. We blasted the stereo. We shook our hips like Shakira. I decided that I would mention the Rob thing later, but for now I would keep things light. Tay was in party-girl mode—silly, happy, whipping her hair all around. I didn't want to jinx it.

At some point Ryan showed up. "Hey, beautiful," he said, wrapping his arms around me from behind, pulling me close. We danced for a few songs before he left to get a soda. Then Kendall and Rae arrived, and a bunch of older girls I didn't know. Before long, the dance floor was packed and my jeans were stuck to my legs like a scuba suit. I needed to get outside. So I left Tay on the dance floor and headed back through the kitchen, where Ryan was now propped against a countertop, bonding with his future teammates.

Ryan's eyelids were droopy—a sign he may have been drinking more than Coke—which surprised me. And not in a good way. Ryan always said getting drunk was stupid. But then I caught his eye through the crowd, and he smiled, sending a spark across the room, straight to me. "Love you," he mouthed silently. Which made everything okay. I knew that later, when we were alone, his breath would smell like Big Red, and his lips would be soft.

But at that moment I needed air. Even though Jarrod had expressly forbidden anyone at the party from going outside—he didn't want the neighbors to call the cops—I ducked out the back door. I braced myself for someone to stop me, but no one did. The night air felt like satin. I rolled up my sweaty jeans and sat on the tile edge of the pool, dangling my feet in the water.

I don't know how long I sat there. Fifteen minutes? Twenty? All I know is when I went back inside Ryan wasn't in the kitchen. I checked the basement, where a bunch of guys were playing Foosball and Ping-Pong . . . no Ryan. The TV room . . . no Ryan. So I headed back to the dance floor to find Taylor.

"Where's Tay?" I yelled over the music to Kendall.

"Bathroom!" Kendall yelled back.

I had a vision of Taylor face-planting a toilet bowl. At every high school party we'd gone to—there had been three so far—we'd seen people throwing up. I knew what I needed to do: check all six of the LeFevres' bathrooms. Just in case Taylor needed me to hold back her hair.

"Tay?" I said each time I knocked. "Taylor, are you in there?"

When I struck out downstairs, I headed up. I checked the guest bathroom. Taylor's bathroom. Jarrod's. Then I did what I would never in a million years have done if Taylor's parents had been home. I walked down the cream-carpeted hallway to the other end of the house, to the master suite. I felt weird doing it, knowing it was wrong. But I needed to find Taylor.

When I reached the end of the hall I turned the corner and there was Heidi. Chubby, frizzy-haired Heidi, standing directly outside the door to Taylor's parents' bedroom. She was wearing the same halter/miniskirt combo as Taylor, but in an unflattering shade of yellow.

"Hey," I said.

Heidi jumped. "Oh! Hey!"

"What are you doing up here?"

She flashed me a big, weird smile. "Nothing."

"Have you seen Tay?"

Heidi shook her head. Then she looked down at the charm bracelet on her wrist and started fiddling with it like crazy.

"Are you sure?"

"What?" Heidi's head popped up. "No . . . I mean—yes! I'm sure."

I watched Heidi's round pink cheeks turn even pinker. I knew she was lying; I just didn't know why. So I told her this was serious. Taylor chugged two beers. *Two.* She could be throwing up right now. Or passed out. Or, worse still, passed out *and* throwing up, inhaling her own barf, just like Mrs. Meechan warned us about in health.

"Yeah . . . I'm pretty sure she's okay." Heidi smirked slightly.

That's when it hit me. "Oh my God, is she with a *guy*? She is, isn't she? She's hooking up in there. . . . Wait—is it *Rob*?" I waited, silently hoping that Heidi would say yes.

But she didn't. She just shook her head.

"Is it another one of Jarrod's friends?"

The corner of Heidi's mouth twitched again. "Maybe."

"*Maybe*?"

"I'm not at liberty to say."

I stared at Heidi, waiting for a straight answer, but it didn't come. All she could do was smirk and yank on her bracelet.

"Well then," I said calmly, "I'm going in."

Heidi sidestepped in front of me, blocking my path. "You don't want to do that."

"Are you kidding me?"

"No."

"Move," I said.

"I promised Taylor I'd guard the door," Heidi said, folding both arms across her chest. Which was downright laughable since I was the best friend in this scenario, and Heidi was only doing what Taylor had told her to do, as usual. Heidi had no clue how annoyed Taylor got with her sometimes. But I knew. And I almost felt sorry for her at that moment.

"Come on, Heids," I said. "I need to make sure she's okay."

"Suit yourself." Heidi stepped aside, and I turned the doorknob. I walked into Taylor's parents' bedroom and there, in an instant, my whole world disintegrated before my eyes. Kneeling on the carpet in the far corner of the room was Taylor. Reclined on a chaise lounge in front of her, boxers around his ankles, was Ryan.

My Ryan.

At first, I couldn't move; the shock was too great. All I could do was stare in disbelief. They hadn't even bothered to turn out the lights.

Seconds ticked by—a lifetime—but they still didn't notice me standing there. Finally, I found my voice. "This cannot be happening," I mumbled. Then, "Tell me this isn't fucking happening!"

Ryan's eyes snapped open. He scrambled for his boxers, tumbling onto the floor in the process. "It's not what you think," he said. Incredibly.

"You've got to be kidding me." The words felt thick in my throat, heavy as stones. "And you," I turned to Taylor, pointing one shaky finger in the air, "*you* . . ." I wanted to call her something awful—the worst name I could think of. Yet nothing came to me.

Taylor's eyes were huge, shocked. She simultaneously shook her head and began walking toward me, stumbling a little. "Lexi—this isn't—"

"Don't," I said, cutting her off. "Don't ever say my name again."

She blinked.

"I hate you, Taylor LeFevre. I will hate you forever."

I knew how stupid those words sounded even as I said them. Stupid and childish. So I did the second best thing

I could think of: I spun on my heel and marched out of the room, slamming the door behind me.

Heidi was still standing in the hall, shaking her head. "I tried to warn you, Lexi," she singsonged, "but you wouldn't listen."

"Go to hell," I told her.

"Lexi!" I heard Taylor calling after me. "Lex, wait!"

But I didn't wait.

Everything that happened next was a blur—a series of hazy snapshots taken underwater. Me, running down the stairs. Me, tripping over an umbrella stand.

A dozen interchangeable guys in white baseball caps, standing around a keg with their red plastic cups. A beer in my hand, the color of pee. *"WHICH ONE OF YOU JOCKSTRAPS WANTS TO GIVE ME A RIDE HOME?!"* The window of Jarrod's Saab, fogged with breath. *"You're so hot, Lexi. Do you have any idea how hot you are?"*

And then . . . darkness.

Pussy Galore

THE IRONY IS, Taylor and Ryan didn't even like each other. Not at the beginning, anyway. I remember the day exactly. It was December 27, winter break, and me, Taylor, Kendall and Rae, Heidi, and a bunch of other kids were skating on the frog pond behind the junior high. When this guy with a hockey stick whizzed past us, every girl over the age of ten did a double take. He was wearing a red Weston Academy jersey, number 24, and—despite the frigid temperature—shorts. His blond hair was messy in that just-rolled-out-of-bed way, like the guy in the Abercrombie & Fitch ad Taylor had taped inside her locker.

"Who is *that*?" Heidi asked as he blew by us a second time.

"Good question," Taylor said.

"He is a major-league hottie."

Kendall rolled her eyes. "You think everyone's a major-league hottie."

"So?" Heidi said. "Am I wrong?"

We watched as the hottie in question spun around in a graceful fashion so that he was skating backward. He raised his hockey stick over his head and rested it on his shoulders. Still skating, he lifted one knee to the opposite elbow, then switched, then switched again. Watching this, I felt a flutter in my stomach that unnerved me. I didn't like show-offs. And this guy was clearly showing off. Yet, hard as I tried, I couldn't make myself look away.

But then, no one could.

"Omigod." Heidi clutched Taylor's arm. "He. Is so. Hot."

"Yeah," Taylor said, pulling away slightly. "We've established that."

"What *I* want to know," Rae said, "is if he goes to Weston Academy, why is he slumming it in Millbridge?"

"They're probably on break," Kendall said, "same as us."

"But wouldn't their rink still be open, like, for players?"

Heidi shook her head. "Weston's a boarding school. They totally shut down over Christmas."

"How do *you* know?"

"I just know."

"Maybe he goes to Weston, but he lives in Millbridge," Rae suggested. "And we just never noticed him over breaks."

"Please," Kendall said. "How could we not have noticed?"

While this debate raged on, number 24 proceeded to do another spin move, lower his stick to the ice, and weave his way toward us again at breakneck speed, dodging every obstacle in his path.

Well, almost every obstacle. Every obstacle except the crater in the ice about three feet away from us, that caught the edge of his skate just right and sent him flying through the air—straight into Taylor.

My best friend was now flat on her butt on the ice, earmuffs askew, looking ticked. This might have been remedied—or at least minimized—if Ryan had said he was sorry. Or asked if she was okay. Or helped her to her feet. Instead, he did something utterly bizarre: he popped up from his own horizontal position, raised one eyebrow, and said, completely deadpan, "Dano. . . . *Ryan* Dano."

Everyone stared at him, blank. Except for me, who half snorted, half choked, because my father was a James Bond fanatic, who once forced me to sit through an entire weekend of "Bonding" with him. Not the recent incarnation of Bond, either. Oh no. I had to suffer through the classics: *Goldfinger, Octopussy, For Your Eyes Only*—

"Omigod!" Heidi let out a shriek and clapped her mittens together. "Ryan *Dano*? I know you!"

"Oh yeah?" Ryan Dano smiled, revealing a slight gap between his two front teeth, which on anyone else would have looked ridiculous, but on him it worked.

"We went to Circle Nursery together!" Heidi said. "Remember? Mrs. Genther's class? The blue room? With the macaroni table and the stall for the horses we made out of broomsticks and pillowcases . . . ?"

Of course *she* would remember this. Heidi is practically a savant when it comes to recalling useless information. When she finished babbling about nursery school, she went on to exclaim what an *amazing coincidence* this was—that *he*, who'd moved to New York City when he was *four*, should be back, skating on *this* pond, on *this* day, and run into *her*!

While Ryan patiently explained to Heidi about his grandparents still living in Millbridge, I snuck a few glances his way, absorbing the blueness of his eyes, the fullness of his lips, the tiny, moon-shaped freckle on his right cheekbone—

"Don't worry about *me*," Taylor cut in. "I'm *fine*, in case anyone was wondering. Which no one was. *Obviously*." As she limp-skated past us, she shot Ryan Dano a look of pure venom. "Thanks for the apology, asshole."

Ryan smiled an adorably crooked smile. "Hey . . . sorry about that."

"Weston Academy, huh?" she said to him, full-on sarcastic. "*Huge* shocker there." To the rest of us she muttered, "I'll be in the cocoa hut. If anyone cares."

Naturally, Heidi sprang into action. "Taylor! Hey! Wait up!"

Kendall and Rae exchanged eye rolls, the way they always did when Heidi annoyed them. But they didn't follow Taylor to the cocoa hut. They didn't have to—not just because Heidi had already volunteered, but because, since the two of them hadn't started hanging out with us until seventh grade, they didn't have the same history with Taylor that Heidi and I did. They didn't have the same allegiance.

I know.

I know I should have followed Taylor to the cocoa hut. I know she was the injured party and I was the best friend. Even in that *second* I knew that I was wrong not to follow her, but I still didn't do it. I don't know why.

Okay, maybe I do. Maybe a tiny part of me didn't want to leave Ryan Dano alone with Kendall and Rae. It wasn't just that they were pretty—tall, willowy Kendall with the legs that stretched on forever, and Rae, whose butt was legendary and whose skin was always tan, even in winter—it was that they could flirt. I knew I was pretty, too, but I always got tongue-tied around boys. Whenever I tried to flip my hair around like Kendall or tell jokes like Rae, I'd end up looking like a goober. And I was determined not to look like a goober in front of Ryan Dano.

So I remained silent. I watched as Kendall and Rae worked their magic. After they introduced themselves, Kendall did her patented move (combination hair flip *with* a giggle) and Rae threw out some obscure professional hockey stats that she must have inherited from her brother, Anthony. Then, in classic Kendall and Rae fashion, they started firing questions: *"So, Ryan, you go to Weston?" "What year are you?" "Do you play any sports besides hockey?" "Where do you live in the city?" "Do you have a girlfriend?" "Yeah, Ryan, are you, like, taken?"*

Ryan Dano grinned. "Who wants to know?"

"We do," Kendall and Rae said in stereo.

"Actually . . ." he said, glancing in my direction, as I did my best to fix my gaze on the ice in front of me, feigning indifference. "No."

"Seriously?" Rae said. "You're single?"

"Seriously."

When I looked up again, there were those blue eyes, staring straight at me. His lashes were long for a boy's—long and dark, which made the blue seem bluer somehow, almost turquoise. In that moment, I remember feeling dizzy, like I might fall over.

"Do *you* have any questions for me?" he asked. Nice voice. Low, warm.

I shrugged.

Little crinkles appeared around his eyes. "Do you at least have a name?"

I wanted my answer to be perfect—something so clever and captivating that Ryan Dano would remember me long after his return to Weston Academy. So I narrowed my eyes seductively, jutted out one hip, and said it: "Pussy Galore."

The words hung in the air like a bad smell. I wanted to die.

Then Kendall burst out laughing. "Pussy *what*?"

And Rae said, "Wow, Lex. I don't think I've ever heard you say *pussy* before." She turned to Ryan, whose eyebrows were raised in, what—astonishment? Horror? "Lexi never swears."

I didn't stick around long enough to hear his response. I was too mortified. I just mumbled something like, "Gotta go find Taylor," and took off.

Later, when it was just me and Tay eating Pop-Tarts in her kitchen, she let me have it. "I can't believe you blew me off."

"I know," I said. "I'm sorry."

"That was *really* uncool."

"I know."

"Kendall and Rae," Taylor continued, "I get. They are beyond boy-crazy. But my best friend?" She shook her head, frowning. "You're supposed to have my back. You didn't even ask if I was *okay*."

It hurt to hear those words from Taylor, but I knew I deserved them—just as I deserved her anger back at the cocoa hut, when, in Ryan Dano's defense, I pointed out the fact that he *had* actually apologized to her. Taylor didn't like that one bit. She accused me of taking his side—of getting sucked in by his Abercrombie looks and choosing him over her. Which wasn't exactly false.

"I'm sorry," I said again. "I really am."

Taylor sighed and went on to make her sub-point: that every guy at Weston Academy was an asshole. She knew this for a fact because her brother had gone to football camp there the summer before, and Jarrod told her, in no uncertain terms: those Weston guys are assholes.

"Maybe it's an admissions requirement," I said.

Taylor smirked down at her Pop-Tart.

"'Must be an a-hole to apply.'"

She was trying not to smile, but I knew I had her.

"'A-hole certification required.'"

She finally cracked, grinned, and threw a chunk of Pop-Tart at me. "You're a big dork, you know that?"

"I know."

"I can't believe you introduced yourself as *Pussy*."

"Yeah, well . . ." I knew Taylor didn't get the Bond Girl reference, just as Kendall and Rae hadn't gotten it when they recapped the story in the cocoa hut. And I wasn't about to set the record straight now. To explain that Pussy Galore was the ultimate Bond Girl would be to admit that I had been trying to flirt with Ryan Dano, which would: A) tick Taylor off even more; and B) be a moot point. Because the guy went to boarding school two towns over. He lived in Manhattan, for Pete's sake. It's not like I was going to see him again.

"So, do you still hate me?" I asked.

"That depends," Taylor said.

"On what?"

"On how long of a foot massage you're going to give me for penance."

Taylor is a freak about foot massages. She'll pay thirty-five bucks for a pedicure, not because she cares about her toenails, but because she wants a foot massage. So—even though the last thing I wanted to do after a day of skating was to rub her hot, stinky dogs—I told her that I would. For one hour.

"An *hour*?" Taylor laughed and peeled off her socks, shoving her bare feet right up on the kitchen table. "Go to town, suckaaa."

I laughed, too. I knew that for as mad as Taylor could get, she never stayed that way. Not like most girls, who could hold a grudge forever. I knew how lucky I was to be let off this easy, and I vowed to myself, right then and there, never to take Taylor's friendship for granted again.

I just didn't plan on Ryan Dano, Round II.

I certainly didn't plan on it happening at church the next Sunday, in front of both our mothers, with him in a blazer and button-down and his hair parted on one side, gelled into submission.

It happened at the refreshment table after the service, while I was pouring myself a cup of punch. "Alexa?" my mother said, approaching from behind and placing a gentle hand on my arm. "Honey, I'd like to introduce you to someone."

I was used to her doing this to me. My mother was the only person in our family who went to church regularly. My dad, being Jewish, went to temple, but only on the holidays, and Ruthie had declared herself an atheist in fourth grade so she didn't go anywhere. Whenever my mom could convince me to join her at church, she had to introduce me to everyone and their dog.

So I picked up my paper cup and turned around slowly, preparing to meet some white-haired biddy in a hat. Instead, it was a blonde in a brown pantsuit.

"Sharon," my mom said, flashing her best hostess smile, "this is my daughter, Alexa. Alexa, this is Mrs. Dano. I just recruited her for the soup kitchen committee."

Out of shock, I sloshed a little punch on the floor. But then I recovered, murmuring, "Pleased to meet you, Mrs. Dano," in precisely the manner I'd been taught.

"Aren't you darling." Mrs. Dano smiled and propelled Ryan forward with one hand. "This is my son, Ryan."

I figured Ryan would say something like, "Actually, we've met," or "Hi again," or—this was almost too horrifying to contemplate—"Wazzup, Pussy Galore?" But he just shot me that crooked little smile and made me slosh even more punch on the floor. "Hey."

"Hey," I said.

At which point Mrs. Dano announced that Ryan would be starting school at Millbridge Junior High next week—ninth grade, same as me—and wouldn't it be great if the two of us could get to know each other beforehand?

While I was reeling from this information, my mom was smiling so hard I thought her face might crack. This was her dream come true: me talking to a boy. Not just any boy, either, but one who dressed in quality fabric *and* went to church with his mother.

Sure enough, my mom and Mrs. Dano turned and

moseyed off together like old friends, even though they'd just met, leaving me and Ryan alone at the refreshment table.

For a minute, I didn't know what to say. Then I was like, *"I thought you went to Weston."* And he was like, *"It's kind of a long story."* And I was like, *"Well, we've got time."*

We talked for an hour. As I listened to Ryan tell me about his dad—how he'd lost his job on Wall Street over a year ago and hadn't been able to find another one—all thoughts of Taylor vanished. I couldn't imagine getting pulled out of school midyear, or leaving my friends behind, or moving into my grandparents' house, but that's what was happening to Ryan.

"I can't believe I'm telling you this," he said at one point, frowning down at the half-eaten muffin in his hand.

"It's okay," I said.

"I don't even *know* you, and I'm unloading all my family crap on you."

"I don't mind."

And I meant it. The more Ryan told me about himself, the more I wanted to know. And the whole time he was talking, all I could think about was reaching out and giving him a hug. It wasn't just the sympathy factor. It was those eyes. That crooked smile. I couldn't explain it; I just had to hug him. And I could tell, just from how Ryan was looking at me, that he was feeling the same way.

"You're not going to say anything, are you?" he asked.

I shook my head. "Of course not."

"Especially not to your friend . . . the one with the attitude."

I hesitated. An image of Taylor flashed through my

mind—that day in the cocoa hut, the expression of anger and hurt in her eyes—but I willed it away. "I won't say a word," I told Ryan. "To anyone."

"Good." He let out a deep breath. "I don't need your friends thinking my family's some kind of charity case . . . especially if I'm going to ask you out."

I plucked a fresh cup of punch off the table, took a casual swig. "Are you?"

"I don't know. Should I?"

I shrugged. "I don't know. Maybe."

For someone who couldn't flirt, I must have been doing pretty well, because a minute later Ryan Dano asked me to the movies.

And I said yes.

In hindsight, that yes was the stupidest answer of my life. If I had said no, I wouldn't have had to hide our first date from Taylor. If there had been no first date, Ryan would not have become my boyfriend. If Ryan had not become my boyfriend, I wouldn't have given a monkey's nut what he and Taylor were doing together at the party, and I never would have gotten into Jarrod's car.

If I had said no when Ryan Dano asked me out, one thing is for sure: I would still have a life.

Talk to Me

SOMEONE AT THE hospital tracked down my parents, who were on the Ohio leg of Ruthie's college tour when they got the call. They took the first flight back to Connecticut and arrived just as I was coming out of surgery. I woke to my mother's smell, vanilla and rosehips. Her face, floating over my bed, was smudgy with mascara.

"Oh, my baby," she said, reaching out to touch the side of my face that wasn't covered in gauze. "My beautiful baby."

Normally, I hated her calling me that, but right then the anesthesia was wearing off and the pain was so bad I thought my head would explode. Literally. Try getting your face bashed in with a crowbar then stabbed with ice picks. Now, add a vat of acid. That's what it felt like. When my mother's fingers touched my skin, I started to cry. I cried and cried, but there was no sound. Then a nurse stuck a needle in my arm and everything drifted away.

When I woke up again, my dad was standing at the foot of the bed, looking rumpled. I'd never seen him look rumpled in my life. "Hey, Beany," he said, reaching out to squeeze my big toe. "How're you feeling?"

I opened my mouth to say my head hurt, but nothing came out. My tongue was a cotton ball.

"Talk to me, Beans. How did this happen? Step me through it."

"She can't talk yet, Mr. Mayer," a voice said—gruff, but kind. "You'll have to wait for the meds to wear off. It could be a few hours."

"I'll wait," my dad said. Then, "You hear me, Beany? I'm not going anywhere."

The next few times I woke up, I felt no pain. Zero. Because when half the bones in your face have been pulverized, and all the king's horses and all the king's men are trying to put you together again, here is what the nurses do: jack up the pain medication. Which makes you feel great. But weird, too. Like one of those giant sea turtles at the Mystic Aquarium, floating around and around in your silent tank, while the people on the outside stare at you and flap their mouths and tap on the glass, trying to get your attention.

Talk to me, Beans. How did this happen? Step me through it.

By the time I could speak, I didn't know what to say. It's not that I couldn't remember what had happened. The image of Taylor and Ryan together was burned in my brain for all eternity. I just didn't know what to tell my dad, who'd been working so hard for the past decade that he didn't seem to realize I'd grown up. To him, I was Lexi Beans. A child. Someone to make pancakes for on Sunday morning. Not just regular ones, either. Animal shapes. Needless to say, I wasn't about to mention the word *kegger* in my father's presence, let alone the words *blow job.*

"Give her time, Jeff," my mother said, pouring a cup of water from the beige plastic pitcher next to my bed. "She's been through a lot."

You have no idea.

"Drink," she said, pressing a straw to my lips. "Hydration promotes healing."

I marveled at the absurdity of her words. "Hydration promotes healing," like she was some kind of expert. Like she actually believed herself. She was putting on a good show—calm, competent mother in the no-nonsense Talbots shirtdress. Perfect hair. Impeccable makeup. But I knew she was wigging out. After my surgery, I heard her talking to my dad. They thought I was still under, but I wasn't. No matter how hard he tried to calm her down, to assure her that I would be fine, my mother kept asking the same hysterical questions, over and over: *"What if they can't fix her?" "What if she's disfigured?"*

"Do you remember anything?" Ruthie asked now. I couldn't exactly see her because she was standing on my right side, and my right eye was swollen shut.

I opened my mouth just barely, like a ventriloquist. "Jarrod hit a tree."

Then Ruthie hit the profanity button, which sent our mother reeling. *"Shhh, Ruth, language. People will think you were raised in a barn!"*

"Your daughter may be scarred for life, all Dickweed gets

is a broken bone, and you're worried about my *language*?"

"Ruth Ann," my mother said, though it was unclear which bugged her more, the "Dickweed" or the "scarred for life."

"Ruthie," my father said gently. "You're not helping."

"Fine. Forget Dickweed. Rank, ill-breeding maggot pie. Yeasty, rump-fed codpiece. Vain, pockmarked—"

"Ruthie," he said again. Not gently. "Knock it off!"

At which point, my sister shut up and my dad explained to me that they'd spoken to Taylor's parents. Jarrod was released from the hospital the morning after the accident, with a broken collarbone and a mild concussion.

"He's going to be fine," my mother said, reaching out to smooth the pill-y blue blanket on top of me. "You both are. Thank God."

"Well." My father cleared his throat. "*Lexi* is going to be fine."

There was a beat of silence. My mother put down the water glass. "What are you saying, Jeff?"

"I'm saying, Laine, that there may be a case here." My father launched into lawyer-speak. *"Reckless driving. Reckless endangerment. Criminal prosecution. Compensable injuries. DWI—"*

He turned to me. "Was Jarrod drinking before he got behind the wheel?"

"No, Dad," I said, which was the truth. Sort of. I remembered Jarrod working the keg, but I couldn't remember him actually drinking anything. In the car, his breath had smelled disgusting, but not like alcohol. More like sour cream and onion.

"Are you sure?"

"I'm sure," I told my father. It's not like he asked me if *I'd* been drinking. And, anyway, I only had one beer. One beer that I didn't even want.

"I need to see the police report. Someone must have administered a Breathalyzer. . . . I'll put in a call to Frank at the station. Just because Jarrod was released from the hospital doesn't mean—"

"Jeff." My mother stared at my father. "You're not *seriously* proposing we *sue* this boy."

"Yes, he is," Ruthie piped in. "That's exactly what he's proposing."

"Ruth, *please*." My father was agitated now. In full public-defender mode, he fired up his lecture on the distinction between criminal and civil litigation, until my mother finally cut him off.

"Think of Alexa," she said. "This is Taylor's brother we're talking about. Her best friend."

Well, I thought, *not anymore.*

My father sighed and then said, "I *am* thinking of Alexa. That's exactly who I'm thinking of. The whole *point* of civil litigation is to ensure—"

"Hello . . ." I cut in weakly. "I'm right here. You can stop talking about me like I'm in a coma."

"Sorry," my dad said, cringing. Then, "It's your call, Lex. Do you want to bring legal action against this kid? Just say the word."

I closed my eyes, trying to will away the nausea that

had suddenly engulfed my body. Taylor and Ryan. The crash. Everything about that night felt like a dream. A sick, twisted dream.

Only it wasn't.

It really happened.

I was actually lying here in a hospital bed, with half my face bandaged and the other half not—like one those half-moon cookies Taylor and I used to bake by the dozens during our fifth-grade baking phase. Vanilla frosting on one side, chocolate on the other. Whenever I ate one, I would start with the vanilla. I'd take my sweet time. Bite after tiny bite, saving the chocolate—the best part—for last. But Taylor? Well, *Taylor* ate hers straight up the middle, plowing through both flavors at once, with no regard—

"Beans," my father said softly.

No regard whatsoever—

I could feel his hand on my foot, squeezing. "Beany?"

NO REGARD.

"Jeff, I think she's asleep."

"No, she's not, Mom."

"How can you tell?"

"I shared a room with her for three years, remember? She snores like a truck driver."

I opened my one good eye and tried to glare at Ruthie, but it didn't really work. My face was too sore and swollen to move. Which sucked. Everything sucked.

"You suck," I muttered, just loud enough for my sister to hear.

"See?" Ruthie patted my arm. "She's awake."

"Lex," my father said. "Do you want me to start making phone calls? Because I will."

"It's your decision, baby," my mother said to me. "Either way, everything's going to be fine. You'll see."

After a long silence, during which I was thinking, *I will never eat another half-moon cookie again as long as I live,* my dad tried once more. "What do you want to do, Beans? Just tell me what to do and I'll do it."

"Nothing," I said finally. "I want you to do nothing."

Because I knew, even then, that the damage had been done. And there wasn't a thing my father could do to fix it.

How Do You Make a Venetian Blind?

EVERY MORNING WAS the same. The nurse on duty would walk into my room with a bag of ice chips, which got Ace-bandaged to my head for twenty minutes. Then I had to rate my pain. Mostly they used a number scale, 0 to 10, with 0 being no pain and 10 being the worst pain imaginable, but one nurse, Janelle, always brought in this stupid laminated chart of facial expressions. "Are we a smiley face or a boo-hoo face today, Alexa?" Like I was three years old or brain damaged, which made me want to yank her perky little ponytail right off her head. But I didn't. I never even said a word. I just pointed to the face that looked the way I felt: horrible.

Depending on my pain level, I got either codeine or morphine, pills or shots. Then the gauze came off, my face got doused with antiseptic, and new gauze went on. If I got pills, they didn't kick in right away, and sometimes it hurt so bad I cried. Other times, I'd bite my lip hard enough to draw blood. To distract myself, I'd close my eyes and replay the images of the party, over and over again, on the miniature movie screen in my mind. *Taylor-and-Ryan, Taylor-and-Ryan, Taylor-and-Ryan.*

The whole time my mother was firing questions. How were things looking? Was the swelling any better? When would it go down completely? What about the scarring? What were they doing now, to prevent scarring later?

Finally, the nurses would cut her off. "Okay. Mrs. Mayer? The doctors will be making rounds in a little while. They'll tell you everything you need to know."

Day Five. The doctors brought in diagrams to explain things to me. 3-D models of the human skull. *"This is the zygomatic bone." "This is the malar." "The lachrymal." "The maxilla."* While they blathered on, I stared out the window at the summer passing me by. *Why couldn't this have happened to me in January? I should be at the beach!* I pictured Ryan's hands, rubbing oil onto Taylor's bare back, as the two of them lay poolside in the LeFevres' backyard, drinking Crystal Light.

"Alexa?" the doctors said. "Do you understand what we're saying about your face?"

"Uh-huh," I'd say, nodding. "Yup."

My face. Everyone in the hospital was obsessed with my face. The doctors, the nurses, the med students, and—worst of all—my mother. Unlike my dad and Ruthie, who ate in the cafeteria and went home to sleep, my mother never left my side. She was too busy hounding the doctors to go anywhere. How was my face healing? Was the swelling going down? What would it look like later? My face was all anyone could talk about. And me, the actual owner of the face? I couldn't have cared less. The only thought in my head was Taylor and

Ryan. *Taylor-and-Ryan, Taylor-and-Ryan, Taylor-and-Ryan.*

"Look at these roses Ryan sent," my mother said when the flowers and cards and balloons started pouring in. "They're absolutely gorgeous."

I pretended not to hear.

The next fifty times my mother commented on Ryan's roses—how gorgeous they were, how thoughtful he was—I said nothing. Finally, without stopping to plan my words, I cracked. "Will you throw them in the trash? Please?"

I kept my eyes on the ceiling, but I could feel my mother's stare.

"I beg your pardon?"

I turned my gaze to the wall. Cards were taped up everywhere. *Get well soon, Lexi. Hope you feel better, Lex. God speed, Alexa. We're praying for you.*

"Alexa," my mother said.

"What."

I expected a lecture on gratitude. Instead, she walked around the bed and pulled up a chair. "What happened? Did you two have a fight?"

Obviously, I couldn't tell her. This was Laine Chapman Mayer, Southern belle, who I am 99 percent sure did nothing more than kiss until she got married. Her idea of The Talk was to hand me and Ruthie a book titled *Abstinence and You: 501 Reasons to Wait.* The notion of telling my mother about Ryan and Taylor's hookup was insane.

"A fight," I mumbled. "Uh-huh."

"Oh, honey."

This was my mother's big opportunity to launch into *her* high school boyfriend story. Landry McCoy, star forward on the basketball team, Laine Chapman, head cheerleader, who, naturally, fell madly in love, applied to all the same South Carolina colleges, and—

"Oh, God," Ruthie said, entering the room with a soda the size of a barrel. "Is this Lifetime Television, The Laundry McCoy Story?"

"*Landry* McCoy," my mother corrected her.

"Who names their kid Laundry? That's just wrong."

"It's *Landry*, and it's a family name."

Ruthie took a sip of soda and grinned. "Good ole Laundry McCoy . . . Well, go on."

It is an old routine with them. My sister mocks our mother's high school boyfriend, but she secretly loves hearing the Landry McCoy story almost as much as our mother loves telling it.

I used to love it, too. Especially the part where my father, the University of Virginia law student, shows up at the UVA-Clemson game and sees my mother for the first time. He is short, nerdy, and not remotely athletic—the opposite of Landry McCoy. But does he let this stop him? No. My father walks right up to my mother after the game and says, "I'm Jeffrey Mayer. I'm just a schmuck from Hackensack, but I'm going to marry you."

"Of course," my mother said, smiling, "I thought he was crazy, but then I started getting these *letters* . . ."

Clearly, this wasn't going to be the abridged version. She was going to rehash my father's entire courtship, play-by-play, right down to the fateful moment when he shows up at her dorm with a guitar and proceeds to serenade her. My mother has no choice. The minute she hears "Carolina in My Mind" she knows she will break Landry McCoy's heart, confessing that she is not only in love with someone else, but she is also transferring to UVA to be with him.

"What's your point?" I asked, cutting my mother off.

"My point?" She looked surprised.

"Your reason. For telling me this."

"It's the Laundry McCoy Story," Ruthie said. "She doesn't need a point."

"Never mind," I muttered. I felt an inexplicable lump in my throat, realizing that my mother had been so busy reminiscing the glory days she'd forgotten what we'd been talking about to begin with.

But I hadn't forgotten. No matter how hard I tried, I couldn't stop thinking about Ryan. It wasn't just the roses. It was the texts he'd been sending, the pathetic attempts to apologize.

> Lx, sry abt wht hapnd sat nite. (You should be.)
>
> I f-d up bg time. (Yeah. You did.)
>
> Let me x-plain. Pls? I lv u.

Lv? Lv??? How much could Ryan love me if he did what he did? If he couldn't even write the whole word?

"Honey," my mother said, obviously catching the look on my face—well, *half* my face. "There's a plan."

"What?" I croaked.

"There's a plan," she repeated, "for you and Ryan. Just like there was for your father and me. Everything happens for a reason."

"What's Ryan got to do with it?" Ruthie asked, giving her soda one last, noisy slurp. I have never known anyone who drinks as much soda as my sister. No wonder she has so many zits.

"Nothing," I told her. The last thing I needed was one of Ruthie's cracks about me and Ryan—one of her Ken-and-Barbie comments.

"Whatever." Ruthie shrugged and tossed her cup in the trash. The perfect ending to a conversation that never should have started.

The whole Ryan-not-showing-up-at-my-bedside situation was easy to explain to my family. We had a fight.

Taylor was harder.

After a week, I was allowed nonfamily visitors, and thirty girls arrived at my door. No joke. Thirty girls, fifteen balloons, eight teddy bears, six *People* magazines, three bags of Swedish fish, one *Sisterhood of the Traveling Pants* DVD, and one fruit basket. But no best friend.

"Lexi! Omigod! You look so good!"

Ironically, it was Heidi leading the pack, carrying the fruit basket. Heidi, whose lifeblood was Little Debbie snack cakes. "This is from me and Taylor," she announced, walking ceremoniously across the room and lowering the basket to the foot of my bed. "We're *so* sorry this happened to you, Lexi. Taylor *really* wanted to be here in person today, but . . ." Heidi paused, trying for an aggrieved expression but not quite pulling it off. ". . . she couldn't make it."

In the silence that followed, thirty arms were nudged, thirty knowing glances exchanged.

Suddenly, I understood why so many of them had shown up—girls I'd gone to school with and played field hockey with but wasn't really friends with, girls I barely knew. It wasn't compassion; it was morbid curiosity. They'd heard about Taylor hooking up with Ryan and wanted to witness the emotional fallout for themselves. Not to mention the carnage.

I took a deep breath, reminding myself that however I was feeling, my face was still bandaged. Whatever I looked like, no one could tell. And I wasn't about to give Heidi the satisfaction of appearing anything but fine.

"Thanks, Heidi," I said. Calm. Cheerful. Then, to the rest of them, "Thanks, you guys."

"You're welcome!" everyone chorused back.

Awkward silence followed. Made even more awkward by my mother launching into hostess mode, bustling around collecting teddy bears, offering Dixie cups of water, while out of nowhere my dad became a stand-up comedian. *How do you make a Venetian blind? . . . You poke him in the eye!*

If Kendall and Rae hadn't burst through the door in their sarongs and flip-flops, swooning over the male nurse they'd just met in the elevator, I might have yanked the IV out of my arm and run screaming out the door.

"Omigod, you guys, he was so hot!"

"He looked like Mario Lopez—"

"But with Justin Bieber's nose—"

"I told him he could give me a sponge bath anytime—"

"Kendall gave him her number on a piece of toilet paper!" Rae shrieked, and everyone laughed. Except my dad, who shook his head, as if to say, statutory rape is no laughing matter.

"Omigod, Lexi!" Rae suddenly said.

And Kendall said, "You look so good!"

As they ran over to hug me, apologizing for being late—they'd been at the beach—I felt a rush of tears that I couldn't explain. "Thanks for coming," I said. Because that is what you say when your friends come visit you in the hospital. And even though I *was* thankful, Kendall and Rae being there only made me feel worse. Their presence made Taylor's absence all the more glaring.

"Where was Taylor?" Ruthie asked as soon as everyone left.

I shrugged.

"Did something happen with you guys?"

"Gee, Ruthie, I don't know. Her brother just decided it would be fun to drive me into a tree."

My dad cleared his throat and said, "Maybe a little distance from Taylor is a good thing. Until we determine the legality of this situation."

"Jeff." My mother frowned delicately. "We've discussed this. We are not going to sue the LeFevres."

"Well, *someone* needs to take responsibility here, Laine. *Someone* is going to need to cover these medical bills. Do you know what our deductible is?"

The minute the conversation stopped including me, I reached for my cell. Just to torture myself, I listened to Taylor's voice mails, starting with the gem she'd left me the morning after the accident. Eight days ago. But who was counting?

"Lex, oh my God . . . I heard what happened. Well, obviously, since Jar was driving . . . I can't believe he was driving . . . anyway . . . I'm freaking out here. Call me when you can, 'kay? I'll keep my phone on."

Oh, you'll keep your phone on? Wow. You are such a good friend. You should win an award.

"Lex . . . it's me again. Still freaking out . . . Call me."

You're freaking out? YOU'RE freaking out???

"Lex, hey . . . My mom talked to your dad and he said something about surgery . . . ? Oh my God . . . I guess that's why you haven't called me back . . ."

Yeah. That's why.

". . . but could you at least text me? . . . I'm sooo sorry about everything. We need to talk. Please?"

It was unbelievable. Taylor spent a full fifteen voice mails pretending to care about my well-being, pretending to care that she hadn't heard back from me. She throws out some lame, generic apology to assuage her guilt, and I'm supposed to call her back like everything's fine? No mention of the party. No mention of Ryan. It was like she thought my brain had been so damaged in the accident I couldn't remember what she'd done. Please.

I drove myself crazy, listening to Taylor's voice mails.

And reading Ryan's texts.

And picturing those thirty girls in my hospital room, nudging each other, exchanging glances.

I went certifiably insane trying to make sense of it all. Why Taylor and Ryan did what they did, how they could live with themselves, whether it was just the one night or if it had happened before. My head was spinning so fast, and my stomach was twisted up in so many knots that I thought it couldn't get any worse.

I had no idea.

A Lifetime Supply of Antimicrobial Soap

THE NEXT DAY I met with a new plastic surgeon, a specialist in reconstruction, who examined my face for all of two seconds before concluding that the skin wasn't healing properly. I would need another procedure, a "split thickness skin graft," taken from my buttocks. While my mother cried, I had one nauseating, hysterical thought. *I'll be a butt-face! Literally!*

As if that wasn't preposterous enough, not thirty minutes after Dr. Ass-Graft dropped his bomb, Taylor's mom showed up. Unannounced. Holding an enormous cellophane-wrapped duck.

Seeing Mrs. LeFevre standing in the doorway of my hospital room, I felt a slow burble of crazy juice rising in my throat. I didn't know whether to barf or cry.

"What is she doing here?" I hissed to my mother, who was perched on a chair next to my bed. *"I told you no more visitors."*

"You know what they say . . ." Taylor's mom called gaily from across the room. "If Mohammed won't answer her cell phone, the mountain will come to Mohammed!" She plopped the duck down on a chair and ran a bejeweled hand through her red, spiky hair. "You would not *believe* how crowded the gift shop was. Everyone and their *dog* seems to be having a baby today! All they had left were ducks!"

I watched my mom glide across the room like an ice dancer, her face morphing before my eyes. "Bree," she chirped as though Taylor's mom were a guest arriving for a dinner party. "It's so good of you to come."

"Hello, Laine."

The mothers clasped fingertips.

"How are you holding up?"

"Fine, just fine. How are *you* holding up?"

You would think, watching the two of them, that they were old pals. But the truth was, even after all the years Taylor and I had been friends, our parents barely knew one another. Whenever they overlapped at school functions and sleepover drop-offs, they would exchange pleasantries, but that was about it. Taylor's mom tried once, when we first moved to town, inviting my mother to one of her ladies' cocktail parties. I never heard what happened. I just I remember my mother telling my dad she wouldn't be doing *that* again.

Laine Mayer vs. Bree LeFevre was like milk vs. whisky. Talbots vs. Juicy Couture. If my mother were a bumper sticker, she would read THAT'S NOT APPROPRIATE. Taylor's mom would read WHY THE FUCK NOT?

"Oh, Lexi." Mrs. LeFevre shifted her gaze to me. "Oh, sweet girl." When she reached my bed, my ex–best friend's mother took my hand in hers, cupping it gently. Her voice dropped three octaves. "I am *so* sorry this happened."

"That's okay," I mumbled. The lie of the century.

Taylor's mom held my hand tighter.

She read my palm once, I remember. It was during a thunderstorm. I was ten and I was sleeping over at Taylor's when a humongous boom woke me up. I was so scared I ran downstairs, where Mrs. LeFevre was sitting alone at the kitchen table, drinking a glass of wine. She took my hand to comfort me, and then she started reading it. My heart line, she said, was the deepest she'd ever seen.

"Taylor is worried sick about you," Mrs. LeFevre said now.

Right.

"She wanted to visit sooner, but since you didn't return any of her calls . . ."

Uh-huh.

Mrs. LeFevre turned to my mother. "Taylor and Jarrod are down in the cafeteria, getting some ice cream to bring up for Lexi."

Ice cream. Sure. That will fix everything.

"Oh!" my mother said brightly. "Alexa's father and sister are in the cafeteria, too."

"Oh?" Taylor's mom said.

"Mm-hm. Maybe they'll run into one another."

Then, right on cue, like some terrible TV sitcom, the door opened. My dad, Ruthie, Mr. LeFevre, Jarrod, and Taylor filed in, one after the other. They reminded me of the conga line at my cousin Jody's wedding. Only this time the band wasn't playing "La Bamba," and my father wasn't laughing. His expression was downright grim. *Reckless driving,* his face said. *Reckless endangerment. Criminal prosecution. Compensatory injuries. DUI.*

The conga line stood there. For a second, my one eye

locked with Taylor's, and a thousand flashbacks came over me. The two of us dressed as carrots in the school play. Sack racing across the green on July Fourth. In matching bubble dresses at the seventh-grade formal. Flopped on the LeFevres' couch, watching *The Exorcist*, grabbing each other's hands during the scary parts. One happy snapshot after another until up pops Taylor in a kelly-green halter and matching miniskirt, guilty as sin, wiping her mouth on the back of her hand as if to erase what she's just done.

Suddenly, there were eight mouths too many sucking oxygen out of the room. Taylor's mouth, shiny with lip gloss. Jarrod's mouth, two slabs of rubber, one slimy, probing, sour-cream-and-onion tasting—*Oh God.*

My throat was squeezing shut.

I focused on the ceiling tiles, trying to breathe, but that didn't help. So I heaved my legs over the side of the bed and lunged for the bathroom, dragging the IV pole along with me.

"Alexa?" my mother called from across the room. "Honey, are you okay?"

No, I am not okay. I am not okay because . . . well, because I just remembered this crazy thing I did.

I kissed Jarrod LeFevre.

Correction, I let Jarrod LeFevre kiss *me.*

We were getting into his car and—given the hideousness of the scene I'd just witnessed between Taylor and Ryan and the beer I'd just chugged in the LeFevres' kitchen—I was feeling more than a little deranged. So when Jarrod looked at me and said, point blank, how hot I was, I sort of giggled. *"Oh, really?"* I said. And he said, *"Yeah. Really."* Taylor's brother had been flirting with me for years, and I had never given him the time of day. Now, I was flirting back. I had the sudden realization that Jarrod was about to kiss me, and when he leaned in to make his move, I did nothing. I didn't say no. Or stop. Or, *"Get off me, numnuts, your breath stinks."* I did . . . nothing.

"Lex?" My father's voice was at the door. "You okay in there?"

I stood at the sink, staring down at a bottle of antimicrobial soap. There was a mirror on the wall, but I couldn't bring myself to look at it. Not yet.

I thought about telling my dad I was sick so he'd send the LeFevres home, but I couldn't give Taylor the satisfaction. Taylor and her stupid cork-soled sandals with the four-inch heels, the same ones she was wearing the night of the party. I wanted to kick her right in the knobby knees.

"Lex?" my dad said again.

I turned on the water. *Screw Taylor,* I thought as I pumped soap into my cupped palm. The smell was so strong my eyes burned. *Screw Jarrod, too.* I dried my hands on the hem of my hospital johnny.

What were they even doing here? That was the question. Probably their parents dragged them, because no way would they show their faces voluntarily.

"*There* she is!" Taylor's father boomed as I emerged from the bathroom. His voice sounded fake, more like a game-show host than a sportscaster. *Let's tell the lovely lady what she's won, folks! . . . A lifetime supply of antimicrobial soap!*

Knowing Mr. LeFevre as I did, his smile was an act. Back home, he must have blown a gasket about the party. Yelled.

Thrown things across the room. He'd probably placed Taylor and Jarrod under house arrest, letting them out just to visit me.

"Beans?" My father's voice was low in my ear. His hand was on my elbow. "You okay?"

I nodded, fixing my gaze across the room. From the waist down, Mr. LeFevre and Jarrod were twins. The same tan, hairy legs. The same shiny brown loafers without socks.

How could a guy who sweats as much as Jarrod possibly justify no socks? The night of the party, his hands were so clammy they left streaks on the dashboard. When he kissed me, I tasted salt—the tang of sweat from his upper lip. Salty, slobbery, jam-it-down-your-throat kisses. Not like Ryan. More like a rabid Saint Bernard. A rabid, sweaty, slobbery—

"Lexi?"

Waffle cone.

"I brought you some . . . uh . . ."

Waffle cone, in my face.

". . . Heath Bar Crunch."

Suddenly, Jarrod was standing beside me. One arm in a sling. The other, tan and bare, holding a waffle cone. He was so close. So close I could smell him. So close I could feel the pressure of his fingers on mine, the heat coming off his skin just like it had that night.

I tried to think of something to say, the perfect insult to hurl. But instead of words, it was ice cream. I didn't *plan* to do it. It just happened. Now, Heath Bar Crunch was splattered all over the wall, an explosion of white and brown, like a Jackson Pollock painting.

The room was dead silent.

Before anyone could speak, I yanked my arm away from my father and stumbled back into the bathroom, locking the door behind me.

When the LeFevres were gone, Ruthie convinced our parents to disappear so we could have some sister time. I don't know what surprised me more: the fact that they listened, or Ruthie's use of the term *sister time.*

Ruthie and I weren't like most sisters. We lived in the same house, obviously, but we didn't bond the way Kendall and her sister, Claire, bonded. We didn't gossip about boys, or swap nail polish, or stay up late talking. And we didn't really fight, either. Because, well, what was there to fight about? We were nothing alike. We had totally different interests. Most of the time we were so busy living our separate lives that we barely noticed each other, let alone engaged in passionate conversation.

I watched Ruthie now, picking up the box of chocolates Mr. LeFevre had brought and tearing open the cellophane with her teeth—a move that our mother would call "crass." But did Ruthie care? No. My sister didn't worry what anyone thought of her. She just let her freak-flag fly. Today she was wearing a variation on her summer uniform: vintage concert T-shirt (The Kinks) and cutoff jeans (stained). Her long, dark hair had zero shape. If you saw her on the street, here is what you would think: drugs. But as far as I knew, my sister had never tried anything stronger than Tylenol. Not that she would tell me if she had.

"So," Ruthie said, plucking a chocolate from its paper skirt and popping it into her mouth. "Are you going to tell me what really happened?"

"What do you mean?" I asked, playing dumb.

"The accident, Lex."

I pushed a finger up under the gauze on my face, trying to scratch. The worst part about stitches isn't the pain; it's the itch. You have to be gentle when you scratch, though. Otherwise it hurts like hell.

"Lex."

"What?" I said. "I told you. Jarrod was driving and we ran off the road. End of story."

"Uh-huh." Ruthie bent over the chocolates, plucking out another. "So what about the *beginning* of the story?"

What was I doing in Jarrod's car in the first place? she wanted to know. Where were we going? And what actually caused the crash? An oil slick, a squirrel in the road, what?

I remember my father saying once that Ruthie would make a great lawyer. I'd witnessed enough debates between the two of them to know that my sister could strip an argument down to its bones, poke holes in any claim. I could avoid Ruthie's questions for a few hours, maybe a day. Eventually, she'd wear me down.

"Fine," I said. "But you can't tell Dad."

Ruthie raised an eyebrow.

"Or Mom."

"Agreed," she said.

So I began at the beginning, sparing no detail.

The only time Ruthie interrupted was when I got to the part about Taylor and Ryan.

"Ah," she said, nodding. "That explains a lot."

"What?"

"Your boyfriend's conspicuous absence, for one."

"*Ex*-boyfriend."

"Whatever. And Taylor acting all weird and twitchy."

"I didn't notice," I said. As if I hadn't been watching Taylor's every move.

Ruthie looked at me. "Are you serious? She was biting her nails the whole time. I'd be surprised if she had any left."

"She can bite off her arms for all I care."

"Tell me how you *really* feel."

I knew I sounded bitter, but I didn't care. I kept going with my story, knowing that when I got to the worst part—the part I'd suddenly remembered when Jarrod was handing me the waffle cone—my sister would go ape. Or catatonic with shock. The last thing I expected was laughter. Ruthie laughed so hard, in fact, she choked, and the half-chewed chocolate in her mouth went flying out onto the floor.

"What's so funny?" I demanded. "He pulled down his pants *while he was driving*. In the middle of the *Merritt Parkway*! He wanted me to touch it!"

"I'm sorry. You're right. It's not funny, it's just—"

"There is nothing *remotely* funny about this, Ruthie! I am in the *hospital*. I'm . . . Look at me! My face is . . . WOULD YOU STOP EATING THOSE STUPID THINGS?!"

I ripped the box of chocolates out of my sister's hands.

Then, without thinking, I popped one in my mouth.

Ruthie blinked at me. "Oh my God."

"What?"

"You're eating candy."

"So?"

"You don't eat candy, like, ever."

I shrugged. Ruthie was right. I couldn't remember the last time I'd eaten candy. Or anything fattening. Now, grabbing an Enzo's Bakery box off the bedside table, I imagined what my mother would say if she could see me. *Remember, Alexa. A moment on the lips, forever on the hips.* Or, *Nothing tastes as good as looking good feels.*

Normally, those words would stop me cold. But right now, the sugar crystals on these blueberry muffins were twinkling like stars. For the past eight days, all I'd been eating was yogurt and oatmeal. "Screw it," I said, lifting a muffin out of the box and shoving the whole thing in my mouth. My jaw hurt, but the taste was worth it.

"Nice," Ruthie said.

Ruthie, who'd never dieted a day in her life, never counted a calorie or a fat gram, never scooped out the guts of a bagel and eaten just the shell. My sister had no idea how lucky she was. She could wear what she wanted, eat what she wanted, and my mother wouldn't say a word. Ruthie was "the smart one," "the gifted one." The rules didn't apply to her.

"So," Ruthie said, getting back to the matter at hand. "*Did* you touch it?"

I shook my head. My mouth was one huge, sweet, cakey gob of muffin, juicy with berries. I couldn't swallow.

"Take your time," she said.

Finally, my throat was clear. "He kept trying to make me, but I kept pulling my hand away. We got in this huge fight. He called me a tease, and I was like, 'All I wanted was a ride home, five blocks, not some joyride across Connecticut,' and the whole time he was still trying to grab my hand and put it on his . . . you know . . . God, what an idiot."

My sister snorted. "I can think of a lot stronger words than *idiot* to describe Jarrod LeFevre."

"Not Jarrod. Me." Suddenly, my eyeballs were burning, but I wouldn't let the tears fall. Instead, I blurted, "I took off my seat belt! In the middle of the Merritt! I took off my seat belt and opened the door and—"

"Wait a second." Ruthie cut me off. "You opened the *door* . . . of a *moving car*?"

"No! . . . I mean, yes, but it's not what you think. I wasn't really going to jump. I was just threatening to . . . you know, to get him to leave me alone . . . but he must have thought I was serious because he kept yelling, 'Shut the door! Shut the door!' And I couldn't . . . I tried, but we were going too fast . . . I didn't want to fall out." I shook my head, pounding my thigh with one fist. "Idiot!"

"Listen to me," Ruthie said firmly. "You are not an idiot. Anyone in that situation . . . I might have done the same thing."

Right. Like "the smart one" would ever go to a party to begin with, let alone hop into a car with the captain of the football team. I remember her saying once, "I don't *get* adolescent social rituals."

But I didn't argue with my sister. I kept going. "Jarrod

tried to shut the door. He let go of the wheel for, like, a second and leaned over me. . . . I saw what was happening . . . we were hitting the soft part . . . the shoulder . . . I tried to grab the wheel, to straighten us out, but he jerked it back from me and we . . . The car just flew off the road. . . ."

Ruthie grimaced.

I fingered the candy wrapper in my hand. "If Ryan was driving . . . he never would have . . . when we hooked up it was always, you know . . . through the clothes. And he was okay with that. I mean, I *thought* he was. And then, Taylor . . ." My voice broke off.

"I'm sorry, Lex," Ruthie said quietly. "I really am. I didn't mean to make light of what happened to you. The whole thing sucks."

"The whole thing *does* suck," I said.

"I know."

"And you know what sucks even more? Tomorrow I have to get this skin-graft thing. They're taking skin off my *butt* and putting it on my *cheek*."

"I know," Ruthie said.

"How twisted is that?"

My sister shook her head. She opened her mouth like she was about to say something, then closed it.

"What?"

"Are you scared?" she asked.

"No," I said.

Because sometimes you lie. You have to, just to convince yourself. Otherwise, here's the thing: you might lock yourself in a bathroom and never come out.

Bogus, Bulimic, Smack Shooters

IRONICALLY, THE DAY of the skin graft was the day I was supposed to be getting professional head shots. Modeling was my mother's idea, based on this one time when we were in New York City and a photographer stopped us on the sidewalk, asking to take my picture.

I will never forget that moment, and I doubt Taylor will, either. We were on our way to the Met to see the Picasso exhibit since Tay and I had both been home with strep throat the week before and had missed the ninth-grade field trip. When we got to the museum, a photo shoot was taking place, right there on the front steps. The models were gorgeous—dressed all in red against the gray stone, with cherry-colored lipstick and bare legs that went on forever. They looked almost too perfect to be real. You couldn't imagine them burping, or stepping in gum, or having a bad hair day—and probably if they ever did, some guardian hair angel would swoop down from the heavens and spritz everything back into place. Taylor, my mother, and I were mesmerized. We stood on the sidewalk for a full twenty minutes, gawking.

That's when this man came up to us. He was dressed in black and holding a camera with the biggest lens I'd ever seen.

"Excuse me," he said to my mother, "is this your daughter?"

When he gestured to me, my mom nodded and smiled.

"She's stunning." The man paused for a second, holding his chin and squinting at me, tracing my body with his eyes, like he wanted to be sure of something. "Yes," he said finally. He extended a hand to my mom. "Zander Kent."

"Laine Mayer," my mother said.

He told her he wanted to photograph me and whipped out his business card—ZANDER KENT, COMMERCIAL AND FASHION PHOTOGRAPHY. Which of course got my mom all jazzed because, in addition to being runner-up to Miss South Carolina three years in a row, she used to do commercials. In fact, she helped put my dad through law school. Tussy deodorant was one, and then a Folgers coffee ad where, inexplicably, she got to dance with a refrigerator.

When she told this to Zander Kent, he laughed, revealing beautiful, pearl-colored teeth.

"Well . . ." My mother smiled, giving her hair a self-conscious pat. "That was a long time ago. It's Alexa's turn now."

At which point, Zander Kent snapped my photo. Me, Lexi Mayer, right there on the steps of the Metropolitan Museum of Art, surrounded by supermodels. Then he snapped another one. And another. It was crazy—like an out-of-body experience. I knew it was happening, but I couldn't believe it was happening to *me*.

Afterward, I felt giddy. I couldn't stop smiling. As we walked through the exhibit hall, I could tell Taylor was annoyed because she pretended to be really interested in Picasso, taking a million notes and even drawing little sketches in the margins of her notebook. Taylor, who never cared about school, let alone art history. So after about an hour of watching her become the world's leading expert on the Cubist movement, I confronted her.

"What's bugging you?" I asked when my mother was safely tucked away in the restroom.

"Nothing's bugging me," Taylor said.

"Obviously something is."

"What?"

"I don't know," I said. "The photo thing? It's not like I *asked* to have my picture taken. He just came right up and—"

"Whatever." Taylor waved her pencil through the air. "Modeling's bogus. Half those girls are bulimic and the other half shoot smack."

"Where'd you hear that?"

Taylor gave me a look like I'd just fallen off a turnip truck. "How do you think they stay so thin?"

"Well," I said, "it's not like I'm going to—"

"*Plus*, they sleep around."

"You think?"

"Of course. That's how they get the big jobs."

Taylor kept going, laying out all the atrocities of the modeling industry. The longer she talked, the more obvious it became that—much as she denied it—the Zander Kent thing had touched a nerve. Big-time. And, bottom line, Taylor's friendship meant more to me than a few photos.

So that night, I nipped the modeling thing in the bud. When my mother wasn't looking, I dug through her purse until I found Zander Kent's business card. Then, I walked to the kitchen sink and stuffed my modeling career down the disposal.

But a few days later, a package arrived in the mail. My mother squealed when she saw the return address and opened it right away. She wouldn't even let me peek at the photos until she'd seen them. Then she got the crazy notion to run to the mall and buy frames so we could surprise my father with the "big reveal" at dinner. I thought this was a horrible idea, but I kept my mouth shut.

Sure enough, after we had eaten my father's favorite dinner—brisket, wilted greens, potatoes au gratin—and we'd reached my mother's "Honey, let me tell you what happened the other day at the Met" portion of the meal, my dad got very, very quiet. He wiped his mouth on his napkin for a full minute. Finally, he set the napkin down. "Tell me you didn't sign anything," he said.

My mother's eyes widened. "What?"

"Tell me you didn't sign your *name* on a piece of paper. A photo release, a contract, anything."

"No," my mom said. "Absolutely not."

My father sighed. "Good." Then he launched in: How could my mother have given our address to a complete stranger? What could she have been thinking? Didn't she watch the news?

"That's how girls end up in Dumpsters," Ruthie chimed in.

"Ruth," my mother said, shocked.

"What? It's true."

"Laine," my father said. "She has a point."

"Well," my mother said, "he wasn't a *stranger.* Zander Kent is a genuine fashion photographer. . . . Look." She reached into the package and whipped out another business card that Zander Kent must have stuck in there. "It's not as if this gentleman—and he *was* a gentleman, wasn't he, Alexa?"

I shrugged. "I guess."

"Well, he was. Very polite. And it's not as if he just approached us out of the blue. He was *already there,* at the Metropolitan Museum of *Art,* on a legitimate photo shoot."

"Or . . ." Ruthie paused for effect, "he was just *posing* as a polite, legitimate photographer. Any pedophile perv with a computer can make a business card."

"Ruth," my mother said.

But my father nodded his approval. "Another great point."

"Thanks, Dad."

It was almost comical, like watching a three-way tennis match. My mother would serve up something along the lines of "Modeling is a wonderful way for Alexa to earn money for college," and my dad would hit back with "She's only fourteen." Then, out of nowhere, Ruthie would drop some gem: "You know, Mom . . . Charles Manson had a camera."

Finally, dinner ended. But my mother's campaign continued. She hung the framed photos of me on the wall outside my father's study. She told him to run a background check on Zander Kent. She clipped out articles bemoaning the rising costs of a private, four-year college education. In short, the woman was relentless. And eventually, she wore my father down. So the two of them came up with a compromise: in nine months, when I turned fifteen, my mother could take me into the city to Zander Kent's studio, to have professional photos taken. *Head* shots, not *body* shots. After that, we would discuss—*as a family*—the next course of action.

I wasn't sure how I felt about this. I knew how keyed up my mother was, and I didn't want to disappoint her. Plus, if I was really honest with myself, a part of me was just as excited. Because . . . what if I ended up on the cover of *Seventeen* some day? Or *Elle*? Then I remembered Taylor, how weird she'd been about the whole thing. How afterward, whenever she was at my house and walking by my dad's study, she'd pretend not to notice the photos of me at the Met.

But as the months went by, I stopped thinking about Taylor's role in my decision. The two of us had been having a blast, riding the wave of our ninth-grade popularity all the way to graduation. Two weeks before school let out, I turned fifteen. And my mom called Zander Kent to book an appointment. And I thought, *Well, what Taylor doesn't know won't hurt her.* I decided I wouldn't say a word unless something huge happened, like me on the cover of *Vogue*. If I made it that far, wouldn't my best friend be happy for me? And if she wasn't, I could always blame my mother. This whole thing was, after all, her idea.

So my conscience was clear. I allowed myself to embrace the prospect of a real, in-studio photo shoot. Zander Kent was an amazing fashion photographer, and my mother was beyond thrilled to act as my agent. Together, the three of us would work to ensure that my future was bright and all my dreams would come true.

Okay, maybe that's laying it on a *bit* thick, but let's just say things were looking up. Until the night of Jarrod's party, that is. When, you know, small detail: My face became roadkill.

Make Yourself Comfortable

I CAME OUT of the graft surgery with cottonmouth and a crazy dream in my head. I dreamt that I ran into Zander Kent in the art room of my old elementary school. He was wearing a beret, and instead of a camera in his hands, he held a paintbrush. Standing beside him, at one of those miniature kindergarten easels, was Ryan. They were discussing a work of art. I moved in closer, to get a better look. It was a portrait—a girl's face—but the closer I got, the weirder it looked. One eye on her forehead, another on her neck. A nose without nostrils. Her skin, a nonsensical jumble of colors and textures that shifted like beads in a kaleidoscope.

Dude, Dream Ryan said, shaking his head. *Girlfriend is messed up.*

Oh no, my boy, Dream Zander Kent replied. *That. Is art.*

The next week brought more pain meds, not just for my face, but also for the graft site—the place on my butt where the skin had been removed. Now, whenever the nurses came to check on me, they weren't just looking at my face, they were looking at my bare behind. It was humiliating.

There were also more balloons, more flowers, more boxes

of candy to eat, more stupid cards to tape on the wall. And a shrink.

"Why do I need a psychologist?" I demanded when my parents told me. "I'm not psycho."

"Of course you're not, baby," my mother soothed. And my father explained that this wasn't a judgment on me personally; it was hospital procedure. *Following a traumatic injury—particularly a traumatic* facial *injury—all patients are required to undergo a psychiatric evaluation to ensure their blah blah blah . . .*

"Well," I said, "I'm not doing it."

I wanted my dad to tell me this was fine, I didn't have to—that he would plead my case to the hospital board, find some loophole in the system. But here he was, shaking his head.

"If you don't do the psych consult," he said, "you can't come home. These aren't my rules, Beans. They're the hospital's. They have to cover their bases, legally speaking."

While I knew he was right, I couldn't bring myself to agree. And, anyway, the tin of shortbread cookies on the table next to my bed was calling to me. *Eat us,* they commanded. *Eat one, eat ten, keep going.* As I stuffed my face, my mother stared at me with barely disguised horror.

"Why don't I take these down to the nurses' station," she said briskly, lifting the tin out of my lap. "And get you an apple?"

Why don't you get an apple and stuff it in your pie hole? I wanted to say. During the past week my mother had been bugging me worse than ever. First, it was Ryan: *Why won't you take his calls? Why won't you let him visit? Why won't you give him a chance to make up?* Then, it was Taylor: *Why won't you take her calls? Why did you throw ice cream at the wall when she was here?*

Now, it was my diet. "This hospital food is pure starch!" she informed me. "Why don't I run out to D'Angelo's and get you a salad? A yogurt? A protein bar?"

What's the point?! I wanted to scream. I would never be a model. I knew that. Even without looking in a mirror, I knew. I could tell by the way my mother glanced away every time one of the doctors or nurses checked under the gauze. By her overly chipper comments. *Things are really healing nicely, Alexa! You'll be back to your old self before you know it!* I wanted to grab a cookie and bean my mother in the head.

But what good would that do? It wouldn't change anything. Short of building a time machine to transport me back to kindergarten, where I could tell Taylor to shove her offer of friendship up her fickle, treacherous ass—which would then, obviously, set my life on a completely different track—I was stuck. And if I was going to be stuck, I might as well be home. In my own bed. In my own room, which didn't reek of disinfectant and canned peas.

So I agreed to the psych consult.

The pediatric psychiatrist was a woman, which I didn't expect. All of the other doctors I'd seen had been men. She was also the first one without a lab coat. Instead, she wore a yam-colored sari and jeans. Her shiny black hair was center parted, pulled back in a bun.

"Hello, Alexa," she said, rising from her desk to greet me. "I'm Dr. Kamath."

"Hello," I said. My voice sounded high and flimsy in the fluorescent-lit office, like Tinkerbell's. If Tinkerbell had a voice . . . Did she? I couldn't remember now. Did she talk or just tinkle?

"Alexa?"

"Yeah."

Dr. Kamath smiled. She gestured to several chairs and told me to sit wherever I'd like. "Make yourself comfortable," she said.

Comfortable. Right.

How comfortable could I be, sitting on one side of my butt? When the other side was covered in gauze so thick I felt lopsided? This was my first time venturing out of my bed and into another wing of the hospital. I'd been wearing a johnny for so long I'd forgotten what it felt like to have on real clothes, to sit in a chair like a normal person.

Normal. There's a funny word. No one in their right mind would be using *normal* to describe me now.

"Alexa?"

"Hmm?"

Dr. Kamath was looking at me expectantly.

"Sorry," I mumbled, taking a seat—awkwardly, with both feet tucked up to the left. "Could you repeat the question?"

"I was asking about the pain. How you're managing physically."

I shrugged, shifting my position. "Okay, I guess."

"Are you uncomfortable? Would you like to try a different seat?"

"I'm okay."

Dr. Kamath nodded, scrawled something down on the notepad in front of her. "Have you looked in a mirror yet?"

Just like that, she said it. Like she was talking about the weather. *Have you been outside yet? Is it warm enough for shorts?*

I cleared my throat. "Not yet. No." I thought about all the times I'd almost looked but chickened out. There was a hand mirror on my bedside table. One of the nurses, Claudia, had left if there, for whenever I felt ready to look. But every time I thought I was, I wasn't. I'd pick up the mirror and then I'd think, *Shit*. And I'd put it right back down.

"Okay," Dr. Kamath said. "What about friends? Has anyone been to visit?"

I let out a snort. I didn't mean to, but there it was.

Dr. Kamath smiled. "Care to elaborate?"

You sound like my mother, I thought.

Every day in the hospital my mother had been hounding me about my friends. Who'd called, who hadn't. Who'd sent flowers, who hadn't. My whole *life*, she'd been hounding me. My friends were a constant source of analysis and discussion. Which was ironic since I never said a word about *her* friends—and there were certainly grounds for complaint. The annoying church ladies who dropped by the house without warning, the high school friends who called in the middle of the night, crying about their cheating husbands. Did I bug my mother about *them*? No. But she had no problem bugging *me*. Why didn't I invite anyone besides Taylor over to our house? That pretty Kendall, or Rae, or Marielle Sisk who went to our church? I made up excuses, like the LeFevres' house being more centrally located than ours or me and Marielle having nothing in common. But the truth was, Taylor was the glue. If it wasn't for her, I never would have met Kendall and Rae.

Without Taylor, I felt weird, even with the girls I'd known since kindergarten. I hadn't forgotten sixth grade, when someone wrote *snob* on my locker. Or eighth, when Heidi invited everyone but me to her sleepover. Afterward, when I asked her why, she accused me of acting "too cool" for the rest of them. My mother always said the same thing: "They're jealous." "I don't think so," I'd say. "Oh, yes," she'd insist. "They're jealous. Because you are a beautiful girl."

Well. Not anymore.

"Alexa?"

I realized Dr. Kamath was still waiting for a response. My palms felt hot and moist against my knees.

"A bunch of people came to visit," I said, shifting my weight in the chair to take more pressure off my left bun. "But they're not really my friends."

"No?"

"Well, two of them are. One of them can't stand me. And the rest are just . . . I don't know . . . other girls in my grade."

"I see," Dr. Kamath said, adding something to her notepad.

I felt, suddenly, as though I were being graded. "Are you, like, not planning to let me go home if I don't tell you exactly what you want to hear?"

"What do you think I want to hear?"

I shook my head. "I don't know."

"Do you *want* to go home, Alexa?"

"Yes!" I said. Then, "Why wouldn't I want to go home?"

Instead of answering, Dr. Kamath cocked her head to one side like some exotic bird. She didn't say anything, just looked at me. And looked at me. And looked at me.

I'll bet she thinks if she looks long enough I'll start spilling. I'll bet this is lesson number one in shrink school.

"Okay," I said finally. "The guy who was driving the car . . . that caused the accident, you know? Jarrod . . . ? He came to visit me, too. He's not a friend exactly, but his sister Taylor is. Well, she *was* . . . I threw ice cream at the wall when they were here."

Dr. Kamath nodded as if this made perfect sense. Then, out of nowhere, she started talking about some author I'd never heard of who wrote some book about dying.

"The process by which people deal with grief can be broken down into five distinct stages. *Denial*, the first stage, is usually a temporary—"

"Jarrod didn't die," I cut in. "He just broke his collarbone."

Silence for a moment. Then Dr. Kamath explained that she wasn't talking about Jarrod. She was talking about me.

I gave her what must have been the world's blankest stare, because she went off on some crazy tangent about grief coming in many forms and traumatic injuries being a kind of death. "Traumatic *facial* injuries," she continued, "like the one you've endured, can be particularly devastating, triggering feelings of loss not unlike those felt after the loss of a loved one."

While Dr. Kamath psycho-babbled on, I focused on her teeth, which at first had seemed just a tad yellowish, but now appeared to be getting yellower by the second. *She must drink a butt-load of tea,* I thought. I pictured the bleaching trays that my mother, also a tea drinker, kept on her bedside table and used religiously. Maybe I should share this information with

Dr. Kamath. She might not realize what an easy fix it was. Just pop 'em in your mouth at night, and in the morning . . . voilà!

"Alexa? Does what I'm saying make sense to you?"

"Mm-hm," I nodded. "Absolutely."

Dr. Kamath jotted something down on her notepad. *Why does patient insist on lying?* Or, *Why are patient's shorts unbuttoned? Are shorts too small for rapidly expanding waistline? What has patient been eating?*

"So," Dr. Kamath said, glancing up from her pad again. "Would you like to look in a mirror now, with me? Or would your prefer to do it back in your room, with your family?"

Um. What?

"It's your decision," she went on, "as long as you take that first step here, at the hospital, where you have a support system."

And if I refuse? I wanted to ask. *Then what? You won't let me go home?* But I already knew the answer.

I thought about the girl I'd seen in the elevator, on my way here. She was maybe seven or eight, and her entire head and neck were covered in pink, shiny scars—thick and raised, like mountain ranges on a relief map. I knew I shouldn't stare, and I tried not to, but I couldn't help myself. I kept thinking, *No* way *can I look that bad. I didn't get burned. I still have hair.*

"Alexa," Dr. Kamath said gently. "Seeing your new self is the first step toward healing. Toward accepting your loss."

I wanted to tell her that I didn't lose anything. I was still here. Still me. "Listen," I tried to explain, making my voice calm, my words deliberate. "I'm not planning to kill myself, so if the hospital's worried about getting sued, they can relax."

Dr. Kamath raised her eyebrows.

"My dad's a lawyer."

"Oh?"

"Uh-huh. A public defender. Which is, like, a really important job . . . He's taking time off to be here. Otherwise, you know, he'd be in court."

"Ah." She nodded.

"Yeah," I said, picking at a stray thread on the hem of my shorts. "So I know all about liability and negligence and . . . you know . . . all that stuff." My voice trailed off. Words seemed pointless, suddenly. I didn't want to talk, yet I didn't know what else to do, so I yanked at the thread on my shorts. Yanked and yanked until it broke free.

"Alexa," Dr. Kamath said softly. "I have a mirror, right here in my desk. Why don't we look together?"

I shook my head, thinking no way was I going to do this. Not here. Not now. No fucking way.

I tried to think of my options, and I floundered. Because there weren't any. What was I supposed to do? Stay in the hospital forever? Break every mirror on Earth?

Finally, I looked up from my shorts and gave Dr. Kamath a tiny nod. "Okay," I told her. "Okay, let's get this over with."

Burnt Toast

FUN HOUSE MIRROR. That's what I thought when I saw myself. *No way can this be real. No way in hell. Fun house mirror.*

It came from this movie I saw once, a true story about a kid who was born with some freaky disease that made his head grow out of control. It kept growing and growing, and he looked more and more deformed, until finally his brain gave out and he died. That isn't the saddest part of the story, though. The part that rips your heart out is when his mom takes him to the fair and he goes into one of those fun houses with all the mirrors—the kind that make everyone's face look warped and hideous. Only for this kid, it's the opposite. When he enters the fun house and sees his reflection, it's like some kind of sick joke. He looks normal.

I hadn't thought about that movie in years, until the moment in Dr. Kamath's office when I saw myself. Despite all the ice and anti-inflammatory meds, the right side of my face was still swollen almost beyond recognition. Puffy and purple as a plum, zigzagged all over with stitches. And right in the middle, the tour de force: a square of graft skin so black and crusty it looked as though a miniature slice of burnt toast had been stapled to my cheekbone.

"Oh my God."

"Alexa," Dr. Kamath said gently. "The sutures will dissolve, the swelling will go down, and the bruises will fade. Keep that in mind."

Something came out of my mouth, a cross between a whimper and a moan. I didn't even sound human.

"Listen to me, Alexa. I know the doctors told you already, but I'm going to say it again. It's perfectly normal for the graft to look this way now. . . . Scabbing is . . . Color changes are . . . It's actually a sign of . . . In a few weeks . . ."

Dr. Kamath's lips kept flapping, but the words no longer registered. I was thinking back to the morning of ninth-grade yearbook photos, when I woke up with a zit on my nose and flipped out. I spent half an hour covering my face with my mother's foundation and powder so my picture would be perfect.

A zit.

A single zit, the size of a poppy seed, which would be gone in two days.

If I could go back in time, I would slap myself so hard my head would spin.

Just Shoot Me Now

WHEN I GOT home from the hospital, the number of reflective surfaces in my house seemed to have multiplied. Not just mirrors, but things I'd never noticed before. Computer screens, shiny countertops, glass doors, spoons, even the well-buffed mahogany of the dining room table. As I walked around the house, they all seemed to be saying the same thing: *look, look, look.*

The best place to be was my room, which only had one mirror, and *that* I had already taken off the wall and shoved in my closet, so . . . problem solved.

I lay in my bed, wearing the same pajamas I'd worn yesterday. And the day before. And the day before that.

Outside my window, the ice-cream truck jingled.

In an alternate universe, Taylor and I would be dashing across the lawn in our bathing suits, dollars in hand. Instead, here I was on this beautiful August afternoon, staring at the ceiling. The same ceiling that Taylor helped decorate. One night when she was staying over, we'd pulled a stack of magazines out of my closet—*Rolling Stone* and *Seventeen* and *Elle*—and we'd cut out pictures and made a giant collage, right there over my bed. I remember the two of us standing on pillows, pounding the ceiling with our fists to make the tape stick.

Tear it down, my brain said. *Rip the whole stupid thing down right now.* But my body wouldn't listen. It was too tired, too comfortable lying here under the covers, with the fan blasting.

Any second now, my mother would poke her smooth, blonde head through the door, insisting that I get out of bed. Take a shower. Grease my face. Because the graft didn't have sweat or oil glands it had to be lubricated, twice a day, to prevent cracking. The whole thing made me want to puke. But my mother wouldn't stop bugging me about it.

So I would ignore her, just as I'd been ignoring my cell every time it rang. I didn't want to talk to anyone. I didn't want to see anyone. I didn't want to do *anything.* All I wanted was to be left in peace so I could stare at the ceiling, straight into Johnny Depp's brown eyes. So what if he was old enough to be my father? Johnny Depp had incredible eyes. Deep. Soulful. I could do without Bar Refaeli the Israeli supermodel, however, squinting down at me from on high. Squinting and judging. *What happened to* you*?* she seemed to say, with her ice-blue stare. *What's with the face? How come the doctors couldn't fix you? How come you're still in your pajamas? Don't you know you never get a second chance to make a first impression?*

I lifted one hand in the air, flipped Bar the bird. She only stuck her boobs out farther.

"Lex?" came a voice at the door. Not my mother this time. Ruthie. "Mom told me to come check on you."

Shocker.

I didn't say my sister could come in, but here she was, anyway, holding a half-eaten bagel in one hand and a phone in the other. "Ryan called—for the fiftieth time."

"So?"

"So, call him back. Put the boy out of his misery."

I stared at Ruthie. "You think I care if he's miserable? He *deserves* to be miserable! I'm *never* calling him back. Ever!"

Ruthie shrugged. "Fine. Call your friends, then. Invite them to the barbecue tomorrow."

"Barbecue," I repeated.

"Hello . . . it's Labor Day weekend. Mom's only been cooking for days."

Oh, just shoot me now.

Ruthie must have seen the look on my face because she laughed. "Come on. You didn't seriously think she would cancel. She lives for this crap."

It was true. There were four times a year my mother lived for: Christmas, Ruthie's birthday, my birthday, and Labor Day weekend, when, for as long as I could remember, she had been hosting her famous back-to-school BBQ for the entire neighborhood. This was Laine Mayer's big opportunity to turn on the Carolina charm and bust out the collard greens. And the chicken-fried steak. And the ribs. And the biscuits. And the corn bread. And the sweet tea. There was such an insane amount of food, and it was all so obscenely fattening, that my mother just threw up her hands in the spirit of gluttony and let me eat whatever I wanted. Last Labor Day, Taylor swiped a pitcher of mint juleps. She and I and this other girl, Meagan O'Hallahan, traded swigs behind the garden shed before my neighbor Mr. Jonas caught us and made us trade it in for lemonade.

"Call your peeps," Ruthie said, shoving the phone in my face. "Sasha can pick them up. It'll be fun."

I stared at her. *"Fun?"*

"Yes, Alexa. *Fun*. Remember *fun*? The other F-word?"

"F-you," I muttered.

But Ruthie just smiled. "That's the spirit."

"I can't go to the *barbecue*."

"Why not?"

"Look at me!" I cried, swatting the phone away, feeling my eyeballs prickle. "I'm a freak!"

"You're not a freak."

"I am. I'm a circus freak. I'm right up there with the bearded lady. I'm . . . the butt-faced girl."

"So wear a hat," Ruthie suggested calmly. "One of those big straw ones of Mom's."

I snorted. "Right."

Ruthie shook her head.

"What?"

"I don't get it. Everyone wants to see you. Your friends keep calling, and you refuse to talk to them."

"Everyone wants to see me," I repeated. "Uh-huh."

I could just imagine what Taylor had been telling people, about my hospital flip-out, my ice cream–flinging fit. I knew why everyone wanted to see me. It was the same reason why, when you see a bum on the street—even though he's crazy and stinky and muttering and he gives you the creeps—you can't stop staring.

When I said this to Ruthie, she frowned. "That's a terrible analogy."

"Easy for you to say," I shot back. "You don't have your butt stapled to your cheekbone."

"What do you want me to do, Lexi? Feel sorry for you?"

I stared at my sister in disbelief. "Yes!"

"Well," Ruthie said slowly, "if that's what you want, then you'll have to find someone else to do it because I won't join your pity party."

I shrugged. "Fine."

My sister was staring at me. I could feel it. But my eyes were back on the ceiling, glued to Johnny Depp. I tried to imagine it was just the two of us. No Israeli supermodels, no sisters. Just me and Johnny. Maybe on a cruise ship. Or a beach. Better yet, a desert island, where no one would ever—

"Lex."

"What." I didn't move my eyes, just my lips.

"Call your friends," Ruthie said. She dropped the phone onto my bed, then turned to walk out of the room.

"You don't understand," I started to say.

Ruthie paused in the doorway. "Try me."

My throat burned. I knew if I said another word I would cry, so I just shook my head.

"Come to the barbecue, Lex," Ruthie said. "Wear a big hat. Make a fashion statement."

My sister, whose idea of a fashion statement was cutoff sweats and the same Chuck Taylor sneakers she'd worn since eighth grade. Whose eyebrows were so thick they practically met in the middle, yet she'd never picked up a pair of tweezers in her life.

"Don't let your face define you," she said.

It hit like a sledgehammer, the irony. I would have laughed, but I could tell from Ruthie's expression that she was dead serious.

"Okay," I said, matching my sister's solemn tone. "I won't let my face define me. I'll let my *butt* define me. Oh, wait. My butt *is* my face."

"Oh, wait," Ruthie said. "Your sarcasm *isn't* invited to the barbecue."

I'm pretty sure she missed my point. Or she was trying to be funny. Either way it backfired, because all I did was yank the covers over my head and close my eyes.

I celebrated Labor Day weekend in my room, in my pajamas. Sitting cross-legged on my bed, I systematically polished off two plates of barbecue, compliments of my dad. *"Are you sure you don't want to join us, Beans?"* he'd said, the first time he came up to check on me. *"Everyone's asking for you out there. It's not the same without you."*

I was sure.

Later, he brought out the big guns. "It would really mean a lot to your mother if you would come outside."

I replied with a long, low, rumbling belch.

"Well, if you change your mind . . ."

My father's false cheer was almost more than I could bear. After he left, I tore into the dessert plate like a starving animal, shoving key lime pie into my mouth with my bare hands. I knew I should stop eating. I wasn't even hungry. But my body had long since stopped listening to my brain.

"Yo, Lex." A voice from the hall interrupted my feeding frenzy. "I'm coming in."

At first, I couldn't place the voice. Then an auburn head popped through the door, and it made perfect sense. Meagan O'Hallahan, the only girl in Millbridge, Connecticut, who used the word *yo*.

Meagan's father, Frank O'Hallahan, was the chief of police and good friends with my dad. Meagan and I would have been closer if she didn't go to Weston Academy for school, and Maine every summer for camp. I liked her a lot, but I got to see her only a few times a year.

"What's shakin', bacon?" Meagan bounded into my room all cheery, ponytail swinging.

Then she got a look at me. "Oh . . . um . . ."

I could only imagine what she saw. For starters, I was still in bed, surrounded by dirty dishes. My hands and pajama cuffs were coated in barbecue sauce and chunks of pie, and my hair hadn't seen shampoo in days. Then, of course, there was the face. No more bandages. Nowhere to hide.

"Gosh . . ." Meagan said. "I'm sorry, I just thought . . . My family's out at the party and your mom said . . ."

Never, in the ten years I'd known her, had I seen Meagan O'Hallahan flustered.

Her dad wasn't just the police chief, he was also some kind of wrestling champion, and her mom was a CEO. She had four older brothers, each one bolder and wilder than the next. The

O'Hallahans didn't *do* flustered. And yet, here was Meagan, stammering away, her eyes flitting from my face to her hands to a spot on the wall above my head.

"It's . . . good to see you," she finished lamely. "You look great."

Right.

"Really," she insisted.

Meagan tried to change the subject, saying she was glad that I was okay. And that Jarrod was okay. Her brothers, Mark and Michael, who played peewee football with Jarrod back in the day, ran into him at the Dairy Freeze, and Jarrod said—

"*Jarrod* said? What exactly did *Jarrod* say?"

Meagan shook her head. "Nothing. Just that he was driving the car when it crashed. And that he and Taylor went to see you in the hospital and you were . . . you know . . . still recovering."

I laughed, a short bark, but Meagan didn't seem to notice. She was too busy trying to avoid looking at me.

"Anyway, my dad said the accident report showed there was no trace of drugs or alcohol in his system at the time of the crash, and he wasn't driving over the limit, so . . . thank God, right? That everything turned out the way it did?"

"Yes, thank *God*," I said, my voice sliding into sarcasm. "Everything turned out just beautiful."

Meagan grimaced. "I'm sorry, Lex. I didn't mean—"

"Especially for Taylor. Did you hear? She has a new boyfriend."

"Yeah . . ." Meagan said. "About that . . . there's someone who—"

"Oh, so you *did* hear. Did you talk to her?"

"No, I—"

"Oh, so you talked to *him*. Of course. Old Weston Academy buddies. I should have known."

"Lexi—"

"Are *you* hooking up with him, too? Is that what you're here to tell me?"

"Lex."

"What?" I snapped.

But before Meagan could answer, a voice from the hall cut in. "Maybe this wasn't such a good idea."

My stomach sank.

I thought about diving under the bed.

I thought about picking up an empty soda can and hurling it at the door.

I thought about doing a lot of things. But instead, I heard my voice ring out, hostess style, "Come on in, Ryan! The more the merrier!"

And now, incredibly, here he was. My lying, cheating boyfriend, standing in the doorway to my bedroom.

Ex-boyfriend, I reminded myself fiercely. Even though Ryan was wearing a shirt I loved—the royal blue polo I'd given him for his birthday, which made his eyes even bluer. Even though his hair was damp from the shower, with comb tracks in it, and I could smell his soap from here. A clean, lemony scent that always made me dizzy. Even though—

"Should I . . ." Meagan started to say, glancing from me to Ryan and back again. "Do you guys want me to, like . . ."

"Oh, no," I said. "*Stay*. Pull up a chair. . . . You, too, Ry . . . Come on. Don't be a stranger."

Ryan took a tentative step forward. "Hey, Lexi."

I said nothing. I was too busy watching the expression on his face as he moved closer. Closer. Close enough to observe the carnage head-on.

"Oh, shit."

I knew he didn't mean to say those words, just as I knew that the flinch in his eyes was involuntary—like a muscle spasm or a sneeze. But that didn't stop the sick feeling that came over me, as though someone were wringing out my stomach like a washcloth.

"Leave," I murmured.

"Lexi, I . . . crap . . . I didn't mean—"

"I don't care. Leave."

"Lex—" Meagan started to say, but I cut her off, too.

"I mean it," I said. "I need you both to get out of my room. Please." My voice was rising, but I didn't care. "Now! Get out of my room!"

Ryan looked stunned. Meagan's face was as red as her hair. You could practically see the thought bubble rising over her head. *She's losing it.*

"You're right! I'm not just ugly now! I'm crazy, too!"

Ryan tried one last time. "Lex, you're not—"

"Shut up, Ryan. Why don't you go find Taylor? I'm sure she'd be happy to give a repeat performance!"

Just as I was bending down to pick up a plate, my mother's head poked through the doorway.

"Alexa *Grace*." Her voice was low, shocked. "*What* is going on up here?"

"Just playing a little Frisbee." I smiled and flung the plate across the room, where it hit the edge of my desk, cracked, and fell to the floor.

"You may experience some anger," Dr. Kamath had said during our last session, the day I left the hospital. *"Anger is a natural part of the grief process."*

I wondered what Dr. Kamath would think if she could see me now, standing on the bed in my barbecued pajamas, screaming and hurling dinnerware. Was this what she meant by "natural"?

You Don't Mean That

THAT NIGHT, I was still mad. Mad at my mother for inviting Ryan to our house, for allowing him to come upstairs. "I can't believe you did that to me!" I said, pausing to take an angry bite of ice cream—my bedtime snack. "You never even asked!"

While my mother sponged down the countertop, she fed me lines about how Ryan and I needed to "talk through our problems," and "put this fight behind us," until I couldn't stand it any longer.

"We didn't have a fight, Mom."

"What do you mean?"

"We broke up, okay? It's over."

"*What?*" she said.

"Okay, we didn't technically break up, but we might as well have. He cheated on me."

My mother dropped her dishrag. "*No.*"

"Yes."

"Ryan wouldn't do that."

"He would," I said, "and he did."

My mother shook her head. There must be some kind

of a misunderstanding, she insisted. The Danos went to our church. Mrs. Dano was on the soup kitchen committee. Ryan was a good boy, a gentleman.

Right. I wondered what kind of "gentleman" my mother would think Ryan was if she saw him with his pants around his ankles.

"I can't believe this," she said.

"Believe it," I told her.

Then, to prove that Ryan wasn't the perfect boyfriend she thought he was, I dropped the Taylor bomb. Not the gory details, just the facts: Ryan hooked up with Taylor. I saw it with my own eyes. *That's* why I wasn't taking her calls. *That's* why she didn't come to the barbecue. It had nothing to do with Jarrod and the accident; it was all about Taylor's betrayal.

"Well," my mother said dryly. "*That* doesn't surprise me."

This wasn't exactly the response I'd expected. "What do you *mean* it doesn't surprise you?"

My mother sighed. "Taylor has always been jealous of you, Alexa."

"Taylor has *never* been jealous of me," I said, feeling a weird flash of defensiveness.

"Oh, yes she has. From the minute she met you."

"Please," I muttered.

"Remember the toe shoes?"

Ah, yes. The toe shoes. I don't know why my mother loves to rehash this story, but she does. Here is how it goes: In second grade, I, like most of the girls in my class, wanted to be a prima ballerina. On Saturday mornings, a whole bunch of us would put on our black leotards and pink tights and sashay across the floor with Miss Decker, while she barked at us to suck in our stomachs and point our toes. Miss Decker was a taskmaster, but I loved her. I loved her long sinewy legs and the way her feet pointed out when she walked, like a duck's. I loved the way she twisted her long, black hair into a bun so tight that not one hair escaped, no matter how fast she pirouetted. I loved how tickly her fingers were when they traced our spines as we bent over the barre, showing us the correct position. And I loved that Miss Decker always used me as the example of how to do things. *"Class,"* she would say. *"Look at Alexa. See how Alexa is reaching her arms up high, like tree branches?"*

On my eighth birthday—a ballet party, of course, at Decker's Dance Studio—Miss Decker surprised me with a new pair of pink satin toe shoes. This was a present no girl in the class had ever received and I had therefore not expected.

"They're really from your parents," Taylor said as she examined the toe shoes in their tissue-paper nest.

"No, they're not," I said. "They're from Miss Decker."

"Nuh-uh," Taylor said. "I've been to a jillion ballet birthday parties, and Miss Decker has never given a single present."

"Go ask my mom if you don't believe me."

"Fine," Taylor said. "I will."

I watched as she marched across the shiny wood floor to where my mother was bent over a table, slicing up triangles of pink-frosted cake. And I saw the look on her face as she heard the truth.

"See?" I said, feeling a surge of triumph when Taylor returned. "I *told* you they were from Miss Decker."

Taylor said nothing more on the subject, but she never took another dance class after that. Within a week she had renounced ballet, calling it "stupid and sissy," and moved on to horseback riding. In my mother's mind, this was sour grapes on Taylor's part, but all I know is after she quit, dance wasn't fun anymore. By the end of second grade, I had quit, too.

"Who cares about the toe shoes?" I said to my mother. "We were kids!"

"That doesn't mean she's any less jealous of you now. That's only one example—"

"Whatever," I muttered, walking to the freezer and taking out the ice cream. While she rambled on, I helped myself to another scoop of chocolate. Then strawberry. Then butter pecan.

My mother stared at me. "Are you planning to eat *all* that ice cream?"

"Yup," I said.

"Didn't you just have some?"

"Yup."

"Well, don't you think you should—"

"Okay!" I said, slamming my bowl on the counter. "Point taken!" I was raising my voice, something my mother abhorred, but I didn't care. "Ice cream is fattening! The whole world is jealous of me! I get it! You've been telling me my whole life!"

"I tell you!" she said, yelling right back. "Because you are a beautiful girl! And I love you! And you need to think about these things!"

For a second, I was so stunned by the intensity of her reaction that I didn't think about her words. Then they hit me.

"Look at my face," I said, a catch in my throat. "You call this beautiful?"

My mother bent to retrieve the dishrag from the floor and resumed her wiping. When she spoke, her voice was calm again, measured. "You need to give it time. You're still healing. It's going to take a few weeks until—"

"Look at me," I said fiercely. "A few weeks aren't going to make any difference."

She shook her head. "That's not true. The doctors said—"

"I was there!" I heard the slightly hysterical rise in my voice that meant I was about to lose it. "'*Skin-graft scars will never look like ordinary skin.*' Direct quote! You act like everything's fine and it's not! You *know* it's not! You can't even look me in the face!"

Before she could say another word, I ran out of the kitchen. When I got to my room, I slammed the door. Instead of crying, I was shaking all over. My entire body. Even my hair follicles.

I climbed into bed, pulled the covers up to my chin, and stared at the ceiling. Johnny Depp stared back. While my eyes stayed dry, his looked as warm and wet as melted chocolates. I held his gaze for the longest time, wishing he would say something—anything—to tell me I wasn't going crazy.

In the morning, my dad knocked on my door. "I come bearing Ovaltine," he said. As he handed me the glass, I felt an unexpected wave of sadness. I remembered all the times when I was little, before he worked eighty-hour weeks, how

I would wake up early and he would make me Ovaltine and cinnamon toast and the two of us would sit together in the breakfast nook, reading the funnies.

My whole life I couldn't wait to get older. But suddenly, in that moment, I wanted to be five again.

"Mmm," my dad said, taking a gulp from his own glass. "Dee-lish . . . Try it, Beans. I made it just the way you like it, extra thick."

I took a sip.

"Well?"

"It's good, Dad. Thanks."

"So . . ." he said, leaning against the wall in his nonwork uniform: khaki suit, seersucker tie. "Taylor called. She said you won't answer your cell and she needs to talk to you."

"So?" My voice sounded cool, but my stomach did a flip-flop.

"So, I've been thinking about what I said earlier, about keeping your distance from the LeFevres, and . . . well . . . I've reevaluated."

I gave him a blank look.

"I think you should call her back."

"What?" I said. *"Why?"*

"Because she's your friend. Because it's not her fault her brother's a reckless—if not criminally negligent—driver. Because you've been sitting in your room, alone, for . . . how many days now?"

I shrugged.

"Beans," my dad said quietly. "I'm going back to work tomorrow, and I'm not going to be around. I need to know that you have some moral support."

Clearly, my mother hadn't shared the news yet, what Taylor did to me. Clearly, he had no idea that Taylor was the last person in the world whose support I needed.

"Dad," I said. "I'm fine."

"Really?" he said like he knew I was lying.

I paused, thinking of all the truthful responses I could give. *No, I'm not fine. I'm horrible. I hate Taylor. I hate Ryan. I'm scared I might be ugly for the rest of my life.* My dad would listen; he wouldn't judge. But whenever I told him my problems in the past, he'd try to fix everything. Struggling in geometry? Let's get you a tutor. Missed three shots in the last game? Let's set up a goal in the backyard. My father was Mr. Fix-it, the ultimate problem solver. His mission in coming to my room this morning: to make me better—to restore me to my former, happy self.

"Why don't you hop out of bed," he said, "and get dressed, and I'll take you and Taylor out for lunch."

"It's lunchtime?" I said. Ignoring the obvious.

"It's one fifteen."

"Wow, I had no idea it was so late already . . . huh. Time really flies when you're—"

"Beans," my dad said gently, cutting me off.

"What?"

"You can't stay in bed forever. You can't keep pushing your friends away. At some point, you're going to have to get up and face reality."

I flinched at the words "face reality." Not that he meant the pun, but still. I didn't exactly need reminding.

"Just give me one more day," I said.

"One more day?"

I nodded.

"All right," he said, reaching out to ruffle my hair. "I'm going to hold you to that."

"Okay."

After my dad left, I noted with satisfaction that I hadn't actually promised anything. *"Give me one more day."* What did that even mean? In the morning I would hop out of bed, clap my hands, and start calling people?

Please.

I hopped out of bed, all right. I hopped out of bed and I moved operations down to the TV room, where I parked myself on the couch for three days straight. The same three days when everyone else was getting ready for school.

"Are you coming tomorrow?" Kendall demanded, when I finally answered my cell phone.

"Tomorrow?" I repeated, marveling at my clueless tone.

"Hello . . . the first day of school?"

"*High* school," Rae's voice piped in. "The first day of *high* school."

"Am I on speakerphone?"

"Four-way call," Kendall said. "Taylor's on the other line."

Sitting on the couch, I felt a gush of hot lava rise inside me. I'd been blindsided! Not that Kendall and Rae were trying to hurt me, but still. What were they thinking? What was I supposed to say? I already told Taylor the night of the party: I hated her, I would hate her forever. To say it again—*By the way, I still hate you*—would be stupid. Besides, I didn't want to sound like I cared. I was beyond caring.

When Taylor said, "Hey, Lex," I said nothing. When she asked in a voice as soft and familiar as the Hello Kitty pillow I'd slept with since I was two, "How are you feeling?" I said nothing. Zero. Zilch.

"Okayyy," Rae said, filling the silence. "So we're meeting at my house at seven. My mom is all, 'I'll drive you girls,' and I'm like, 'Hell no, woman! We are *not* showing up in a minivan, we are taking the *bus*.'"

"Right," Kendall said. "We are *busin'* it."

Last year, Taylor and I walked to school. The junior high was half a mile from my house, and the LeFevres were on the way, so I would pick up Tay and the two of us would walk together. Even if it was raining or frigid cold outside, even if one of our parents offered to drive, we still walked. We liked to walk. But this year was different. The senior high was all the way across town, so anyone on our side of the highway who didn't have their license yet took the bus. Correction: anyone who *planned to attend high school* and didn't have their license yet took the bus.

I did not plan to attend high school. The day after the barbecue, I'd made my position clear. *"Hire a tutor,"* I told my parents. *"Sign me up for GED courses online. Homeschool me. I don't care. But I am not going."*

And that is what I said now, to Kendall and Rae and Taylor: "I'm not going to school tomorrow."

"So, what," Kendall said, "are you starting next week?"

"No."

"Did the doctor say you had to wait?"

"It has nothing to do with that," I said. The truth. At my last checkup I'd learned my face was healing "beautifully," and as long as I kept the graft hydrated and wore sunscreen every day I didn't even need bandages. I could resume all of my "normal" activities.

"So . . ." Rae said.

"So, I just don't want to go back to school."

"Like . . . at all?"

"Right."

"Are you serious?" Taylor sounded genuinely shocked. "Is this because of what happened with me and Ryan?"

It's the first time she's mentioned his name, and suddenly I'm like the girl from *The Exorcist,* head spinning around and puke flying from my mouth. "Because of what *happened*? With you and *Ryan*? What *happened* with you and *Ryan*, exactly? Enlighten me."

"Here we go," Rae murmured.

"Lex," Taylor said quietly. "Let's not do this over the phone. We need to talk in person."

I gave a snort that said, *Never gonna happen.*

"What do you want me to say?" Her voice was low, pleading. "Tell me and I'll say it."

"Tell you what to *say*? You want me to hand you a *script*?" I hated the way I sounded. I hated it, but I couldn't help myself.

"It's not that complicated, Taylor. A baby could do it! A newborn baby could apologize better than you can!"

Then she actually had the nerve to get mad. "What do you think I've been trying to do? Why do you think I've been calling you every five minutes for the past month? What am I supposed to do when you keep blowing me off?"

"Oh, this is *my* fault now?"

"It's not like I haven't been punished," Taylor said, her voice rising. "My dad grounded me for two weeks!"

"Oooo. Two whole weeks."

"Come on, guys," Kendall said. "Don't do this."

"Yeah," Rae chimed in, "life is too short. And you've been friends for too long."

When I heard those words, they hit me literally. *"You've been friends for too long."* "You're right," I said. "This friendship is beyond over."

"You don't mean that," Rae said.

"Yeah. I do."

My throat thickened, but I pushed past it. I told Taylor that I meant what I said. I told her to stop calling me. I told her to stop texting me. I told her, for the very last time, to stay out of my life.

I didn't even give her a chance to respond. After I hung up, I sat on the couch, holding the phone in my lap and waiting for it to ring.

It didn't.

Delinquent

ON THE FIRST day of school, I watched from the kitchen as Ruthie the senior backed out of the driveway in her VW clunker. A few minutes later, a big yellow school bus—my big yellow school bus—slowed to a stop at the end of my street, idled, then pulled away.

Hence my mother's sigh, her sideways glance in my direction. Was I sure I didn't want her to drive me? It wasn't too late. If I hopped in the shower right now we could still make it.

"I told you," I said. "I'm not going."

"Well, if you change your mind . . ."

"I won't."

"But if you do . . ."

"I *won't*. God, Mom. How are you not getting this?"

"All right." My mother nodded, rubbing the counter with her dishrag. "All right, I understand."

"Good," I said.

I couldn't believe she was pushing the school thing. Last night, in the Mayer Family Debate about Education, my mom had been my biggest ally. While my sister threw out terms like *pity party* and *enabling*—and my father reminded me that when he took the job in Connecticut, he chose Millbridge specifically for the *quality of the public schools*, public schools that have an *anti-truancy statute*—my mom was the one who insisted I have time to heal.

But now, with Ruthie back to school and my dad back to being a workaholic, maybe she didn't know what to do with me. Maybe me staying home all day was cramping her style.

"I don't need a babysitter," I told her. "Whatever you need to do, errands or whatever, just do it."

"Well," my mother said, "I already went to the market . . . and the dry cleaning won't be ready until tomorrow . . . and—I know!" Her face lit up. "Why don't the two of us go into the city? We haven't done any back-to-school shopping yet, and the stores won't be crowded. We could grab a bite, get you a few cute outfits for fall. . . ."

"Cute outfits for fall." Ha!

What was the point of shopping if I was going to spend the rest of my life in my pajamas? Besides, the thought of me and my mother in a dressing room together—under fluorescent lights, surrounded by mirrors—made me sick. I literally couldn't stomach the thought. Yet I couldn't stomach the thought of her at home, either, hovering over me.

"Thanks," I said, "but I don't think I'm up for the city today."

"Well," my mom countered, "how about just Lord and Taylor? We could find you a little dress, some heels. . . ."

I stared at her. "Why would I want a *dress* and *heels*?"

She smiled, swinging her dishrag through the air like a pom-pom. "Homecoming!"

"What?"

"Homecoming!" she repeated, gesturing to the calendar on the wall. "October twenty-fourth!"

Of course. The minute my mother started planning an event, or whenever she received something in the mail—a baptism invitation, a tooth-cleaning reminder, a school calendar—she would document it, in color code, on the kitchen wall. Every upcoming occasion in our lives from here to eternity.

"You and Ryan will make up," she continued, "or another boy will ask you. Either way, you'll want to look your best at the dance."

Oh, there were so many things wrong with this I didn't know where to begin. How could my mother, who was born in 1972, still think we were living in the 1950s? Nobody went to dances as couples anymore. Not to mention the fact that there was no way in hell I would show *this* face on a dance floor, high school gym or otherwise. I hated to rain on my mother's homecoming parade, but . . .

"I'm not going to any dance. Ever."

"Of course you are," she said brightly.

I told her no, I wasn't, and if she thought otherwise then she was in for a lifetime of disappointment.

"Oh, honey," my mother sighed as I grabbed a bag of Chips Ahoy! from the pantry and marched right back to the couch.

I turned on the TV and started flipping around—one stupid game show and soap opera after another, reminding me of how I was wasting my life sitting there. Finally, I stopped on 61. I watched a bunch of girls wearing cheerleading uniforms and shiny, wholesome smiles, standing at their lockers, talking about the big game. *"Omigosh, you guys! Isn't high school the best?!"*

What a crock, I thought as I started to cry. I pictured my face on one of their bodies. Not that I ever wanted to be a cheerleader; that was my mother's dream, not mine. I just wanted to see what I'd look like—the butt-faced girl, standing at her locker, trying to act normal.

It was a vision too pitiful for words.

Day two . . . Day five . . . Day seven . . . Day ten.

In all my years as a student, from nursery school to elementary school to junior high, I had never missed so many days in a row. Not for sickness. Certainly not for playing hooky. And now here I was, two weeks into my high school career, already a delinquent. And bored out of my mind.

In my former life, if I ever got bored, I would call Taylor. My best friend, the boredom buster. Needless to say, I wasn't doing that now. Which left me with three options: daytime TV, food, and feeling sorry for myself.

Lying on the couch, all I could think about was the fact that I was stuck at home like some kind of leper, while Taylor and Ryan were living it up on the sports fields. I knew from Kendall and Rae, who'd texted me from the gym as soon as the team rosters were posted, that Ryan made varsity football, and Taylor made varsity field hockey.

Well, I thought bitterly. *At least Mr. Dano will be happy.* Ryan's dad used to play Division 1 football for Notre Dame, and whenever I was over at the Danos', that's all Mr. Dano could talk about. Football, football, football. He cared about football, it seemed, more than he cared about finding a job. No way would he have been satisfied if Ryan only made JV.

Taylor making varsity wasn't a shock, either. She and I were the best players on our ninth-grade team. Up until the accident, the two of us had practiced every day of the summer—running drills, even timing each other in the two-mile, to ensure we were in the best shape possible for tryouts.

Tryouts that I missed.

A team that, even if the coach took pity on me and let me try out late, I would never play for. Because the mere thought of running down the hockey field—my hair in a ponytail, my face bare to the world—filled me with dread.

The longer I thought about it, the worse I felt. Why should Taylor get to play when I couldn't? Why was I the one to end up looking like this when she deserved the punishment? And why, for God's sake, did I *defend* her to my mother?

This tsunami of self-pity swept me off the couch and down the hall to the bathroom, where I stood in front of the mirror for a long time, squeezing my eyes shut.

Finally, I opened them.

Even though the stitches had dissolved since the last time I'd looked, and the bruises had faded from a deep purple to a sick, yellowish green—even though the entire right side of my face was no longer swollen up like a puffer fish—I still looked horrible. Worse than horrible. *Hideous.* All you could see when you looked at me was the graft. It drew your eyes in like a target. A two-by-two-inch target of angry, red butt-skin with a crispy maroon border, about two millimeters higher than the rest of my face. It was the ugliest, most wretched thing you have ever seen in your life.

"I hate you," I said to my reflection. "I hate you so much."

The girl in the mirror glared at me. I took a few steps back, trying to see the big picture. I was still wearing pajamas, but since my mother forced me into the shower last night, my hair was finally clean. Clean and thick and shiny as ever, the color of corn silk, down to my shoulder blades. "Barbie hair," Taylor used to call it. "Rapunzel hair."

All I could think now was how incongruous it was. How could someone so ugly have such beautiful hair? It made no sense. It was absurd.

The girl in the mirror smirked at me. *You know what to do, silly.*

I opened the medicine cabinet and peered inside. Lying on the second shelf from the top, in their faux-leather carrying case, were my mother's good scissors. I remembered how bossy she always was about these scissors—how Ruthie and I were never allowed to use them for craft projects, not even for cutting thread—like they were made of thousand-year-old crystal.

Now, holding them in my hand, I felt their power. The metal was cool and slick against my skin.

I reached for a hunk of hair. As I cut, the blades of the scissors made a soft, satisfying swooshing sound. An eight-inch stretch of blonde fell to the sink.

Never in my life had I seen so much of my hair *off* my

head. For fifteen years, my mother wouldn't let me get more than a trim, no matter how hard I begged. Well, who was she to dictate what I did with my own hair?

I reached for another hunk.

Swooosh.

Then another.

Swooosh.

Then—

"Oh. My. God."

I jumped, just as the silhouette of my sister appeared behind me in the mirror.

"Jesus, Ruthie!" I said, whirling around. "You almost made me stab my eye out!"

She stared at me. "You're pulling a Deenie."

"What?"

"Deenie," she repeated. "You're channeling Deenie."

"Who the hell is *Deenie*?"

"You know," Ruthie said. "Pretty girl with the messed-up spine? Hacks off her own hair when she gets the back brace?"

I shook my head.

"You've never read *Deenie*?"

"No," I said, annoyed. *"So?"*

"*So,* it's only one of the greatest books of all time. Vintage Judy Blume . . . *Please* tell me you know who Judy Blume is."

I shrugged.

Ruthie gasped. "Blasphemy!"

"Did you come in here to lecture me on literature?"

"Actually, I came in here to pee, but—"

"Then pee," I snapped, turning back to the mirror. "And get out."

I grabbed a fresh hunk of hair, lifted the scissors again.

"Oh, no," Ruthie said. "No, no, no." She whipped out a hand so fast I didn't have time to stop her.

"What are you *doing*? Give those *back*."

"No."

I lunged for the scissors. Ruthie hopped up on the toilet, holding them over her head.

"What the *hell*, Ruth!"

"Trust me. You'll thank me later."

"No I won't!"

"Yes," she said calmly. "You will. . . . Now get dressed. We're going for a ride."

"I'm not going anywhere."

Ruthie sighed. She tucked the scissors into the back pocket of her jeans and hopped down from the toilet. She took two steps forward, grabbed both my arms, and leaned in so close I could smell the peanut butter on her breath. "If I have to drag you out of this house, I will do it."

Brush your teeth, I thought.

"I'm serious, Lex. You need to get out of here."

"Whatever," I said, even though she had a point. I was going stir-crazy. Spending the first two weeks of school in exile was one thing. But the first official weekend of fall? In New England? If I didn't smell some of that good, leafy air soon, I might shrivel up and die.

"Is that 'whatever,' you're coming?" Ruthie asked. "Or 'whatever,' I have to drag you?"

I looked at her fingers gripping my arm, the ragged cuticles, the bitten-down nails. "You need a manicure," I told her.

"Don't change the subject."

"I'm not."

Ruthie squeezed harder.

"Fine!" I said. "I'll come! You don't have to break my arms off!"

"You'll get dressed?"

"Yes," I said. Then I thought better of it. I would get in a car with my sister, let her drive me around, but no way was I showing my face in public. I would exit the front seat when, and only when, we were home again, which meant there was no point in changing out of my pajamas.

"What you see is what you get," I said.

Ruthie nodded. "Fair enough."

"Okay then."

"Where are you taking me?" I asked as my sister merged onto the highway, heading north.

"Just sit back and relax," Ruthie said. "You're supposed to trust me, remember?"

"That's what I'm afraid of."

"Relax," she said again, reaching over to click on the radio. Some crappy classical station.

I sighed loudly.

"What?"

"Can't we listen to something else?"

"What's wrong with Mozart?"

"There's nothing wrong with Mozart. I'd just like to listen to music from this century."

"Expand your horizons," Ruthie said. "Try a little culture." She turned up the volume. Violins soared.

"C'mon!" I said.

"Shhhh . . . listen . . . it's soothing."

"It sucks!"

Ruthie smiled serenely. "My car, my tunes."

"I hate you," I muttered, pulling the hood of her sweatshirt tight over my ears. At first, when she'd made me put it on—to smuggle my hair past our mother—I'd protested. Nothing screams "dork" like an Interlochen Arts Camp sweatshirt.

But hoods do come in handy. Especially if you pull the cords tight, so all that's left is a tiny nose-hole. The rest of your face is cocooned in soft, dark fleece. You're not just cozy, you're practically invisible.

The next thing I knew, the car had stopped. I poked my head out momentarily, blinking in the sun. "Where are we?"

"Westerly, Rhode Island," Ruthie said.

"Why?"

"Because nobody knows us here. *And* . . . to visit what appears to be a fine haircutting establishment with an even finer name: Mar's Hairy Business."

"What?"

"You heard me."

"Oh no," I said, shaking my head. "No way."

"Yes way. Someone's got to fix your hair . . . what's left

of it . . . I'd offer myself, but I have *zero* skills in that department, so—"

"I told you. I'm not getting out of the car."

"Well then," Ruthie said, "I'll just have to ask Mar if she'll come to you."

"That's ridiculous."

"Yes," Ruthie said. "It is."

I knew my sister was trying to reverse psychologize me, but I wasn't about to fall for her tricks. No way, no how. She might have been the budding lawyer in the family, but my position was firm.

Okay, the only reason I was following Ruthie into Mar's Hairy Business was this: bribery. If I agreed to let some stranger fix my hair, Ruthie had to let me decide what would be done to *her.* Hair, face, nails, the works. I could have my sister shaved, plucked, pierced, tattooed, anything I wanted. That was why I was walking up the steps and through the tinkly glass door right now. Payback.

"Hi there." Ruthie marched right up to the reception area. "Are you Mar?"

The girl behind the counter shook her blue, spiky head. "Mar's in Florida. I'm Luna."

"Well, Luna," my sister said, "I'm Benny, and this is my sister, Brandy. And we'd like to get our hair cut."

I stifled a snort. Benny and Brandy were the hamsters Ruthie and I got for Christmas when I was six and she was eight. We used to dress them up in doll clothes and pull them around in Ruthie's Radio Flyer wagon. When they died, we held a hamster funeral of epic proportions. Programs. Refreshments. Even a song-and-dance routine we'd choreographed ourselves.

"Brandy," my sister continued, grabbing my hand and yanking me toward the counter, "has a bit of a hair issue that needs addressing."

"Uh-huh," Luna said, nodding, taking in my hooded head and my pajama bottoms. "Okay."

"And *Benny,*" I squeezed Ruthie's hand so tight the bones scraped together, "has *several* issues—as you can see—all of which will need to be addressed today. That is, if you have time . . ."

Luna gestured to the back of the salon, which was empty except for a white-haired lady with a bad perm, hunched under a dryer. "I think I can squeeze you in."

"Great!" Ruthie said, grinning at me.

I shot her my dirtiest look.

Then, before I could stop it from happening, she reached over and tugged down my hood.

"Oh my God," Luna murmured, one purple-manicured hand flying to her mouth. "What happened?"

"Bear attack," Ruthie said, glancing at me and shaking her head sadly. "When we were in Maine a few weeks ago, camping."

"Seriously?" Luna's eyes were wide, staring at my face, my hair, the whole ensemble.

I shrugged, as in, *These things happen.*

"Oh my God," Luna said again.

Ruthie nodded solemnly. "Every day's a gift."

✦ ✦ ✦

By the time Luna was finished with us, our mother had left four voice mails on Ruthie's cell. She wanted us to know that she was "worried sick" and that "the least her daughters could do" was to answer their phones.

"Why is she having a conniption?" I said. "She was *thrilled* I was leaving the house. She practically pushed me out the door!"

Ruthie shrugged. "Maybe she thinks we got in an accident."

"Please," I muttered.

I wanted to blow our mother off, pretend we didn't get the messages. It's not like we were doing anything wrong. We'd said we'd be back for dinner.

But Ruthie pointed out that it was already five o'clock. If we didn't call now, by the time we got home our mother would have summoned not only the state police, but also the National Guard.

"Good point," I said.

Ruthie handed me the phone.

"No way!" I told her. "This whole thing was your idea." Which was a tough line of reasoning to refute, even for Ruthie.

It took a full five minutes for her to calm our mother down. Violation number one: not answering our cell phones. Violation number two: driving out of state without her permission.

When Ruthie hung up, I said, "You think she's flipping *now*? Wait until she sees my hair."

"Are you kidding?" Ruthie said. "You look great."

"Right," I said.

My new hair—short and spiky on the left (thanks to my

hack job), chin-length layers on the right (to cover the graft)—was bizarre. And eerily reminiscent of Taylor's bi-level 'do, circa fourth grade.

"I'm serious," Ruthie insisted, shifting in her seat to face me. "It's cool. Funkified."

"Whatever."

I felt an unexpected pang, looking at Ruthie. For the first time in her life she had groomed eyebrows. And a sleek, side-parted hairstyle that made her nose seem more delicate, even regal. Ruthie seemed to have noticed, too. Ever since we got in the car she'd been sneaking little glances at herself in the side-view mirror. I wished suddenly that I'd told Luna to do something unflattering. A buzz cut. Or a Mohawk. Then I felt bad. "You're the one who looks great," I told my sister.

She shook her head. "No, I don't."

"Yes," I said, a bit of an edge in my voice. "You do."

Ruthie shrugged, looking uncomfortable. She turned the key in the ignition. "I guess we should get going, huh?"

"I guess so."

"Bye, Luna," Ruthie said. "Thanks for the memories." She gave a little salute as we pulled away, showing off her nails—Aphrodite's Pink Nightie, my signature color. Subtle. Classy.

I shifted my gaze to the passing scene, the storefronts and Saturday afternoon shoppers. Part of me was glad that we'd taken this trip. But a bigger part of me felt worse than ever. I wasn't Brandy the bear-attack victim with the great attitude and the heart of gold. I was a bitch, jealous of my own sister—a role reversal if ever there was one.

"There's a Subway in a few exits," Ruthie said as we entered the highway. "You hungry?"

"Not really," I said. "Are you?"

"I guess not," she said.

After a few minutes of silence, Ruthie flipped on the radio. Classical music again, but this time I didn't say a word. I just pulled my hood over my head and stared out the window.

We arrived home as the sun was starting to set. Ruthie pulled into the driveway and unsnapped her seat belt. She shifted in her seat to face me. "So. What are you planning to do on Monday?"

I knew what she was asking, but I pretended not to. "The usual. Eating bonbons, watching *Ellen* . . . organizing my socks."

My sister's face stayed serious. Gone was the fun-loving Benny of yesteryear. "Lex," she said, looking me straight in the eye. "You need to go back to school. I understand why you don't want to, but you need to. It's too important."

The way she said it—with such conviction—made my stomach hurt. I could try to argue with her, but deep down I knew she was right.

I heard myself murmur, "Okay whatever."

"Okay whatever?" Ruthie raised her new eyebrows.

"Dad's going to make me, anyway. You were there. His whole 'truancy is a criminal offense' speech?" I made my voice deep and lawyerly. "'*Twenty unexcused absences warrants a blah blah blah*' . . . I already have ten."

"So, is that a yes?"

I shrugged. "Whatever."

"*Whatever* is not an affirmative," Ruthie said. "I need an affirmative."

My sister the walking thesaurus. How we were even related was beyond me.

"Fine," I said.

"*Fine* you'll go to school on Monday?"

"*Yes,*" I said. "I will go to school on Monday. Is that affirmative enough for you?"

"Yes, it is."

"But I am *not* taking the bus."

"No bus," Ruthie agreed. "I'll drive you."

"Good," I said.

For a second, I imagined the two of us walking into high school together, with our new haircuts and killer attitudes. Benny and Brandy, the Mayer sisters: a force to be reckoned with.

For a second, I let myself believe it.

Ifonlyifonlyifonly

ON MONDAY MORNING, I woke with a pit in my stomach. *Why did I agree to this? What was I thinking?* Then came a rap on my door and my mother's voice. "Rise and shine!" Her chipper tone—plus the Lord & Taylor gift box in her hands—made me want to dive out the window.

"Happy first day of school," she said, beaming. "I bought you a little outfit. . . . I hope you like it. . . . If you don't . . . well . . . we'll just go back and exchange it later."

I nodded, afraid that if I opened my mouth I'd barf.

"Here!" She handed me the box. "Take a look!"

I nodded again, trying to smile. But when I lifted the lid and peeled back the layers of tissue, I felt sick. Inside was a floaty, cream-colored blouse and a lavender skirt embroidered with tiny, cream-colored flowers.

"Thanks, Mom," I murmured.

"Don't you love it? I thought the blouse was darling. And the detailing on the skirt makes it special without being too busy. . . . I wasn't sure about sizes. . . ." She hesitated. "But we'll just take it back if it doesn't work."

I nodded, feeling ten times worse.

My mother hadn't said a word about my weight since the accident. Food comments, yes. Hair comments, definitely: she *freaked* when she saw what Luna had done to me. But she hadn't yet crossed the line to weight. Even now she was back-pedaling. "I'm sure you're still a size two, honey."

"Uh-huh," I said, knowing that I wasn't. Knowing that she knew it, too.

"Do you want to try them on?" she asked.

"Not right now." As I placed the clothes back in the box I mumbled something about gym being first period and not wanting to get my new outfit sweaty, which was, of course, total BS. I hadn't even seen my schedule. "I'll try them on later," I added.

Satisfied, my mother changed the subject to something even worse. "Have you done your oil yet?"

Just like that, we were back to the face. I said I hated the oil; she said I had to do it, anyway. I asked what difference did it make? She asked did I *hear* what the doctor said about scar prevention? Then she whipped out a beige-colored bottle—some kind of miracle foundation she'd discovered at the Lord & Taylor cosmetics department, especially for scars. She told me that after I did my oil, she would be happy to do my make-up. "How does that sound?" she asked.

I shrugged.

"I think this will really make a big difference, honey. Why don't we try it?"

"Go nuts," I said, suddenly too tired to argue.

It's not like I could look any worse.

✦ ✦ ✦

Here is a picture: sophomore girl, walking through the double doors of Millbridge Senior High School on her first day—a moment she has imagined a thousand times before. In her mind, it has always been her and her best friend, and they have always looked amazing—strutting down the hall like they own the place, hair flowing out behind them, legs tan and strong from running the two-mile, senior guys staring, senior girls frowning.

But that is only a picture.

That isn't real.

Real is walking into high school two weeks late, with your sister and her trombone. *Real* is a haircut from hell, ten extra pounds, and eyes so red from crying that even the Visine your mother gave you before you left the house didn't make an ounce of difference. *Real* is incomprehensible.

Not that my mother didn't try. She tried the special foundation. Then her regular foundation. Then powder and blush. She even tried bright pink lipstick and dramatic, kohl-lined eyes, to distract from the graft. Nothing worked. The minute I got in Ruthie's car I scrubbed it all off with a paper towel. I stuck on four Band-Aids, even though they looked ridiculous, and combed every possible strand of hair in front of my face.

Now here I was, a hideous freak, slumped against the wall outside the guidance office, wearing my sister's pants because nothing else fit.

"You okay?" Ruthie asked as I stared down at my schedule.

"No."

"Everyone's nervous their first day. . . . Trust me . . . you'll be fine."

I shook my head, feeling fresh tears spring into my eyes.

Ruthie unzipped her backpack and pulled out some mini tissues. "Here," she said gruffly. "Take these."

My sister wasn't a fan of emotional displays. Of any kind. Whenever she saw people making out, or screaming, or bawling—even on TV—she would get all weird and twitchy.

Like now. While I dabbed at my eyes, Ruthie shifted from foot to foot, buckling the chest strap of her backpack. The chest strap. Who buckles the freaking *chest strap* of their *backpack*?

"First bell's about to ring," she said, glancing at her watch. "You know where sophomore hall is, right?"

"Uh-huh," I said, wiping my nose. Last spring, the ninth grade had been bused over from the junior high for Step Up Day. All morning, we toured the building. Then, while everyone else was eating lunch, Ryan and I snuck into the janitor's closet and made out in the dark, surrounded by mops.

"Good." Ruthie's tone was brisk, businesslike. "So you know where you're going. Locker, homeroom, library—all in sophomore hall. You've got your schedule. You're good to go."

Good to go. Did she not see that I was having a breakdown here? That I was not qualified to "go" anywhere?

"Hey." Ruthie punched my arm lightly. "You'll be fine."

I gave her a look to indicate that no, I would not be fine, and that she was the worst sister ever. But before she could respond, Sasha and Beatrice appeared out of nowhere, which is what they do. Whether they are suddenly holding a séance in your backyard or watching the SyFy Channel in your basement. I have seen their fashion sense evolve through the years—from combat boots to dreadlocks to capes. When I was in the hospital, they showed up with Guatemalan worry dolls (Sasha) and oolong tea (Beatrice). They have never been anything but nice to me, but still. Words cannot describe how weird they are.

"Hi, Ruth," they said. "Hi, Lexi."

I managed a watery smile.

"Do you want us to walk you to your locker?" Sasha asked. Her voice was kind, her eyes soft. Her suspenders an arresting shade of orange.

I shook my head. "That's okay."

"You sure?" Beatrice squinted at me through her cat's-eye glasses.

"Yeah."

Ruthie glanced at her watch just as the bell rang. "Gotta go," she told me. Then, "I'll look for you at lunch."

"Okay," I said.

But as the three of them took off down the wall, I had the crazy urge to sprint after my sister and grab her by the leg, like I was a little kid. I don't remember this, but my mother says I used to follow Ruthie everywhere. I called her "Woofie," and I would get insanely jealous whenever anyone tried to play with her. We were at the playground once and some girl asked Ruthie to go on the slide. Apparently, I went ballistic, screaming, "*My* Woofie! *My* Woofie!" so loud that half the park came running over, just to make sure I was okay.

Where was my rescue team now, when I actually needed it? MIA. There were people everywhere—laughing, shouting, scurrying to their lockers—but they weren't my people. I *had* no people. No best friend. No boyfriend. I was, for the first time in my life, totally alone. I could walk right back outside, and no one would notice. I could call my mom, and she would come and get me, and in twenty minutes I would be home in my pajamas, eating ice cream.

But something stopped me.

It wasn't the pitiful vision of myself festering away in front of the TV, getting fatter and uglier by the second. It wasn't dignity. It wasn't pride. It was a voice.

"Omigod! *Lexi?*"

A voice so grating I would know it anywhere.

"I barely *recognized* you! What are you *doing* here? I thought you weren't coming back! Taylor said—what *happened* to your *hair*?"

I shrugged, reassuring myself that Heidi—whose jeans were so tight you could see the fat bulging out over her waistband—was in no position to talk.

"I cut it," I said.

"Wow!" Heidi said, a big, fake smile plastered on her face. "It looks *really* good!" Her eyes darted from my hair to my face to the rest of me. I watched as everything came into focus: not just my Band-Aids, but the popped-off button on my shirt and Ruthie's khakis—which, while new, were the high-rise, butt-widening variety.

"*Love* the pants," Heidi gushed in the manner of a preschool teacher telling a three-year-old how awesome her scribbles are.

It was the last straw. Worse than the pain of a hundred pulverized bones, a thousand skin grafts. Heidi was happy to see me like this.

Well, fuck her.

As the second bell rang, I didn't even think about it; I just took off running down the hall, blowing past Heidi and all the other stragglers—so I wouldn't be late for homeroom.

LeFevre, Mayer. L, M.

We'd been in the same homeroom since seventh grade so it shouldn't have come as a big shock, but when I peered through the window and saw Taylor—sitting in the second row, between J. P. Melillo and Elodie Love—I froze. There were new highlights in her hair, a bright coppery color that matched her shirt. My first instinct was to run over, tell her how good she looked.

Then I remembered. When you hate someone, you take a seat in the back row—as far away as possible—and hope that she doesn't notice.

But of course she noticed.

Everyone noticed.

As soon as I opened the door, eighteen heads turned.

I'd imagined it a hundred times, the looks on people's faces when they saw me. The options were limitless: Shock. Horror. Disgust. Pity. Glee. (This was the one I'd envisioned for Heidi, and for Jenna Morelli, who once told me I was so stuck-up she hoped I got run over. Even though that was sixth grade, I hadn't forgotten.)

"Lizbeth Lunn?"

Mr. Ziff was taking attendance.

"Here."

"John Lynch?"

What was I going to do, stand there like a moron?

"Here."

"Cecilly Macomb?"

I climbed over Jenna Morelli's backpack, taking the nearest seat I could find.

"Here."

"Alexa Mayer? . . ." Mr. Ziff—who was tall and skinny, with a bobbing Adam's apple and Harry Potter glasses—glanced up from his clipboard. "Alexa?"

At first, I couldn't catch my breath. The air felt too heavy, too warm. But finally, like a chicken that's been trying for a year to lay a single egg, out it popped. "Here."

Here. Gawk away.

As the eyeballs bore into me, the room grew hotter. Or maybe it was my face. If I blushed, the graft would be even more obvious. I pictured myself sweating so hard the Band-Aids fell off. All people would see was a red square on an even redder background. The thought made me nauseous. It killed me not to dive under my desk, but I made myself look straight ahead at Mr. Ziff. Not at his face, but at the impressive collection of ballpoint pens clipped to his shirt pocket.

"Welcome, Alexa," he said.

"Thank you," I mumbled.

How much did he know? I thought about my father's phone call to the principal, explaining my absences. A whole scene played out in my mind: the principal calling a staff meeting, informing my teachers about the accident, describing what had happened to my face, encouraging everyone to treat me as "normally" as possible.

Out of the corner of my eye, I could see Taylor staring. *Everyone* staring. I bent down, pretending to need something out of my backpack. While Mr. Ziff finished attendance and moved on to announcements, I riffled around, thinking, *If only I could zip myself inside my backpack and never come out.* Then I started to spiral.

If only I never met Taylor.

If only Ryan never moved here.

If only the party never happened.

If only I didn't get into Jarrod's car.

If only I didn't take off my seat belt.

Ifonlyifonlyifonly.

The instant the bell rang, I jumped up. I couldn't wait to get out of there—out of my own head. I had just made it to my locker, just opened my combination lock, when Kendall and Rae descended out of nowhere.

"Lexiiiiii! We heard you were back! It's *so* good to see you! Your *hair* looks *awesome*!"

The tears were just behind my eyeballs, pricking away. But then I felt the warmth of bare, tanned arms around me. I smelled Kendall's Juicy Fruit, Rae's coconut shampoo, and somehow I could talk. "Hey, you guys."

"You look *great,*" Kendall said, taking a step backward. "Doesn't she look great?"

Rae's head bobbed. "She does. You look great, Lex."

"So great."

I knew they were trying to make me feel good, but their smiles were a little too wide, their words a little too sweet. Where were Kendall's usual snarky comments? She had plenty to snark about. My lack of return texts. My not telling them I was coming today. Something.

But no. "What do you have first period?" Kendall asked, scanning my schedule. "Sophomore Lit with Bardo. Me too!"

"Me three!" Rae said.

"We'll walk you!"

"Great!" I said. "Thanks!"

I stretched my face into a smile as fake as theirs, and I let them walk me down the hall, surreptitiously fingering my Band-Aids to make sure they hadn't slipped off.

The day only got worse.

In trigonometry, the unthinkable happened. Mrs. Silver had assigned seats and I was next to Ryan. Ryan, who last saw me throwing plates. In the heat of the moment, let me tell you, throwing plates feels incredible, but in retrospect it is mortifying. Pathetic.

Even more pathetic, the minute I saw him sitting there, doodling in his notebook, my stomach flipped over just as it had back in December, when he skated past me for the first time.

He looked so good. He was tan from coaching tee ball, and his hair was even blonder than usual. He'd just gotten it cut—I could tell from the white line at the nape of his neck and above his ears—but the top was still long, flopping onto his forehead just the way I liked it. Shaggy, but not sloppy.

I instantly regretted cutting my hair. Ryan always told me how much he loved my hair, how sexy it was—how, when I blew it out and put in hot rollers, I looked like a Victoria's Secret model.

Now, I was a freak. A freak with a patchwork face and clown clothes. When Ryan looked up from his desk, he did a double take, his expression morphing from *Who are you and why are you sitting there?* to *Holy shit.*

"Lexi . . ." he mumbled, flustered. "Hey . . . you're back."

I shrugged. Actually, it was more of a muscle twitch, which made me look like an even bigger freak.

Was it my imagination or had everyone stopped talking? Except for the squeak of Mrs. Silver's marker on the white-board, all sound had ceased. I could see Annalise Jankoff—the biggest gossip in our grade—a few desks over, a half smile playing on her lips. By lunch, whatever happened next would be all over school.

"Are you . . . feeling better?" Ryan asked.

I snorted, not just for him, but for the peanut gallery. "Yeah, Ry. I'm feeling better. I'm feeling *awesome*." I unzipped my backpack to take out my trig binder, and my pencil case clattered to the floor. Pencils flew everywhere.

Crap.

Mrs. Silver spun around. "Everything all right?"

Oh, yes. Everything's peachy.

As I squatted to retrieve my pencils, a vision of Ryan and Taylor flashed across my mind—her coppery highlights, his tan legs. If only Ryan were wearing flip-flops right now: I would stab him in the foot. Which wouldn't be nearly as bad as getting stabbed in the *back*, but still. You had to start somewhere.

After trigonometry, I tried to shake it off. I tried to pay attention to my teachers, but I couldn't. Seeing Ryan again triggered all sorts of memories I didn't want to think about.

Like this one time when he and I were hanging out at his grandparents' house and he dragged their old tandem bicycle out of the garage because I told him I'd never ridden tandem before. He told me not to worry, he'd steer; all I had to do was pedal. He took me to the top of this really steep hill. I told him to go slow, and he promised he would. But when we started going down, he did the opposite. He went kamikaze: all pedals, no brakes. "Slow down!" I kept screaming. "Slow down!" I was so scared. But Ryan just yelled back, "Hold on!" When we got to the bottom of the hill, he was laughing. Then he saw that I was crying, and he said, "Shit." He pulled me into this big hug and told me he was sorry. Probably, I should have slapped him. A lot of girlfriends would have done that, to get their point across. But I didn't. I stayed right where I was, my face pressed against his shoulder, breathing in the grassy-sweet smell of his shirt, feeling safe in his arms.

My throat hurt, thinking about that moment. *See, dumb-ass?* part of me was saying. *He was always a jerk.* While the other part of me was saying, *No, he wasn't. He loved you.*

"These burritos smell like armpits," Rae announced as we settled into our seats in the cafeteria.

"Why do you buy?" Kendall asked. "Why don't you *bring* your lunch like a normal person?"

Heidi set her tray next to Rae's and squeezed in beside her. "I *like* cafeteria food."

"Shocker," Kendall muttered. This was a clear reference to Heidi's weight, a running joke that made me uncomfortable and the other girls at the table—a mixture of field hockey and soccer players—snigger.

"Seriously." Piper Benson smirked into her Diet Coke. "Carbs much?"

Heidi, oblivious as always, started chowing on burritos. At the same time, Rae asked me how it felt to be back—was it weird?

"It's okay," I said.

And what about this random table we'd been relegated to, now that we were lowly sophomores?

"It's different," I admitted, more to my sandwich than to Rae.

"We've been demoted!" Kendall cried in faux outrage, like losing our center-table status was the worst thing that had ever happened.

I could feel my old teammates, Kelly Bartells, Ariana Ramos, and Laurel Popovich sneaking glances at me.

So I asked the obligatory question: "How's field hockey going?"

Laurel, who'd played left wing to my center since seventh grade, said that the season was off to an awesome start, that—even though they were only on JV and didn't have me or Taylor—they'd already won their first two games against Greenwich and Darien, which was *huge*, and that their coach, who looked like Angelina Jolie, used to play Division 1 for Boston College.

"Wow," I said, not knowing what else to say.

"Yeah."

Both Ariana and Kelly nodded and smiled in my direction, but they didn't exactly meet my eyes.

"So," Laurel said, "are you getting a late tryout?"

I was about to answer no when Heidi suddenly shrieked, "TayTayyy!" Which meant that Taylor, her lifeline, had arrived.

"Where have you *been*?" Heidi demanded. "I waited for you at your locker for, like, *ever*."

Every cell in my body froze as I waited for Taylor's next move. *If she sits next to me I'll leave,* I thought. *I will stand up and I will walk straight out the door without a word.*

But Taylor took the seat between Heidi and Ariana. "Sorry I'm late," she murmured. "Jarrod had a doctor's appointment, and my mom was dropping him off. I wanted to find out how it went."

Suddenly, the whole table was buzzing. "What did the doctor say? Can Jarrod play football yet? How's his collarbone?"

I'd forgotten all about Jarrod and his collarbone. But

clearly no one else had. Which, okay, I know not everyone felt the aversion to Taylor's brother that I did. In fact, most of them worshipped him. But all this concern over how he was doing, when *he* was the pervert behind the wheel, driving us into a tree? Come on.

"Well," Taylor said, glancing tentatively at me, then back at everyone else, "the collarbone is healing fine, but apparently he separated his shoulder, too, which they didn't realize at first. That's why he's been in so much pain."

Pain? Jarrod doesn't know pain.

"Does he still need the sling?" Rae wanted to know.

"Yeah, for a few more weeks. Then he'll start physical therapy. But it looks like he's out for the season. He'll still be captain, but . . ." Her voice trailed off and a chorus of *ohhhs* and *poor Jarrods* commenced.

Taylor grimaced, glancing at me as if to say, *I know. I'm sorry. You have it a million times worse.*

I knew what she was doing, trying to get back on my good side. As if that were even possible. As if I could ever, in a million years, forgive her for what she did.

Just as I averted my eyes from Taylor's, the lights in the cafeteria flicked off, then on again. My head swiveled like everyone else's, to see Jarrod at the far end of the room, standing on a chair.

"Omigod," Heidi squealed. "Speak of the devil!"

We watched as he lifted a megaphone to his mouth with his non-sling arm. "Three words, people: Friday. Night. Lights. Millbridge versus Fairfield."

That's six words, moron.

"Be there."

Eight.

Jarrod made a sweeping gesture with his megaphone and every football player in fifth-period lunch stood up. Taylor's crush, Rob. A bunch of guys I recognized from the LeFevres' pool. Kyle Humboldt. Jason Saccovitch. Ryan.

Slowly, and in complete unison, they began to clap.

Clap . . .

Clap . . .

Clap . . .

Until the entire cafeteria was clapping along with them. Clapping and cheering. Clapping and screaming.

My table, it seemed, was the loudest in the room—everyone shrieking and jumping up and down, like groupies at a rock concert. I wanted to feel it, too. But somehow this collective burst of Wildcat pride had the reverse effect, sucking the spirit right out of me.

Taylor's face was lit up like Christmas morning. It hurt my eyes to look. It hurt my hands to clap.

It hurt.

It hurt.

It hurt.

The Point of Baked Chicken

"YOU MEAN YOU weren't moved by the Wildcat Spirit?" Ruthie said in the car on our way home. "You weren't tempted to bust out Mom's old pom-poms and start straddle jumping?"

"Please," I snorted, thinking of the cedar trunk in our mother's closet—the one that held her most prized memorabilia. Beauty pageant sashes. Prom corsages. Pom-poms.

"You realize," Ruthie deadpanned, "that football players are our heroes. Right up there with firefighters and Jesus. We're *supposed* to worship them at mealtime."

"Well," I said, "Jarrod killed my appetite. *And* Ryan. The whole thing made me want to barf."

I knew, even as I spoke, that I was being a hypocrite. Two months ago, I would have been cheering as loud as anyone. Louder. And the sad thing was that I actually *wanted* to be cheering. I *wished* that my only care in the world was whether Millbridge beat Fairfield on Friday night.

"Other than that, Mrs. Lincoln," Ruthie said, lifting an eyebrow at me, "how was the play?"

"What?"

"It's a joke . . . Abraham Lincoln? Assassinated in the Ford Theater by John Wilkes Booth?"

"Whatever," I muttered.

"I'm drawing a parallel to your day," Ruthie explained, college professor to janitor. "Trying to add some levity."

"Can you ever just talk like a normal person?"

"I don't know, Lex. How does a normal person talk?"

I rolled my eyes and told her, "Never mind."

"No, no. I want to be *normal*. I want to be just like everybody else."

I knew she was messing with me. Ruthie loves to mess with people to make a point. It is one of her patented lawyer-in-the-making moves, designed to bamboozle her opposition.

"I hereby pledge," Ruthie said in her best-little-Girl-Scout-in-the-world voice, "to avoid all historical references and multisyllabic words, so all the cool kids will like me—forever and ever, amen."

"Good luck with that," I said, letting the sarcasm flow right back at her. Which was better than tears, at least, which I'd spent most of sixth period shedding in the locker room while I avoided gym class. And Taylor.

And the whole world.

As soon as we got home, my mother began her interrogation. Ruthie pleaded physics quiz and took off for her room. I considered doing the same. I had a legitimate excuse—two weeks worth of homework to catch up on—but I knew that nothing would stop my mother. Wherever I went, she would follow.

"How was your day?" she asked the second I entered the kitchen. There were after-school snacks on the counter. Carrot and celery sticks arranged in the shape of a fan. Grapes. Ice water with slivers of lemon. My mother smiled, gesturing to a stool. "Why don't you sit and tell me all about it?"

I sat. "What do you want to know?"

"Everything! How are your teachers? Your classes?"

"Okay."

"How are your friends?"

I thought about Kendall's and Rae's forced smiles. The weird, sideways glances of my field hockey teammates at lunch.

"They're okay," I said, plucking a grape from its stem and holding it in my hand. I'd barely eaten all day, and I was starving, but I didn't want rabbit food.

My mother raised her eyebrows, waiting for information. For fifteen years she'd been doing this. Hounding me for every last detail of my life. Who did I sit with at lunch? Which boys were cute? Who liked who? This time, I didn't feel like giving her anything.

"Well," she said in her infuriatingly chipper tone, "great! I'm glad the day went well."

"Why?"

"Why?" She frowned slightly.

I rolled the grape between my fingers. "Yeah."

"*Why* am I glad you had a good day?"

I shook my head. "Never mind." My mother hates when people say never mind; she thinks it's the height of rudeness. "Forget it," I muttered.

There was a beat of silence. My mother picked up a carrot then set it back on its plate. "Do you think I don't know how hard this has been for you, Alexa? Do you think I don't see those Band-Aids?"

I stared down at the counter.

"Well, let me tell you something . . . it hasn't exactly—" Her voice cracked. For a moment I thought she was going to lose it, but then she recovered. "It hasn't been easy for me, either."

It was the craziest thing I had ever heard. It was even crazier than Kendall and Rae telling me I looked great. This hasn't been easy for *my mother*? This wasn't *about* her. It had nothing to do with her! I made my voice dead calm. "Oh. Right. I'm sorry this has been so difficult for you."

"Alexa." My mother shook her head. "I didn't mean—"

"No, no," I said before she could finish her sentence. "You must be devastated . . . to have a daughter who's never going to be Miss Connecticut or prom queen or homecoming queen . . . or . . . you know . . . queen of any kind." I was babbling now, a complete idiot. "I'm sorry I ruined your dreams for me!"

"Honey, no." My mother's voice was shocked, her eyes shiny. Any second now there would be waterworks, and I wasn't about to stick around to watch.

"I have homework," I said, realizing, as I turned to leave the kitchen, that the grape in my hand was now a pulpy mess.

I couldn't call Taylor, obviously. Taylor, who had always been my go-to girl in times of angst—the ultimate giver of pep talks. I couldn't call Ryan because . . . well . . . Ryan was dead to me. My dad was in court. Which left Kendall and Rae, who, although they had always been closer to Taylor than to me, seemed to be taking my side right now. I shouldn't have faulted them for acting fake in school. At least they were showing some loyalty—walking me to class, saving me a seat at lunch. If that wasn't friendship, what was?

I picked up my cell to call Kendall, but it went straight to voice mail. Rae, same thing. That's when I remembered they had soccer practice.

So I left messages, and an hour later Kendall called me back.

"Lex!" she said. "I've been thinking about you. What's up?"

"My mom is driving me *nuts*," I said.

Kendall's battles with her own mother were legendary—like the time in eighth grade when Mrs. Kinsey showed up in the cafeteria with Kendall's retainer in a Ziploc bag, telling her she was supposed to be wearing it, and a screaming match ensued, right there in front of everyone. Kendall knew just what to say to me now. "Moms are the worst."

"Tell me about it," I said.

"What did she do?"

"It's not so much what she *did*," I explained, "as what she *said*. She tried to tell me how hard it's been for her . . . you know . . . since the accident. Like *she* was the one it happened to."

"Oh . . . uh-huh."

I kept blathering. "It's like my face is a reflection on *her* and . . . I don't know . . . it's taking everything in her arsenal just to get through the day. Meanwhile, I'm the one who—" I paused, hearing noise in the background. "Where are you?"

"JB's," Kendall said. "A bunch of us came here after practice. . . . Hold on a sec, will ya? I'm putting you on mute so I can order."

"Okay," I said. Just thinking about JB's made me drool. They had the best mozzarella sticks in the universe. And the best chicken fingers. And fries. And—

"Omigod, you guys."

Just like that, my food reverie was over.

"Someone take the phone."

I wasn't on mute.

"I don't know what to say to her."

I was on speaker.

"She's, like, freaking out."

I was on speaker, listening to my friends talk about how they didn't want to talk to me.

"Rae, you do it."

"What? I don't know what to say, either."

"Laurel, take the phone."

"Uh-uh."

"What did she do to her hair, anyway?"

"I know, right?"

As I sat there, frozen, the reality of my new life came into focus. I had no friends. I had. No friends. I. Had. No—

"Hey. Sorry about that," Kendall finally said in the same phony, over-cheerful tone she'd used in school. "New guy behind the counter, doesn't know his ass from his elbow . . ."

"What did you order?" I managed to ask.

"What? . . . Oh, mozzarella sticks . . . Hey, listen, Lex . . . I'm really sorry, but I have to go. . . . Wish you were here with us."

I could tell she'd tacked this on at the end to make me feel better, like the obligatory postcards I used to send my grandmother from Florida. *Wish you were here! Weather's great!*

"Me too," I murmured, wondering what Kendall would say if I told her it wasn't mute she'd pressed, it was speaker. Would she make up some excuse? Fall all over herself apologizing? Would she—

"Lex?"

"Yeah."

"I'll see you in school tomorrow. . . . Take care of yourself, 'kay?"

"'Kay," I repeated.

And the phone went silent.

For the next hour, I lay in bed thinking about Sylvia Plath, this poet we studied in ninth grade, whose life got so bad that one day she sealed off the rooms between herself and her children, left out some milk and bread, turned on the gas, and stuck her head in the oven. Then I remembered this woman I saw on *Dateline* who, after her husband divorced her, made herself a Gatorade and Windex cocktail.

It's not like I was planning to kill myself. It's just that I needed some real friends, and a new face, and a different mother, and—

"Hey."

I looked up, startled.

"Beans in your ears?" Ruthie said. "It's dinnertime."

"I'm not hungry," I lied.

"Mom made baked chicken. Your favorite."

"What's the point?"

"The point of baked chicken?"

I shook my head. "Forget it."

"Suit yourself." Ruthie shrugged, and turned to walk out the door.

I felt my eyes burn, realizing that I needed a new sister, too—a sister who wasn't an emotionless robot. "Thanks a lot!" I blurted after her.

Ruthie turned around. "What?"

"You're just *leaving* me here?"

She raised her eyebrows. "Um . . . it's your *room*?"

I felt a stirring of anger. "Obviously, Ruthie, I'm in my room for a reason. Which is my life basically sucks right now. Which maybe you, as my *sister*, could *notice* without me having to spell it out for you. . . ." I paused, giving her ample opportunity to say that she *had* noticed and she was sorry. When she said nothing, I kept going. I told her about the fight with our mother and the phone call with Kendall. "I'm telling you, I can't even look at Mom right now. And I can't go back to school, either. I'm way too humiliated."

That's when Ruthie had the nerve to suggest that perhaps my friends were acting weird because *I* was acting weird.

"Me?" I pointed to my chest in disbelief. "You're blaming *me* for the way they're acting?"

"I'm not *blaming* you, Lex. I'm just saying . . . you chop off your hair, you don't want to talk on the phone anymore, you suddenly hate pep rallies. . . . Should I keep going?"

I opened my mouth, but nothing came out.

"They're not necessarily bad friends," Ruthie continued. "Maybe they just don't know how to act, how to treat you after the accident. . . . It's like when Jenny Albee's brother died, remember? And Mom made five thousand casseroles because she didn't know what else to do?"

I stared at my sister. "Who cares about casseroles?"

"You're missing the point."

"No, *you're* missing the point!" I cried. "I hate my life!"

"So," Ruthie said calmly, "get a new one."

I snorted. "Great. Thanks."

"I'm serious, Lex. If you hate your life so much, stop wallowing and change it. Change *yourself.* No one's going to do it for you."

At first, I was too furious for words. I leapt off the bed, ran to the door, and shut it in my sister's face.

But later, when I really thought about it, I saw the genius in Ruthie's idea. It was so simple and yet so brilliant. I would change my*self,* and in so doing I would change my *life.* But this wouldn't be a Sandy-Dumbrowski-from-*Grease* type of transformation, where she goes from cute goody-goody to leather-clad hottie just to impress the Pink Ladies and win back Danny Zuko. Oh no.

This would be the opposite.

There Must be a Reason You're Dressed that Way

IN THE MORNING, while Ruthie was in the shower, I went straight to her closet. Riffling through my sister's clothes gave me a feeling of hope I hadn't felt yesterday, when I was stuck wearing her khakis by default. Yesterday, because my mother was dictating everything—from makeup to clothes to every bite of food that entered my mouth—I felt powerless. But starting today, things would be different.

For half an hour, I was all about creating the perfect outfit, determined in my mission to ditch the old, pathetic Lexi and welcome the new one. I opened a drawer and found a pair of leggings with a rip in the knee. Then I unearthed a box of ratty, oversized cardigans I remember Ruthie buying at the Salvation Army. I picked the best one: mustard yellow with a distinct old-man smell. As I laced up a pair a combat boots, I felt almost giddy, imagining the look on my mother's face—on *everyone*'s face when they saw me.

I closed my eyes and pictured my new life. . . .

Gliding through the hot-lunch line of the Millbridge High School cafeteria, tray balanced casually in one hand, I select my favorite foods: pepperoni pizza, side of fries, Yoo-hoo. As I pay the cashier, I spot my ex-friends flagging me down. But I breeze straight past Taylor, Kendall, and Rae—past Heidi, whose jaw is on the ground from seeing my outfit, past Ryan and Jarrod and the football guys, who don't even give me a second glance. Finally, I arrive at my destination: a table that, in a million years, no one would ever expect me to sit at. A table that—

"What are you doing?"

I opened my eyes and there was Ruthie, wrapped in a towel, hair dripping. "What are you doing," she repeated, "in my closet?"

"Getting dressed!" I said, springing to a stand. "You like?" Then, before she could answer, I added, "As a wise woman once told me, 'change your life, change yourself.'"

Ruthie shook her head. "That's not exactly what I said."

"Yes, it is." I quoted back her other gemstones: "don't let your face define you" and "stop wallowing." "See?" I smiled, gesturing down at my outfit. "I'm taking your advice."

Ruthie shot me a funny look, but that didn't stop me from sharing the list I'd written the night before—my RULES FOR BECOMING THE ANTI-LEXI—that I happened to have brought with me into her closet.

1) Eat what you want.

2) Stop worrying about looks, aka no more makeup, scales, or *Elle* magazines.

3) Get some real friends (who aren't fake, obnoxious, or boyfriend stealers).

4) Forget guys (they're more trouble than they're worth).

5) Boycott all football games, pep rallies, dances, and other nonacademic after-school activities aimed at the so-called "popular" crowd.

6) Study!

7) Stop letting other people (aka Mom) dictate your life.

Then, because I'd just thought of this one and I knew Ruthie would appreciate the sentiment, I threw out:

8) Care more. (Become more "globally aware.")

"Wow," Ruthie said when I was finished. "You've really thought this through."

"Yes, I have."

She was giving me the strangest look—like she wanted to say something but wasn't sure she should.

"What?"

Ruthie shook her head. "Nothing." She reached up to a hook on the wall. "Here . . . the fashion police will hate this."

"Oh, yeah." I smirked at the barf-green scarf she held out to me. It looked like something one of the old ladies at church would knit for the Christmas bazaar. "This is hideous."

"Right," Ruthie said, shrugging as she turned to walk out of the closet. "I made it."

I started to apologize and then stopped myself. Apologizing was an old-me move, because the old me never wanted to offend anyone. But the new Lexi didn't let other people dictate her life (Rule number seven). She spoke her mind. Besides, my sister didn't care if I thought her scarf was ugly. Those things never bothered her. And, anyway, Ruthie was smart enough to understand that—starting today—ugly was whole the point.

My mother's reaction was even better than I'd hoped. When I walked into the kitchen she took one look at me and sloshed her tea on the floor. Then, after she'd cleaned it up and regained her composure, she asked, "Are you doing a skit in school today? Some kind of performance?"

I played completely dumb. I flopped onto a chair, helped myself to a piece of toast, and said, "What do you mean?"

"Your clothes."

"What about them?"

"There must be a reason you're dressed that way."

"Yes," I said, spreading butter on my toast—not just a thin coating, either. Hunks. "I'm going to school."

My mother shook her head. "No. No, you are not going anywhere dressed like that."

I took a bite. "Why?"

"*Why?*" she repeated in disbelief. "Because you look like a ragamuffin . . . a . . . homeless person."

This was exactly the opening I was waiting for. "Ruthie dresses like this all the time, and you don't even blink!"

My mother hesitated then said, "We are not talking about your sister. We are talking about you."

"I wore her khakis yesterday!" I cried, spraying crumbs through the air. "And you didn't have a problem with *that*!"

"Those pants were new. I bought them just last week. They didn't have rips, or stains, or—"

"Right, *you* bought them. *You* picked them out. If *you* pick something out for me, it's fine. If Ruthie picks something out for *herself,* it's fine. But if I want to choose my own clothes or get my own hair cut I need your *approval*? That's just . . ." I paused for a second, wracking my brain for the best word.

"Lunacy! And I am not doing it anymore!" Then, for good measure, I threw out, "And you can take that scar makeup back to the store because I'm not doing that anymore, either!"

I grabbed three more pieces of toast before marching out of the kitchen, down the front steps, and into Ruthie's car.

Minutes later, my sister opened the door and got in.

"Did you hear me telling off Mom?" I asked.

She nodded, turning the key in the ignition.

"You should have seen the look on her face. . . . She *hated* my clothes . . . and I really got my point across about her not telling me how to do everything all the time, how just because she wants me to look a certain way doesn't mean her way is the be all and end all. . . ."

The whole time I talked, Ruthie didn't say a word. She just drove. When I stopped talking and looked at her, she stayed silent.

"Well?" I said.

"Well what?"

"Aren't you proud of me?"

Ruthie turned the steering wheel and sighed. "Is that why you're doing this? To make me proud of you?"

"Doing what?" I said.

Ruthie gave me that look again—the one from the closet. I could see in her eyes that she had something to say, but she couldn't bring herself to say it. Which wasn't Ruthie at all. Never, in all her seventeen years, had my sister kept her mouth shut about anything. "*What?*" I said, exasperated.

I waited.

Finally, Ruthie shook her head. "Nothing," she said quietly. "I'm glad you're feeling better, Lex. I'm glad you're back at school. Let's just leave it at that."

I stared at her.

"I know how you feel about the bus," she continued, "and I'd love to help you out, but stage band starts today. It goes until five o'clock. You can hang out in the library until I'm done or call Mom to pick you up or . . . whatever you want to do."

"Library," I said.

Ruthie raised an eyebrow.

"What? An afternoon among the books will do me good."

"It's not just one afternoon, Lex. I have rehearsal every day but Friday, every week of the school year."

I frowned. "Seriously?"

"Seriously. Stage band, marching band, jazz band. Trombone is a serious commitment."

It's a serious waste of time, I thought to myself. But instead of saying that, I shrugged. "Fine. I'll hang out in the library four days a week. Rule number six, remember? Study!"

"Yeah," Ruthie said, pulling into the parking lot. "I remember."

When the car stopped, I combed my hair in front of my face but resisted the urge to look at myself in the side-view mirror. I knew what I looked like, and I didn't need to be reminded. I wasn't about to let anything ruin this perfect day.

For the first four periods, everything went great. I successfully ignored Taylor and Heidi, avoided Kendall and Rae, and, in trigonometry, didn't look at Ryan once. I was the model student: attentive to my teachers, oblivious to the superficial chatter around me. I knew people were staring at my face. I knew they were whispering. I just refused to let it bother me.

But fifth period, after I'd dodged Laurel and Ariana in the hall and ducked into the girls' room to steer clear of Jarrod LeFevre, I was in the lunch line, waiting for a tray and listening in on the conversation taking place a few feet ahead of me. It was football players, I could tell—even before I saw their sweats, MHS muscle shirts, and gold chains. As I contemplated fries versus onion rings, I heard one of them vow to "kick Fairfield's pansy ass" on Friday night and the other complain about his "bee-atch of a mother," who wouldn't let him drive her car. Then the question arose, "Dude, have you seen that sophomore with the smokin' bod?"

"Which one?"

"The blonde chick with the fucked-up face."

"The one LeFevre hooked up with?"

"Yeah . . . lucky bastard."

"*Hell*, yeah. She's hot as shit from the neck down."

"All she needs is a bag over her head."

There was laughter, a high five, but I no longer heard what they were saying. Words were bouncing around my skull like pinballs. *Fucked-up face. Bag over her head. The one LeFevre hooked up with.*

Jarrod told people we hooked up? We barely kissed. Hooking up could mean anything. It could mean *everything*.

My brain went numb, and I forgot all about the new Lexi. The walls were caving in and I couldn't breathe and I needed to get out of there and I pushed my way back through the line and walked faster and faster until I came to a room and in that room was a door and I threw it open and—

"Hey!"

I froze.

"Shut the door!" a voice barked. "Shutthedoorshutthe-doorshutthedoor!"

I shut the door.

"It's called a darkroom for a reason."

Darkroom, I thought, my heart pounding against my rib cage. *Right.*

There was a sharp, chemical smell in the air. I steadied myself against the wall, feeling my nose burn. But after a few breaths I got used to it. My eyes adjusted to the blackness. I didn't care how dark it was. I didn't care who else was in here. I was just happy not to be seen. I slouched against the wall, letting the darkness wrap me like a quilt, feeling my muscles loosen, my pulse return to normal.

"Damn," the voice muttered.

"What?"

"My film's ruined."

"Oh," I said.

"Didn't you see the warning light? The big red one outside the door?"

It was a stupid question, because obviously I hadn't. "Why don't you just use a digital camera?"

"That," the voice said, "would defeat the purpose."

"Why?"

"Film development is an *art form.*"

Then, out of nowhere, the lights flicked on and a boy was squinting at me. A boy with black, wiry hair and skin so pale it looked like he hadn't spent a single day of his life outside. He was two heads taller than I was, so I felt like a child looking up at him. Which, after the humiliation I'd just endured in the lunch line, was the last thing I needed. I felt my eyes sting, and I hated myself for being such a baby.

Don't cry. Don't cry, you idiot.

"Hey," the boy said, his eyes softening. "I'm not mad at you."

I shook my head, feeling my face grow hot, which made me remember my graft and the fact that I wasn't wearing Band-Aids, which made me want to fling open the door and run.

I didn't want to run.

New Lexi wouldn't run.

She would do this: stare straight into Photo Boy's eyes without moving a muscle, until he turned away. I needed to train my brain, make it completely blank.

Forget your face.

Forget what Jarrod said.

Forget the lunch line.

Just stare.

For a second, I was doing it—mind over matter. But then, for some reason I got distracted and realized I was in a small, enclosed space with a boy whose eyes were an unnerving shade of green, and he was staring at my face.

I ran because I couldn't stand another second.

✦ ✦ ✦

I stayed out of sight until the end of the day, avoiding everyone—except for the nurse who gave me Band-Aids—by skipping sixth, seventh, and eighth periods, holing up in a carrel in the library. At five o'clock, Ruthie found me.

"Oh my God. Are you *studying*? Alert the presses!"

I shut the random book I'd grabbed from the stacks, the same one I'd been staring at for the past four hours without reading a single word. "How can I be studying? I don't even have my backpack."

"Why don't you have your backpack?"

"You don't want to know."

"It wasn't a rhetorical question."

"Never mind," I told her. "Just walk me to my locker."

Ruthie shrugged. "Whatever you say." She picked up her trombone case. Then, as soon we got out into the hall, she started whistling.

What are you *so happy about?* I thought, trudging along behind her. *You've never whistled a day in your life.* When we got to my locker, she was still whistling. "Could you stop?" I snapped. "That's really annoying."

"Well, excuuuuuse me," Ruthie said. But she didn't look offended. In fact, she was smiling.

"What's *wrong* with you?"

Now, she laughed. "What makes you think something's wrong?"

I slammed my locker. "Never mind."

We started walking again.

"Ask me about band," Ruthie said suddenly.

"What?"

"If you really want to know, ask me about band practice."

"Why?" I asked, with growing annoyance. "Who cares?"

"Thanks a lot."

"Look, I've had a horrible day. I'm not in the mood."

Ruthie nodded, no longer smiling. The whole way to the parking lot, she didn't say word.

"What—now you're mad?" I said as we got in car.

"I'm not mad."

"You seem mad to me."

Ruthie sighed, turning the key in the ignition. "I'm not mad. I'm not anything. Let's just go." This from the girl who loves to argue, who never backs down without a fight.

Now I *knew* something was wrong.

We drove all the way home in silence, during which I replayed, over and over, the events of my day.

By the time Ruthie pulled into the driveway, I couldn't take it anymore.

"Jarrod told the football team we hooked up!"

"Well, didn't you?"

"No! All we did was kiss!"

Ruthie nodded. "Okay, but hooking up's a continuum, right? Anything from kissing on."

I stared at her, amazed she even knew this.

"If he told people you guys hooked up—if he used that precise term—he wasn't necessarily being inaccurate."

"Are you *defending* him?" I demanded.

"No. I'm just being logical."

"There's nothing *logical* about it," I said. And I replayed the conversation from the lunch line, in sordid detail. "How could they say those things about me?" I cried. "How could they say those things about *anyone*?"

"I don't know, Lex. It's how they roll."

"It's how they *roll*?" I stared at my sister. "Do you even *know* any guys on the football team?"

"Yes."

I snorted in disbelief.

"What—you think because I'm in band I couldn't possibly interact with anyone *popular*?"

I shrugged. "Your words. Not mine."

"Ty Mastrobattisto," Ruthie said. "Marcus Burns. Jason Godomsky. Rob Stiles, Peter Moskowitz, Brendan Sutcliff . . . Do you want me to keep going? Because I'll keep going. . . ."

I shook my head, dumbfounded.

"You think you're the only one they've ever insulted? Try getting called Godzitla every day for three years. You'll get to know them really well."

"Godzitla?"

"Yeah."

"Because of your—"

"Yeah . . . forget it."

"That's the stupidest name I ever heard. Your skin isn't even that bad." I was saying this to be nice, but I realized, looking at her, that Ruthie's face was clearer than I'd seen it in a long time.

"Forget it," she said again a little sharply. "I don't care.

Those guys are Neanderthals. They run around head-butting each other all day and treating girls like pieces of meat. Their opinion means nothing to me. That's my whole point."

"*What's* your whole point?"

Ruthie sighed, like this conversation was suddenly too exhausting for words. "Get over it, Lex. Grow a backbone. Just like the rest of us."

Specks of Dust, Atoms

WHEN RUTHIE AND I walked in the house, our father was waiting on the couch in the mudroom. He did not look happy.

"Tough day in court?" Ruthie asked.

But he didn't even answer. He looked straight at me and said, "Alexa. My study. Now."

I'd never heard him speak to me that way. As I took off my backpack and followed him down the hall, I felt a mounting sense of dread.

There were only two chairs in my dad's study—both dark leather with cracked armrests—and he'd set them up to face each other.

"Sit," he commanded.

I sat.

"I received a phone call from your principal this afternoon," he said, "and do you know what he told me?"

I shook my head.

"He told me that in the two days you have been back in school—of the sixteen class periods you have been expected to attend throughout those two days—you have been absent a total of five class periods. Five."

He looked at me, as though waiting for me to question his math.

I didn't.

"While I understand, and your teachers understand, that this is a time of readjustment for you, *you* need to understand that skipping classes is absolutely unacceptable. The anti-truancy statute in the state of Connecticut is irrefutable. Your mother and I have given you plenty of leeway by allowing you to miss the first two weeks of school, but that grace period is over. You are too smart to repeat your sophomore year. Am I making myself clear?"

I nodded.

"I cancelled a court appearance to come home and have this discussion with you. Your mother is very upset."

I looked down at my fingernails to hide my annoyance. If my mother was so upset why wasn't she a part of this lecture? Why was she hiding in the kitchen? Why was she making my father do the dirty work?

"Alexa."

"Yeah."

"You need to be more respectful of your mom."

My head snapped up. "I need to be more respectful of *her*? *She* needs to be more respectful *me*!"

"How so?" He was using his lawyer voice, calm and measured. "Give me a for instance."

"For *instance*, she won't get off my back! She won't stop hounding me! She won't get a life and stop trying to run mine!"

I was only getting started, but my dad held up his hand to stop me. "Your mother loves you very much."

"What's *that* got to do with anything?"

"Her heart is in the right place. . . . Look, I'm not asking for a miracle. I'm just asking for a concerted effort."

I heaved a sigh.

"Beans."

"What."

He looked at me. "Throw me a bone here."

"Fine," I said.

"Fine?"

"I will make a concerted effort."

Even though it made me mad to say it. I'd vowed not to let my mother rule my life, and now here she was, using my father to lay a guilt trip on me. Which I couldn't be mad at him for. It wasn't his fault.

Watching my dad now, removing his glasses and rubbing the bridge of his beaky nose, I felt horrible. There were bags under his eyes. A day's worth of stubble on his cheeks.

"I'm sorry, Dad." I hesitated. "I'm sorry you missed court. I won't skip any more classes."

There was a lump in my throat the size of a golf ball when my father got up from his chair and hugged me.

"I know you won't, Beans," he said, scruffing his chin against the top of my head. "I know you won't."

Fucked-up face.

Bag over her head.

The one LeFevre hooked up with.

I couldn't stop thinking about it. I lay in bed, watching the words crawl across the screen in my brain, over and over—like the ticker tape at the bottom of the TV when you're watching CNN.

I mean, what are you supposed to do when people are saying, essentially, that you are an ugly slut? I'd been called things before—snob, stuck-up—but I'd always had someone to defend me. Taylor, Ryan, my mom. Someone to assure me those accusations weren't true.

Now I had no one. No one but myself.

"Dad?"

"Yeah?"

It was 10:30, and he was still in his study.

"Can I borrow your credit card?"

"Hmm?" He looked up from the stack of papers on his desk.

"Can I please borrow your credit card?"

He lowered the glasses on his nose and looked at me. "What do you need?"

I shrugged, focusing on the diploma framed in gold on the wall. JEFFREY CHARLES MAYER, JURIS DOCTOR, UNIVERSITY OF VIRGINIA. "Just some stuff online. For school."

"Define *stuff*."

"Just . . . you know, clothes . . ."

"Didn't Mom already buy you everything you need?"

"No, she did. It's just . . ." I hesitated, then heard the words come tumbling out. "None of my jeans fit and I only have one hooded sweatshirt, which isn't even mine, it's Ruthie's, and the thing is . . . I don't want to go into any stores and I need to wear hoods now, so . . . I won't spend a lot. I promise. I'll shop around. Just tell me what the limit it is and I'll stick to it."

The room went silent.

I shifted my gaze from the wall to my dad and saw the shine in his eyes. What, I wondered, did he see when he looked at me? Whatever it was, I knew that in a second he would reach into his briefcase and pull out that credit card. Whatever he could do to fix the problem, he'd do it.

"Beans?" His throat sounded full of marbles.

"Yeah?"

"You know I love you, right?"

"I know, Dad."

Over the next few weeks, THE RULES were in full effect.

To prove that I no longer cared about my looks (Rule number two), I wore only jeans and hooded sweatshirts, pulled as tight around my face as possible, leaving just enough room to see. Hoods were against dress code, but not a single teacher called me on it. Shocker.

To prove that popularity was the least of my concerns (Rule number five), any time I saw Taylor, Ryan, Jarrod, Kendall and Rae, or any of the field hockey girls or football guys, I would pretend they were nothing. Specks of dust. Atoms.

I became a walking Homeland Security Alert System, constantly on the lookout, scanning the halls through my hood hole for Taylor's coppery highlights, Ryan's baseball cap, so I could be prepared to ignore them.

Vigilant though I was, I couldn't avoid everything. Like the time Taylor stepped out of the bathroom stall as I was washing my hands. Our eyes met in the mirror and her mouth opened as if to say something, but I quickly walked away, wiping my hands on my jeans and repeating the mantra: *You are nothing. A speck of dust. An atom.* Meanwhile, my heart was pounding and every nerve in my body screamed, *Code Red!*

Or the time Jarrod suddenly appeared in the doorway of my English class just as I was coming out, and we both froze like deer. Then, without a word, we brushed past each other, silent as branches.

Or the time I turned a corner in the hall and bumped smack into Kendall and Rae. "Lexiiii!" they squealed, pretending they were happy to see me. "How *are* you?" Kendall asked, all low and concerned. And Rae said, "We never *see* you anymore!" Their insincerity—their two-facedness—was mind-boggling. I didn't know what to say, so I mumbled something about needing to find a teacher, and I hightailed it out of there.

I tried making new friends (Rule Number Three). For a week, I sat at a lunch table where, in my old life, people would have laughed hysterically to see me sitting. With Marielle Sisk and Robyn Pinover and those girls. They weren't exactly unfriendly. Marielle, with her Little-House-on-the-Prairie dresses and her pocket Bible, was too well mannered to be mean. And Robyn barely spoke a word. She just stared at me through her Coke-bottle glasses. I felt like a bug under a microscope, especially when this other girl, Lynn—"Lithpy Lynn" we used to call her in elementary school because she couldn't say her s's—started firing questions. Why was I sitting with them? I never sat with them before. What happened to my friends?

I stopped going to the cafeteria.

Lunch wasn't technically a class, so I didn't feel guilty about skipping it. I'd dodge any teachers in the hall, find an empty room, and wait there until the bell rang. The language lab. The auditorium. Anywhere but the darkroom. The last thing I needed was another encounter with Photo Boy. I spotted him twice, once with two other guys—bow-tie-wearing, pencil-behind-the-ear types—and once in the gym while I was playing badminton. Both times he had a camera around his neck and an intense expression on his face, like he was trying to solve the climate crisis.

I pretended not to notice.

At the end of each day, I would drag myself to the library to study (Rule Number Six) until Ruthie finished band. Then she would drive me home, or we'd stop at Dunkin' Donuts for a Coolatta, followed by a painful dinner where my mother asked too many questions and all of my answers were one word. By the time my dad got home, I'd already be in bed, dog-tired but unable to sleep—the movie reel in my brain spinning overtime.

No one seemed to care that I was blowing them off. I wanted Taylor to be miserable, but every time I saw her she looked fine. Perfectly content to be walking down the hall with Heidi instead of me. Heidi, who seemed to have taken up residence on Taylor's hip like a giant, frizzy-haired burr.

I tried not to let this bother me. The two of them deserved each other. Still, whenever I spotted them together, I felt a pang. Heidi would never be Taylor's best friend, I told myself. If it weren't for their mothers, Taylor wouldn't give Heidi the time of day. If Heidi's dad weren't richer than Oprah, no one else would put up with her, either. She wasn't pretty. She wasn't funny. She was just annoying. Kendall and Rae, Kelly, Ariana, and Laurel, Piper and the other soccer girls—none of them could stand Heidi. They only tolerated her because Taylor did, and because Heidi had an eight-person hot tub right in the middle of her kitchen.

Then there was Ryan, who seemed to have moved on spectacularly. For about a week, he tried talking to me in trig. The conversations went like this:

Ryan: Hey, Lexi.

Me:

Ryan: How are you?

Me:

Ryan: How's it feel to be back?

Me:

Ryan: Are you going to keep ignoring me?

Me:

Ryan: (annoyed sigh) Whatever.

After those first feeble attempts, he started ignoring me right back. Then Mrs. Silver changed the seating chart, and we were on opposite sides of the room, which should have made things easier.

It didn't.

I knew I should forget Ryan, not just because of Rule Number Four but because I had my pride. Only I couldn't help myself. I watched him all the time when he wasn't looking.

Wrestling with Kyle Humboldt and Jason Saccovitch in the hall. Buying Cokes from the vending machine. Laughing with some ponytailed girl at his locker.

I wondered what was so funny.

I wondered if he was comparing her to me.

I wondered whether, if I had just gone farther with Ryan, all of this could have been prevented.

He tried once. It was the day after graduation. We were down in his grandparents' basement and he started to unbutton my jeans, but I stopped him. Then he tried putting my hand on his zipper, but I pulled away. At the time, he was cool about it. He said he would wait until I was ready. "You're not mad?" I said. And he said, "It's no big deal." But if it was really no big deal, why would he hook up with Taylor? Was it all about sex? Did he get something from her just because he couldn't get it from me?

I lay in bed for hours asking myself these questions, waiting for answers that never came.

"So, what are you girls wearing tonight?"

It was Saturday morning, ten o'clock, and already my mother had popped her head through Ruthie's door three times—each time with a new excuse for interrupting. First, it was to deliver our folded laundry, then it was to open the windows and let in fresh air. Now, here she was again, placing a tray of iced tea and orange wedges on Ruthie's bedside table.

Ruthie, blasting away on her trombone, didn't hear the question.

"What are you girls wearing tonight?" my mother repeated, louder.

From my spread-eagle position on Ruthie's bed, I gave her a blank look. "What's tonight?"

As if I didn't know. As if there hadn't been a million posters plastered around school for the past month. HALLOWEEN HOMECOMING, OCTOBER 24! MASQUERADE BALL! BE THERE OR BE . . . A LOSER!

"Band uniform," Ruthie announced, propping her trombone against the wall and helping herself to iced tea.

At first, I thought she was joking, but then I remembered. The marching band played at halftime.

"*After* the game," our mother clarified. "The dance . . . I heard from Mrs. Gillespie at church that the theme is masquerade, and I have a few dresses that would be perfect. I even picked up a couple of masks at the costume shop, with feathers and glitter and—"

Ruthie shook her head, muttering that she had other plans.

"What kind of plans?" I asked. My sister's idea of a fun weekend was watching the SyFy Channel with Sasha and Beatrice or hanging out at the coffee shop with all the other band geeks.

She ignored me, proceeding to gulp down the first glass of iced tea and then to pour herself another.

"Since when do you have *plans* on a Saturday night?"

"It's a band thing."

"What *kind* of band thing?"

Ruthie shrugged and started drinking again.

"Alexa?" My mother smiled tentatively. "Would you like to take a look at what I have?"

"No, thank you," I said, in the polite-but-distant tone I'd mastered since promising my father I would make an effort. "I will not be attending any homecoming festivities." (Rule Number Five.)

"Oh." My mother nodded. "Well, that's fine." She busied herself with the orange wedges, then with a stack of books on Ruthie's desk. Then, because she couldn't stand it a second longer, she blurted, "Not even the game? . . . I thought your father and I would take you out for an early dinner and then the three of us would go to the game and watch your sister march. . . ."

"Mmm-hmm," I murmured, like I was actually considering this. Then, "Thank you for the offer. Maybe next time."

"Next time," she repeated.

"You and Dad should go, though," I said, thinking how nice it would be to have the house to myself. "Be Ruthie's cheering section."

Ruthie rolled her eyes just as our mother took the bait, murmuring, "Of course. We wouldn't miss it."

Jackpot.

As it turns out, having the house to yourself is not as great as you would think. The second Ruthie and my parents left, I blasted the stereo and started bumping and grinding around the living room, but without anyone to laugh at my dance moves, I got bored. So I raided the kitchen for ice cream, chips, cherry Coke. I settled into my mother's best chair—the white one with the pink roses—that we were never allowed to sit on. For maybe five minutes I was in heaven, stuffing my face, sprinkling barbecue-potato-chip dust all over. Then I started feeling sick. No one was here to reprimand me or to suggest that I have celery instead. I didn't know why I was doing it. So I put everything back.

The house, I realized as I walked from the kitchen back to the living room, was too quiet. I might as well turn on the TV and visit my old friends—Hannah Montana, Ellen, Sponge-Bob, and Dr. Phil—just to have some company. So I flopped down on the couch with no regard for my dirty sneakers resting on my mother's hand-embroidered Peruvian throw pillows.

I forgot it was Saturday. None of my favorite shows was on. I was a little annoyed, but then I remembered the movie channels. I found one of the Batmans, which I wouldn't normally be into, but this one had Christian Bale, and who doesn't love Christian Bale? So I settled in.

I think it's no coincidence that my lightbulb moment occurred during this particular movie. You can't watch a kid's parents get murdered before his eyes and feel nothing. You can't watch him put on his armored suit and start fighting bad guys and not cheer. If you have any shred of human decency, you want Batman to win, not just to avenge his parents' death, but also to show the miserable jerks of this world what it feels like to lose.

I didn't even watch the whole thing. When inspiration hit, I just went with it. With no friends and no parents around to drive me, I pulled my bike out of the garage for the first time since July Fourth, when Taylor and I rode to the fireworks.

The wind on my face felt good and crisp. I pedaled like a crazy person, until my legs burned and the air in my lungs felt like needles. On the highway, cars whizzed past me. A few of them beeped. Mothers, probably. I wasn't wearing my helmet, and my own mother would be having a conniption if she saw me, but I didn't care. For the first time in a long time, I felt free.

The guy behind the counter at Costume City was greasy haired, pock faced, and mean looking—the last kind of person who should be working in customer service. To the woman in front of me in line, who was searching for a Strawberry Shortcake wig for her daughter, he snorted, "Strawberry *Shortcake*? Are you kidding me? She sucks."

The woman demanded to speak to the manager.

Greaseball said, "I *am* the manager."

After she stormed out, he rolled his eyes toward me and said, in the most bored manner possible, "Can I help you?"

I almost chickened out because I knew what was coming. *Batman? Are you kidding me? He sucks.*

Instead, the guy nodded approvingly. "Batman is the shit."

I felt a surge of relief.

"We're all sold out, kid. Halloween's a week away."

Crap.

Then he grinned, showing a surprisingly nice set of teeth. "How do you feel about Catwoman?"

Meow

THE GYM DIDN'T look like a gym, that was for sure. Whoever was in charge of decorations took their job seriously, what with the endless strands of Christmas lights and the gold and silver balls hanging everywhere. Tables were set up along the perimeter, with champagne glasses for punch and vases full of what looked like tree branches sprayed with metallic paint, and millions of glass pebbles. Even the bleachers had been covered in shiny paper. Because the overhead lights were turned off, the whole room had a shimmering, otherworldly feel—as long as you ignored the basketball hoops and the lingering smell of sweat socks.

After half an hour of standing in a corner, observing the scene, it occurred to me how stupid I was to be nervous. I was Catwoman. Every square inch of my body—and most of my face—was shielded in black Spandex. If ever there were a time to be fearless, it was tonight.

Walking around the gym, I noticed that other girls' "costumes" weren't much different from the dresses they'd wear to a regular dance. Short or long, shiny or lacy, strapless or not. But the masks changed everything. You had to look at bodies and hair for clues.

Right away I spotted Taylor. I knew her so well—her knobby knees, the way she tipped her head to the right when she was talking, her low, gravelly laugh—it didn't matter what she was wearing. (Which tonight happened to be a gunmetal gray sheath dress with sky-high strappy sandals, an updo, and a glittery silver mask.) I could pick Taylor out of a crowd in Grand Central Station. In the middle of rush hour. During a power outage.

Which made it all the more ironic that she walked by me three times without so much as a clue—each time carrying a champagne glass and hanging all over Heidi, making me wonder what she was drinking besides punch.

Ryan was nowhere to be seen. But then, most of the guys were impossible to identify. While a handful had skipped dressing up altogether or had thrown on the token skeleton T-shirt, others were wearing full costumes. There was a gorilla, Darth Vader, Jack Sparrow from *Pirates of the Caribbean*, four President Obamas, one Bush, vampires, mummies, Beavis and Butthead, and probably thirty grim reapers—complete with skeleton masks, black robes, and bony hands holding knives. Fake, plastic knives, but still. They were freaky.

At one point, a few of them sidled up to me and—because there was no way I could possibly know who they were—said things they otherwise wouldn't have had the guts to say. Like, "Hey, Catwoman, looking for something to lick?" On any other night, in any other context, this would have been mortifying; which is to say, if I had been *me*, I would have been mortified.

But I was not me.

I was Catwoman.

For the first time since the accident, I liked what I looked like. A) My face was covered, and B) my newly acquired fat, disgusting in regular clothes, was compressed into submission by my cat suit. I was curvy in all the right places.

The word *meow* actually rolled off my lips, and instead of sounding dumb, it sounded hot. Which is what a disguise does. It gives you permission to act however you want—to not care what people say, to become someone else.

The girls' room, too, was a whole new experience. I could actually look at my reflection without cringing. I could reapply my lipstick in front of the mirror and feel completely at ease.

"I *love* your costume," a girl from my English class gushed as she added a layer of mascara to her lashes.

I couldn't tell if she recognized me, but I thanked her.

"Why didn't *we* wear costumes?" asked another girl in a pink tulle dress and black mask. "We should have worn costumes."

"Seriously," her friend said. Then, to me, "You look awesome."

"Thanks."

I double-checked my mask in the mirror, making sure that the graft was completely hidden and no stray blonde hairs had escaped.

Perfect.

As I walked out into the hall, something stopped me. A

few yards away, bent over the water fountain, was one of the grim reapers. He was holding his mask in one hand, and when he stood up and tossed his bangs out of his eyes, I saw who it was.

Jarrod's friend Rob, Taylor's greatest crush of all time.

That's when this idea started taking shape in my mind. *Right here, right now is my chance to get back at her.*

I could picture it exactly. I could see myself walking over to Rob and taking his hand, leading him into the nearest classroom, shutting the door behind us.

"What are we doing?" he would say.

But I would say nothing.

Instead, I would push him into a chair.

I would lift up his robe.

I would unzip his jeans.

I would do *exactly* what Taylor did to me.

Rob was a senior, and he was probably as much of a perv as Jarrod. I'd seen him in his bathing suit at the LeFevres' pool. He had a line of thick, black hair leading from his belly button downward. His "treasure trail," Taylor called it. He'd probably had sex a hundred times.

But so what? Tonight, I was Catwoman. If he tried to touch me, my cat suit would be like a force field between us. I, however, would be touching the real thing.

The real thing.

I suddenly remembered this Halloween party Taylor had once, where her mom dressed as a witch and we all wandered around the LeFevres' pitch-black basement, sticking our hands in different bowls, shrieking as we touched the lizard eyeballs (which were really cherry tomatoes) and rat intestines (cold spaghetti).

I wondered what a penis would feel like. I'd never touched one, so I could only guess. Cucumber? . . . Hot dog? . . . Twinkie?

I tried to stifle a laugh, but it didn't work. I was picturing X-rated things, but my mind was still stuck in third grade.

"What's so funny?"

Rob was looking at me curiously.

I only sniggered harder.

"Come on. Share."

I shook my head.

"Lexi, right? Taylor's friend?" He took a step toward me. "I'd know you anywhere."

I shouldn't have been surprised. Why look at a girl's face when you could look at her body? Every guy at the dance probably knew who I was. Still, the realization hit me like a wrecking ball. How could I have been so stupid? How could I have thought that a little spandex would make me invisible?

Rob took another step toward me, smiling. "Hey," he said, cocking his head toward the gym. "You going back? I'll walk with you."

But I didn't answer.

Slick as the jungle cat I was, I turned and ran in the opposite direction. I darted around a corner and down the darkened corridor. The weight room, I remembered, was somewhere in senior hall. I could get back to the gym through there.

✦ ✦ ✦

The first thing I noticed was her feet.

Two sky-high, strappy sandals propped on a weight bench, pointing in opposite directions. I couldn't see the rest of her. The lights were on, but black robes, like the one Rob had been wearing, obscured my view. There were four of them, standing in a semicircle, all holding—not plastic knives this time—cell phones.

It took me a minute to work my way around the bodies, but when I did, there she was. Taylor, flopped on a wrestling mat, head lolling to one side. Her dress was pulled up to her chin and so was her bra. Her rainbow underpants—a pair I recognized because we'd gone shopping together and bought the same ones—were halfway down her hips.

At first, I didn't realize what was happening. What the cell phones were for. Then, it hit me. "Are you taking *pictures*?"

All four skeleton heads turned.

"Easy, kitty cat," one of them muttered.

And another said, "She's wasted."

I felt a mean, hard spark of triumph in my gut. *Serves her right*, is what I thought. *Karma.*

But then one of the grim reapers bent down to take a close-up picture of Taylor's bare boob. "My new screen saver!" he announced.

The rest of them cracked up.

Taylor didn't make a sound.

And I don't know why, but something in me snapped. I started hissing, "Stop that! Get away from her!" With all the strength I had, I shoved my way in. "Taylor?" I knelt beside her and started yanking her clothes back into place, too rough, but I couldn't help it. I needed to cover her up. "Tay?"

"Oh, shit," I heard someone mutter. "Is that LeFevre's sister?"

"Tay!" I said again.

She didn't respond. Not even when I shook her. Not even when I screamed her name. Panic rose like bile in my throat, but when I turned around for help, the black robes were gone.

Not knowing what else to do, I heaved Taylor up from the wrestling mat and onto her feet, where she collapsed like a Slinky. I tried again, this time planting myself beside her, wedging my right shoulder under her left armpit and wrapping my arm around her waist. Somehow, I managed to drag her out the door.

We didn't make it two feet before a teacher materialized in the hallway. At first, I thought it was a student because she looked so young, but then I saw her chaperone badge.

"I'm Ms. McCann?" she said, like she was asking a question instead of stating a fact. "The library media specialist?" She hesitated, glancing at Taylor, then back at me. "Someone said they heard screaming?"

I knew that this was the luckiest break ever, Ms. McCann being the one to find us, and I knew that she couldn't identify me, but I was still tongue-tied. I felt the same way I did at Girl Scout camp when I was ten. My counselor, Lacey, was only six years older, and all the girls in my cabin acted like she was our annoying big sister, but to me, Lacey was an adult whose rules I needed to obey. Ms. McCann may have been wearing a ponytail and jean skirt, but she was still in charge.

"My friend's sick," I blurted—the first lie that popped into my head. "I think it's that flu bug. You know . . . the one that's been going around? I just got over it myself. . . . Anyway, she's so tired she can't even keep her eyes open. We're heading outside for some fresh air."

Ms. McCann frowned like she wasn't sure this was such a great idea.

"It's just a twenty-four-hour thing," I babbled on. "The best thing for her is rest. . . . I already called her parents. They're on their way to pick us up."

Either I was an incredible liar, or Ms. McCann was a total pushover. In any case, she must have believed me.

Because she let us go.

"Ruthie? I need you to pick me up. . . . Because I do . . . *Because* . . . Because I rode my bike and I can't put Taylor on the back. . . . Because she's *passed out*, okay? She's completely wasted. . . . I'll explain later. . . . No . . . *No*, I am *not* calling Mom. . . . What could you possibly be doing right now that's more important than helping your own sister? . . . Just get here, okay? . . . Fine. The courtyard by the parking lot."

After I hung up, I walked back toward the cluster of bushes where I'd left Taylor, curled up in the fetal position on a bench.

Only now she wasn't alone.

At first, when I saw a pair of horn-rimmed glasses glinting at me, I panicked. I thought it was the computer teacher, Mr. Canto. But then, in the glow of the security light, I saw the camera around his neck. And the same intense expression he'd worn in the darkroom.

"What are *you*—" I started to say before I caught a whiff of something horrible emanating from the bench. "Oh God. Did she throw up?"

Photo Boy nodded. "I won't be wearing these shoes again."

I grimaced.

He shrugged. "They're just shoes."

Before I could respond, Taylor suddenly revived herself, sitting straight up and squinting at him. "Who are *you*?"

"I'm Theo."

"You're cute," she said. Then she slumped sideways and ralphed all over his jeans.

The smell was so overpowering, for a second I thought that I, too, was going to be sick. But I managed to breathe through my mouth, and the moment passed.

"Well," Theo deadpanned, "I guess I won't be wearing these jeans again, either."

I laughed. I didn't mean to. There was nothing funny about this situation, but still, I laughed.

Theo bent down in front of Taylor's face. "She's breathing. . . . Probably just needed to get it out of her system . . . How much did she drink? Do you know?"

"No . . . She's only been drunk one time before. I've never seen her like this."

Theo nodded, then stood up. "So, is this your superpower?"

"What?"

"Rescuing your inebriated friends."

I shook my head. "She's not my friend." Then, like a moron,

I kept going. "She used to be. But she's not anymore."

"Rescuing inebriated *ex*-friends?" Theo raised an eyebrow. "Now I'm impressed."

I thought, *Don't be.*

"I'm Theo," he said, extending a hand.

"Catwoman," I said, shaking it.

I was glad again, to be wearing the costume. Relieved that Theo didn't recognize me from the darkroom.

"So," I said, "what's *your* superpower? Taking pictures?"

But before he could respond, my phone rang. It was Ruthie, saying she'd just left the party and was on her way.

"A *band* party?" I said.

"Screw you, Lex," she snapped, and hung up.

I turned to Theo. "My sister just hung up on me. Can you believe that?"

"I don't know. Who's your sister?"

"Ruth Mayer. She's a senior. You probably don't know her."

"Sure I do," Theo said. "She's the queen of chocolate chip cookies."

I gave him a blank look.

"I'm a senior, too. She was my home-ec partner last year."

I nodded as though this made perfect sense.

"Your sister's cool," he added.

I scanned his face to see if he was joking. He wasn't.

"Yeah," I said, covering my surprise. "She plays a mean trombone."

When Ruthie pulled up and saw Theo standing next to me she looked confused.

"Clark Kent?" she said through the driver's side window.

And he said, "Ruth Wakefield?"

"What are you doing here?"

Theo held up his camera.

"You're covering the dance?"

"I was. Until I ran into Catwoman."

Ruthie's forehead crinkled at me. "What's with the unitard?"

"What's with the hair?" I retorted.

My sister—who'd never used a styling product in her life—seemed to have busted out the gel tonight. And the weird thing was, it actually looked good. Parted to one side, slicked down and clipped into place by a sparkly barrette.

I stared at her for a second before shaking my head. "Never mind," I said. "What took you so long? I told you Taylor's drunk. She's been throwing up and everything. She could have alcohol poisoning for all we know! What are we going to *do*?"

"First of all," Ruthie said, "chill. We are going to take Taylor home. Her parents will decide if she needs to go to the hospital. You and Theo get her in the backseat."

The ride to Taylor's house was worse than I could have imagined. She threw up twice, both times with me holding her head so she wouldn't choke. Most of it landed in my lap.

Ruthie didn't say much. I filled her in on the essentials of what had happened, and Theo interjected once to say "Never trust a grim reaper," but Ruthie's responses were minimal. To my sister, our job was to get Taylor home; that was all. Her frowns in the rearview mirror spoke volumes. She was disgusted with the whole thing.

By the time we pulled into the LeFevres' driveway, Taylor was still too drunk to walk. When Ruthie and I tried to drag her out of the backseat, she opened her eyes and suddenly shrieked with excitement.

"Woofie!" A glob of something flew out of her mouth and onto Ruthie's chin. "Hiiii!"

"Hi, Taylor," my sister said grimly, wiping her face with one hand and clasping Taylor's elbow with the other. "You're home."

"Woofiewoofiewoofie," Taylor chortled. "Where's Theo?"

"Theo's in the front seat," Ruthie said.

"Hey, Taylor," Theo said, walking around to our side of the car.

"The-ooooo! You're cute."

"Thanks. Hey. It's time to go in now."

"That's right," Ruthie said. "It's bedtime."

Taylor tried to yank her arm out of Ruthie's grasp. "Nonononono."

"Yes. It's late. Everyone's tired."

Shaking her head wildly, Taylor finally noticed me standing there and started crooning like an idiot. "Hello, kitty. Kittykittykitty. Niiice kitty."

I don't know what possessed me to do this, but for the first time all night, I pulled off my mask.

"It's me, Tay. Lexi."

Taylor's face crumpled and a string of nonsense came out of her mouth—something about me hating her, and Ruthie hating her, and boys hating her, then some rant about high heels, which by that point she'd pulled off her feet and was holding in her hands.

Then she started bawling.

Ruthie turned to me. "Go ring the doorbell."

She said it in a way that meant *don't even think about arguing.* But still, I hesitated.

"You too," Ruthie said to Theo.

"Me?" he said.

"Yeah. Make sure Catwoman doesn't wimp out."

Theo shrugged. "Okay, boss."

The two of us trudged up the brick walkway.

I knew exactly what was going to happen next because Taylor's mom went out every Saturday night to play bunco. Taylor's dad would come to the door, take one look at her, and hit the roof. If there was one thing I'd learned about Mr. LeFevre over the years, it was this: he hated surprises. One night when I was over for dinner, Taylor's mom forgot to turn on the oven for the meat loaf. When she brought it out of the oven, cold, Taylor's dad got so mad he threw the whole thing against the wall.

My finger hovered in front of the buzzer. I tried to imagine the look on Mr. LeFevre's face. No way was Taylor going to pull this one past him. He'd already grounded her once, after Jarrod's party. Now there was puke in her hair. The smell coming off her was flammable.

"Hey," Theo said as my finger continued to hover, "if you can bust into a darkroom, you can ring a doorbell."

Only then did I remember that my mask was off. Of course

he recognized me. I glanced at him and saw that he was smiling. For a second, I forgot what I was doing. Maybe it was the glasses, but I noticed that his eyes, which I had thought were just green, were actually flecked with gold. His skin, too, looked different in the porch light. Less pale, more—

"They'd rather have her drunk than dead," Theo said.

"Do it," Ruthie commanded, suddenly appearing behind us, Taylor slung over her shoulder like Santa's sack.

When I didn't move fast enough, my sister grabbed my finger and pressed it to the buzzer, holding it there.

"Shit," I murmured.

And the door swung open.

Petty Little Problems

"DID YOU SEE the look on his face?" I asked as we backed out of the LeFevres' driveway. "He's going to kill her."

"Isn't that the point?" Ruthie said.

"What?"

"You wanted payback. Now her dad's going to kill her. You should be dancing a jig right now."

I shook my head. Of course I wanted payback. Taylor deserved serious punishment, but still—

"Why are you shaking your head?" Ruthie asked. "You wanted this to happen. *You* called *me*, remember?"

"Yeah, but not to bring her *home*. Her dad is a complete lunatic."

"In fact," Ruthie said, ignoring me, "I seem to remember you *begging* me to come." She made her voice high and squeaky. *"I need you, Ruthie! Tell me what to do, Ruthie!* I left Sasha and Beatrice stranded at the party. For *you*."

"That's not . . ." I spluttered. "It wasn't like . . ."

"What did she do?" Theo, who was sitting in the passenger seat, turned around to look at me.

"What?"

"Taylor. What did she do that was so bad?"

I opened my mouth to answer, but Ruthie beat me to it.

"She seduced Lexi's boyfriend."

"Ouch," Theo said.

I shot Ruthie a look in the rearview mirror.

"What?" she said innocently. "Am I wrong?"

I thought about jabbing my sister in the back of the head. I would have, if she wasn't driving.

"Where to, Mr. Kent?" Ruthie said, like this was some kind of TV sitcom, and she was playing the butler.

"Geneseo Lane, Ms. Wakefield," Theo said. "Number sixty-seven."

His tone was amused, but I bet he couldn't wait to get out of the car. And who could blame him? Who likes listening to other people fight, especially people you barely know?

It wasn't easy, but I managed to keep my mouth shut for the rest of the ride, stewing silently in the backseat.

After Ruthie and I thanked Theo for his help, he disappeared into his house, probably collapsing with relief that he was free.

"What's this Clark Kent business?" I muttered, climbing into the front and buckling my seat belt.

"Hello," Ruthie said, like I was a moron. "Superman's alter ego?"

"I know *that*."

"Clark Kent is a reporter for the *Daily Planet*."

"So?"

"So . . . Theo is editor of the *Millbridge Monitor*. Which, if you ever bothered to read anything besides *Seventeen*, you might know."

My heart pounded with indignation, but my voice stayed calm. "Well, who's Ruth Wakefield then?"

Ruthie heaved a sigh. "She invented the Tollhouse chocolate chip cookie."

"Since when do you *bake*, anyway?"

"Since I needed an elective and I didn't want to take metal shop. Okay? Are we done with Twenty Questions?"

"Oh my God!" I cried. "Why are you being such a wench?"

Ruthie snorted. "Why am *I* being such a wench?"

"Yeah. Why are *you* being such a wench?"

"Why am *I* being such a wench." She slowed to a stop in front of a red light and shook her head. "That's rich."

"What is your *problem*?" I shouted.

My sister turned to me and said, without a drop of kindness in her voice, "Can you think about anyone but yourself for one minute?"

"What's that supposed to mean? The whole reason I called you to pick me up was to help Taylor!"

"Uh-huh." Ruthie pressed on the gas.

I knew what *uh-huh* meant: she didn't believe me.

"What—" I cried, exasperated, "I was thinking of *myself* when I dragged Taylor out of there? If I was thinking of *her*, I would have left her there, passed out naked while a bunch of guys took pictures of her? That makes absolutely no sense!"

Ruthie shook her head. "I wasn't talking about Taylor."

"Well, who *were* you talking about?"

"Me, Lex! . . . I was talking about me!"

Then suddenly, out of nowhere, my sister started going off: saying how she was having a great time tonight when

I called, how she didn't want to leave, but I goaded her into picking me up.

"*Goaded* you?"

Ruthie ignored me and kept going. "You're always doing that. Putting yourself first. Like whatever I'm doing—whatever I'm interested in—doesn't matter. Band is a waste of time. Classical music sucks. My friends are geeks. How could *I* possibly have *plans* on a Saturday night? Well, let me tell you something that may shock you. . . . Are you ready for this? . . . I actually have a *life*, and it doesn't revolve around you."

"Well, that's . . . I know *that*," I said, stumbling on my words, feeling my face grow hot.

Ruthie kept going. She was on a roll now, pounding the steering wheel for emphasis. "Every time you come to me with one of your petty little problems, what do I do? I *listen*. I give *advice*. I try to make you feel *better*."

"*Petty little problems?*" I sputtered. "You think my problems are *petty*?"

"Yeah, Lex. I do. On the scale of things that actually matter, I think your problems rank pretty low."

I stared at her in disbelief.

"I'm sorry, but it's true. You just can't look past yourself long enough to see it."

She then proceeded to hop in her time machine and fly back to August, where her college tour got interrupted by my accident—and to tell me how disappointing that experience was for her.

"Let me get this straight," I said. "You think I ran into a tree on purpose, just to ruin your trip?"

Ruthie shook her head. "No."

"Because that's sure what it sounds like. It sounds like you think I *deliberately* rammed my face through Jarrod's windshield, *deliberately* shattered my own bones just to—"

"No," Ruthie said, more fiercely. "That's not what I'm saying. You're twisting my words."

"Well, untwist them then."

"I *will* . . . Jesus . . . if you could stop interrupting me for one second. . . . I *know* you didn't hurt yourself on purpose. Of course I know that. I was scared shitless when it happened. I prayed for you—literally *prayed*, on my knees, in the middle of the hotel bathroom, that you would be okay. And I don't even believe in God! . . . But that's not the point. . . . The point is that ever since you got home, Lex, you've been front and center. Everyone comes to your rescue, and I just get left in the dust. 'Oh, don't worry about Ruth. She's so smart. She's so competent. She can handle it.'"

I opened my mouth to say something, but my sister kept ranting, through traffic circles and stop signs and blinking yellow lights. "After the accident, I thought you might open your eyes a little, gain some perspective. But you know what? You're more self-centered now than you ever were before."

"That's not true," I murmured, only half believing myself.

"Do you realize you never once asked me about my trip? Never once asked which colleges I'm thinking of applying to?"

I got a little snarky then, telling Ruthie I'm sorry, but I was a little busy getting jacked up on enough pain medication to stun a buffalo, and, you know, having my *ass* stapled to my *cheekbone*.

"Lex. No offense—because I don't want to minimize the pain you felt in the hospital—but that was over two months ago. The victim act is getting old."

"Easy for you to say!"

"No," Ruthie said, pulling into our driveway and cutting the engine. "Not easy for me to say . . . and Dad's going to kill me for saying it because he asked me to cut you some slack, which I have, for a long time. But I'm sick of this shit, Lex. I'm really sick of it. I'm sick of you lambasting Mom and Dad when all they're trying to do is help. I'm sick of you barging into my room whenever you feel like it, and putting on my clothes without asking—"

I started to defend myself, saying that I hadn't worn her clothes in days. Not since my new jeans and sweatshirts arrived in the mail.

But Ruthie just kept ranting. "Clothes which, for your information, I happen to *like*, even if you're wearing them to make some kind of statement about how little you care what people think. Which is a joke because it's so obvious how much you care."

"No, I don't," I said weakly.

"Whatever your 'Rules' are," Ruthie continued, scratching quotes in the air with her fingernails, "you're obsessed with your face, you're obsessed with how people perceive you, and you're obsessed with Taylor and Ryan, to the point that your life has become . . . well . . . pathetic. . . . I mean, why did you even go to the dance tonight?"

An image of Rob popped, unbidden, into my head. Had I

really imagined leading him into an empty room and sticking my hand down his boxers? Had I really thought that hooking up with him would hurt Taylor? It didn't even make *sense*. How would she find out what I did unless I told her? And then, why would she believe me?

"Well?" Ruthie said.

A hot flicker of shame licked at my chest. I couldn't tell my sister about Rob, so I mumbled a half-truth. "I wanted to feel like me again."

"By dressing as *Catwoman*?" Ruthie looked at me like I'd just sprouted horns.

I shook my head miserably. "I don't know."

"Lex," she said, no longer sounding like Cruella de Vil. "Do you really think you're so different now?"

"Yes."

"How?"

I stared at her. "Isn't it obvious?"

"Not to me."

"I have no friends . . . and Ryan's completely moved on."

"Ken doll?" I could tell from her voice that she couldn't believe what she was hearing.

"I loved him," I said pitifully.

"Well," my sister said, sighing and unbuckling her seat belt—a sign that she might finally be finished tearing me to shreds. "As far as I can tell, Ryan has never done much of anything to deserve your love. Taylor's been your friend forever, but Ryan? . . ." She shook her head. "Whatever. You can make your own judgment about those two. I've said my piece."

Then she announced that she was going inside—her car smelled like a barf factory, and she couldn't breathe through her mouth anymore.

After Ruthie left, I sat in the car for a long time, wearing my rancid cat suit. Licking my wounds. Replaying her tirade over and over, trying to make sense of what she'd said.

Finally, it hit me. This whole time, I'd been wrong about my sister. Ruthie wasn't jealous of me, not even close.

I'd Rather Be Cleaning Litter Boxes

I WOKE AT five in the morning with an unsettled feeling—the kind you get when you know something bad happened, but you can't remember what it is. Then I remembered.

Taylor on the wrestling mat.

The grim reapers.

The look on Mr. LeFevre's face.

Ruthie's litany of insults.

Taylor again.

I checked my cell: nothing.

Without even thinking, I found myself walking down to the living room in the dark. Sitting at the computer, logging on to MyPage. I used to MP every day—write on people's blackboards, update my news flash—but this was the first time since the accident. I felt like I was opening a time capsule, or walking into Jenny Albee's brother's bedroom. Even a year after the funeral, Mrs. Albee didn't touch a thing. Teddy bears still on the bed. Tonka trucks littering the floor. She left everything exactly where Caleb had left it the day he died.

The picture on my page was like a relic from another life. Smiling, scarless Lexi, face pressed up against smiling, rosy-cheeked Taylor. Both of us have our pointer fingers raised in the air, signifying to the world that we are number one, having just beaten New Canaan 3–2 in double overtimes.

We looked so young and happy it made my stomach ache. It made me remember a simpler time—a time before Ryan, before parties where people started drinking beer and tearing each other's clothes off, before everything got so messed up.

There were a bunch of notes on my blackboard from the days following the accident. I scrolled down to the bottom and worked my way up.

OMG, Lexiiii!!!! What happened last nite? (Kendall)

R u ok??? R u really in the hospital? (Rae)

Y r u not ansring ur cell??? We have 2 talk! (Taylor)

R u getting my texts? (Ryan)

We r all thinking of uuuuu! Call usssss!!! (Laurel)

The most up to date was from Meagan O'Hallahan on September 1. *R u not on MP anymore? Wazzup w/ that??? Coming 2 ur BBQ on Sat. Cant wait 2 c uuuuuuu!*

There was nothing on my board from last night. There were no new messages in my in-box. For a second, I thought about calling Heidi or Kendall and Rae, but then I changed my mind. They'd probably say, "Why are you calling so early?" or worse, act all fake and thrilled to hear from me.

So I clicked NEWS FLASH. That is the beauty of MyPage. You can see what people are doing without them even knowing.

If only you could un-see something after you've seen it.

If only you could wave a magic wand and erase a single night from collective memory.

That's what I wanted to do as soon as I saw Jason Saccovitch's post. He and Kyle Humboldt were legendary for their perverted links. Usually, I ignored them, but this time, when I saw *You have to check this out*, I clicked it. The realization that I couldn't delete what popped up—that Taylor and her rainbow underpants were on display for the whole world to see—made me nauseous.

Apparently, I wasn't alone because someone behind me gasped. "What in the *world* . . . ?"

I jumped a foot in the air. "Oh my God! Are you *spying* on me?"

My mother gasped again, leaning in for a closer look. "Is that *you*?"

"No!" I made a crazy attempt to cover Taylor with both hands before realizing all I had to do was press a button and the window would disappear.

"Well, are you . . . was that . . ." My mother grasped for words. "What I mean to say is . . . it's perfectly natural for you to be curious about—"

"Oh my *God*," I moaned, realizing what she was getting at. "You think I'm looking at *porn*? . . . Gross! It's Taylor, okay?"

"Taylor?"

"I told you last night, she got a little drunk at the dance. That's why I called Ruthie."

The bare minimum. That's what I'd given my parents when I got home. Just enough to get them off my back.

Now my mother was folding her arms across her chest, waiting.

"Okay," I conceded. "She wasn't a little drunk. She was a lot drunk. She passed out, and a bunch of guys took pictures of her and now someone posted them on MyPage. You can't tell it's her because she's wearing a mask, but I know it is because I saw it happen and . . . I can't believe I'm telling you this!"

My mother's expression changed from shocked to disdainful. "I knew something like this would happen . . . with the amount of alcohol in that house . . . and the irresponsible parenting. . . ."

"What are you *talking* about?"

My mother sighed. "Let's just say that Bree LeFevre is not exactly a role model when it comes to drinking. And with Taylor's poor judgment, not to mention poor self-esteem, something like this was bound to—"

"Oh my God!" I stared at her. "Are you blaming *Taylor* for what these guys did to her?"

My mother wrapped her bathrobe more tightly around her waist. "Of course I'm not *blaming* Taylor. I'm just making the point that—"

"Well, *don't*, Mom. Okay? Don't make points about things you know nothing about. You don't know these guys. You don't know anything!"

With that, I sprang to a stand, roughly pushed the swivel chair back under the desk, and marched out of the living room. Because there's nothing like your mother getting on her high horse to suddenly inspire you to defend your ex-BFF and her stupid choices.

✦ ✦ ✦

Later, when my mother came up to my room to apologize and to bring me my freshly laundered cat suit, I was still mad. But I had to bite my tongue. I'd promised my father I would make an effort.

"I didn't mean to spy on you, honey," she said.

"Uh-huh."

"The reason we keep the computer in the living room is so Daddy and I will always know that you and your sister are safe. With the world the way it is today . . . Internet bullying, predators . . ."

"Right."

"You did the responsible thing, calling Ruth last night," she continued. "I want you to know that . . . and I also want you to know . . . if you ever find yourself in a situation like that again, I'm here for you. . . ."

"Uh-huh."

"Thank you for leaving me and Daddy a note to let us know you were going to the dance, so we wouldn't worry. . . ." She hesitated, gestured to the cat suit draped across the foot of the bed. "Did you at least have fun getting dressed up?"

"A blast."

My voice wasn't sarcastic. It was flat. Totally devoid of emotion.

"Alexa."

"Mother," I said, realizing I was mimicking her.

She gave me a look, and I looked right back at her.

I could tell she was losing her patience, but she kept her voice calm. She loved me very much, she said, but she didn't appreciate my attitude.

"Well . . ." I said, scrambling for a comeback. "I don't appreciate the *attitude* of guys who post photos of drunk girls on the Internet."

It was a complete non sequitur, but somehow it worked.

"Those boys did a terrible thing," my mother said, frowning. "Taylor is a very lucky girl that you found her when you did."

"Yes," I said. "She is."

All day, I waited to hear from Taylor. A phone call, a text—anything to acknowledge what I'd done for her.

But nothing came.

By Monday morning, I still hadn't heard from Taylor—or from anyone else. This made me anxious to get to school, but not so anxious that I was about to get in a car with my sister.

I'd managed to ignore Ruthie for the past thirty-six hours. I'd almost cracked last night, when I walked into the bathroom to brush my teeth and there she was, standing in front of the mirror. She didn't notice me; that's how hard she was staring at herself. Staring and poking at her face with her fingers. At one point, she took a step backward and stood on her toes, to see her whole body. She lowered her shoulders, turned to side, and smiled at her reflection. Smiled!

What are you doing? I wanted to say.

But I already knew. I knew because I'd done it a million times myself: turned sideways in front of the mirror to see how I looked from a different angle. But my sister? Watching Ruthie check herself out was so weird I had to leave the bathroom. Without her even noticing I'd been there.

Now, Ruthie was sitting at the breakfast table, drinking coffee. Which I will never understand. She and Sasha and Beatrice think coffee is the coolest thing ever, even though it reeks and turns their teeth brown.

"I don't need a ride today," I announced, scraping my chair against the floor as I sat. "I will be taking the bus."

Ruthie's eyes widened over her mug. "Really?"

I nodded.

"But you hate the bus."

"So?"

"I would be happy to drive you," my mother said, gliding over to me with a glass of juice.

"No, thank you," I said primly. "I don't need anyone to rescue me."

The corners of Ruthie's mouth twitched, like she was trying not to laugh.

I shot her a look. "I'm glad you think this is funny."

"I don't think it's funny—"

"What's funny?" my father said, appearing in the doorway in full court uniform: navy suit, red tie.

"Nothing," I said.

Ruthie smirked into her coffee.

"That's right," I said, "keep it up."

"I didn't say anything!"

"And for the record," I added, taking a sip of juice and setting it down with a bang. "I am not wearing *any* of your clothes. This is *my* sweatshirt, and these are *my* jeans."

"Congratulations," Ruthie said.

My father glanced from me to my sister and back again. I

guess he read something in my expression because he didn't push it. He just walked over and kissed the top of my hood, wishing me a great day at school.

Unfortunately, "great" is not the word to describe it.

At my locker, there was a surprise waiting for me.

Initially, seeing the triangle of orange paper sticking out made me smile. It made me think of junior high, when Taylor and I used to leave each other notes all the time. She wrote the best notes, always on the orange paper that she kept in her backpack. Multiple-choice questions like, *If there was a nuclear war and you could only choose one boy to share your bomb shelter, who would it be?* And fill in the blanks using dirty words. Sometimes she drew cartoons of our teachers, with thought bubbles rising over their heads, saying things like, *I'd rather be cleaning litter boxes.* Taylor's notes always cracked me up.

This time, not so much.

Alexa [not Lexi, not Lex; Alexa],

Thanks to you, I am forced to write this letter on a piece of paper instead of in a text or e-mail. Thanks to you, my father threw my cell in the pool and locked my computer in his car. He also called my coach, so now I am off the field hockey team for the rest of the season, even though we could be heading to sectionals—so again, thanks. By doing what you did on Saturday night, I can only assume you were trying to punish me for Ryan. Well, guess what? It worked, because I am grounded until Christmas and my parents are barely speaking to me. So congratulations! You have officially ended this friendship. I'd hoped for a while that we would be able to get past what happened, but now I know we never will.

I tried. I really did, to explain about the night of Jarrod's party. But you wouldn't even let me talk. So I am going to set the record straight right here and now. Not for your sake (I'm so mad at you right now I could punch a window) but for mine. I'm tired of feeling guilty. Guilty, #1, for getting drunk that night. (This is not an excuse for what happened, but it is the truth.) That is what gave me the courage to do it.

I don't expect you to understand this because you don't have a brother, but I was actually trying to help Ryan. You don't know the things guys make each other do, especially in football. And the new recruits HAVE to do it if they want any chance of making the team. When Jarrod was a sophomore, the seniors were a-holes and he got it even worse. He got stripped, shaved, covered in eggs and shaving cream and had to sit in Scotty Fieron's tree house all night in the freezing cold. All Ryan had to do was get a BJ, and he had too much respect for you to ask you to do it, so . . . that is what happened.

I know you hate me, and I know you probably think I'm a slut and a horrible person, but I was only trying to help Ryan's chances of making the team, which I thought is what you wanted for him, too. No matter what you think, I was NOT trying to steal him away. Do you really believe I would do something like that to you? Anyway, Ryan would never go for me because I am, well, ME, and you are YOU and there is just no comparing. I know better than to ever try to compete with you, Lexi.

I am crying while I write this because I still can't believe that the girl who used to be my best friend in the entire world, one of the best overall PEOPLE I have ever known, would turn me in to my father. You know how he is. You know how mad and crazy he gets. How could you do that to me???

I guess you could say that we are even now. (Although what you did was for spite, whereas my actions—however drunken and misguided—were from the heart.) You got what you wanted, at least. I hope you are happy.

—Taylor

P.S. I'm not even going to get into what you did with my brother, except to say that it's pretty ironic how mad you got at Ryan when you were doing the exact same thing that night.

I felt like I'd just opened a letter from a terrorist. Taylor had hijacked my anger and made it her own.

By the time I finished reading my hands were shaking. I just stood there, staring at the paper, stunned.

Ryan had too much respect for me? How much respect could he have? He'd never even *told* me—his own girlfriend—what the seniors asked him to do, let alone given me the chance to say no. And Taylor thought she was *helping*? Like hooking up with her best friend's boyfriend was some kind of *sacrifice*? Her way of "taking one for the team"?

It was too mind-boggling for words.

I hate her. That was all I could think.

I was in the girls' room, between first and second periods, when I ran straight into Taylor's guard dog, Heidi.

"It wasn't enough to get her grounded, was it, Lexi?" she said in a voice loud enough for all of sophomore hall to hear. "You had to humiliate her, too?"

"What are you talking about?" I said.

Heidi sneered at me. "Did you really think you could get away with taking those photos?"

"Get *away* with it?" I said in astonishment. "I had nothing to do with it!"

Heidi's arms were crossed over her chest. Her face had the pinched look of disgust, bordering on pure hatred. "You're the only one with a motive."

Two girls at the sink exchanged looks and left. Another skittered out of a stall and out the door without even washing her hands.

"Heidi," I said with as much calm as I could muster, "you had better check your facts before you go accusing people of things they didn't do."

That's when Taylor walked out of the handicapped stall, her eyes redder and puffier than I'd ever seen them.

I looked straight at her. When I spoke, my words were

like shards of glass. "You *know* I had nothing to do with those photos. *I'm* the one who got you out of there! You should be *thanking* me!"

"I don't know what I should be doing," she whispered, more tears welling up. Then, "I think I'm getting a migraine."

Taylor had been getting migraines since fifth grade, right around the time her parents started fighting 24/7. Stress brought them on, the doctor said. I used to feel bad for her. Not anymore.

"Come on, Tay," Heidi said, swooping in and throwing her arm around Taylor's shoulders. "I'll walk you to the nurse. *Some* people should lock themselves in a stall all day so they don't ruin any more lives."

I nodded. "Good one." To Taylor I said, "You're a piece of work, you know that? Nice letter."

Taylor said nothing, just blinked at me with those red eyes.

After she and Heidi left, I collapsed against one of the sinks, feeling my heart thump and my head spin.

Did Heidi really think I took those photos? What if she told everyone? Then I wouldn't just be the girl with the fucked-up face, I'd be the girl with no morals.

Could this day get any worse?

I found out the answer to *that* question after school. Somehow I'd managed—by hiding behind my hood and steering clear of anyone who might confront me—to make it to the final bell. I was about to step onto the bus when I suddenly remembered my bike, which I'd ridden to the dance but forgotten to put in Ruthie's car.

Minutes later, standing at the bike rack by the parking lot,

I wanted to scream. There was glass all over the ground—which of course I'd failed to notice on Saturday night. Now both my tires were flat. Not just soft. Completely, undeniably flat.

I knew that Ruthie would give me a ride after band, but that would mean swallowing my pride and letting her rescue me, which I was *not* about to do. The second-worst option was calling my mother.

Which I would have done.

If my cell were in my backpack where it was supposed to be.

Instead of at home, on my bedside table, charging.

Arrrrrgh!

I wanted to punch the brick wall of the school building. That's how mad I was. But the rational part of my brain took over and marched me back inside in search of a pay phone, which I finally found in senior hall, wedged between a bank of lockers and a trophy case. I scavenged my backpack for quarters and was just starting to dial when something made me jump.

"No!" a voice barked. Then, "Whose life do you think this is?" Followed by, "It's not your decision!"

It was none of my business. I knew I should keep dialing. But I was too curious.

I hung up the phone and crept toward the nearest classroom—the one with its door half open. I stepped inside and, there, sitting at a desk piled high with newspapers, laptop balanced on his knees, was Theo. He was wearing a plaid shirt with the sleeves rolled up, and some kind of weird hat—like a baseball cap only puffier, with a shorter brim. On the wall above his head was a quote: JOURNALISM IS THE FIRST ROUGH DRAFT OF HISTORY.

"You're not listening to me!"

At first, I thought he was arguing with the computer screen, but then I saw the cell clutched to his ear.

"Bullshit!"

I started to back away.

"Complete bullshit!"

Theo slammed the phone on the desk at the same time the strap of my backpack snagged on the doorknob and I stumbled.

When Theo looked up, his mouth was a grim line. His eyebrows were two black slashes.

"What?" he snapped as though I was the one he was mad at, which threw me.

"Nothing," I said.

"You want me to go to college, too? Huh? Get in line!"

I paused for approximately one second, then whipped around and started walking away, straight past the pay phone.

I thought *I* had problems? This guy had *problems*.

I made it all the way down the hall and out the double doors before I heard footsteps behind me. Another yard before I saw, out of the corner of my eye, a plaid shirt.

"Hey."

Theo's voice was calm now, but I didn't respond.

"Sorry about that . . . back there . . . I was mad at my dad. I shouldn't have taken it out on you."

I kept walking. Straight to the bike rack. Ignoring him.

"Hey," he said again. "Did you hear me? I just apologized."

"I heard."

I knew how I sounded, but I didn't care. After the day I'd had, I was too pissed to be nice.

I yanked my bike out of the rack.

"Whoa," Theo said, looking down. "What happened there?"

When I didn't answer, he said, "You'll ruin your rims if you ride on them."

I shrugged, throwing one leg over the seat.

"Seriously," he said. "It's not good for the metal. It'll warp."

I turned to face at him. "What are you, some kind of bike whisperer?"

Theo shook his head, and I saw the flicker of a smile appear on his lips. "Just a concerned citizen."

"I didn't ask for your concern."

He shot me a look, halfway between puzzled and annoyed.

"Sorry," I muttered. Then, "It's not you. I just had a crappy day. . . . I mean a *really* crappy day. I think I might need to punch something."

"Really?" Theo said. "Because I could arrange that."

I gave him a blank look.

"My dad . . . the horse's ass I was talking to on the phone? He owns a boxing ring. I work there after school."

My expression must not have changed because Theo raised both fists to his chin. "You know"—he threw a jab in the air—"boxing? Muhammad Ali? Oscar De La Hoya?"

"I know boxing."

"So if you want to go hit something, my truck's over there. Your bike'll fit in the back."

I squeezed my handlebars. "I don't know. . . ." I pictured what was waiting for me at home. *English essay. My mother. Celery.*

"Come on." Theo jerked his head toward the parking lot. "We'll have fun."

We'll?

Like a doofus, I felt my face grow hot. To cover it up, I shrugged and said, "Okay, whatever."

Theo started to lift my bike over his shoulder, then stopped. "Just so you know . . . I don't invite any old girls to do this."

"Oh no?"

"Nope. Only the ones who dress as Catwoman and perform daring rescues . . . and you know . . . bust into darkrooms in their spare time."

He grinned.

And I don't know why, but my face got even hotter. As we walked across the parking lot together, I thanked God once again for inventing the hooded sweatshirt.

The First Breath Is the Worst

FROM THE OUTSIDE, Barbuto Boxing Gym looked more like a warehouse, but when you walked in, the smell gave it away. *Pungent* was the first word that came to mind, followed by *hockey gloves*, which Ryan once forced me to smell. Everyone in there—pounding on bags, jumping rope, dodging each other around the ring—was male and sweating bombs. You could almost taste the testosterone.

Theo must have seen the look on my face because he said, "The first breath is the worst."

Within seconds, a man who could only be Theo's father came bounding up to us. He was a few inches shorter than Theo and barrel-chested, but he had the same wiry, black hair and green eyes. When he embraced Theo and kissed him on the neck—not just once, but three times—Theo tried to pull away. "Get off me."

But his dad wouldn't let him go. "Still mad at your old man? Huh? Still mad?"

"Off!"

"Don't bite the hand that feeds you. Arrrr." He pretended to bite Theo on the shoulder. "Arrr."

"Pop!"

This went on for some time, the two of them wrestling around, until Theo's dad finally let him go and turned to me. "You believe this kid? Who doesn't want to go to college, huh? He's a smart boy. Talented. He'll get a scholarship. His guidance counselor says—"

"Jesus, Pop." Theo's voice sounded strangled. "Don't drag Lexi into this."

"Lexi?" His dad jumped back suddenly, eyes widening. "*The* Lexi?"

He knows who I am?

I glanced at Theo and saw, to my complete shock, that he was blushing. "Pop, this is Alexa Mayer. . . . Lexi, this is my dad."

Theo's dad pumped my hand up and down. "Vince Barbuto," he said. "Father to this stubborn son of a gun who won't listen to reason. In this financial market—"

"*Pop,*" Theo groaned. "For Christ's sake."

"Okay, okay," his father said, holding up his hands in surrender. Then, "Where are your manners, Taddeo? Get the lady some gloves!"

"Oh, I'm not a boxer," I said, and immediately felt like a moron. "I mean . . . I just came to watch."

"There's no watching here," Theo deadpanned.

And his father said, "That's right. Everyone suits up."

Before I could open my mouth to protest, I was whisked off to a room that smelled—thankfully—more like detergent than sweat, and Theo handed me a pile of clothes.

I took a quick inventory: shirt, shorts, boxing gloves. Nothing to protect my face.

"Are you serious?" I said.

"I am."

"You really want me to . . ." I hesitated. I knew Theo had seen my graft, but I couldn't bring myself to mention it. ". . . put these on?"

"I do."

I took my time getting ready, making sure the door was locked behind me so no one could barge in while I was changing. The room didn't have a mirror. All I could do was look down at my standard-issue, gray T-shirt and navy mesh shorts and grimace at how big my boobs had gotten and how my thighs—which used to have an inch of space between them—now rubbed together when I walked. I decided to put my sweatshirt back on. The hood, I told myself, tying it tight around my face, made me look more like a prizefighter.

Theo knocked just as I was opening the door.

"How'd you do?" he asked.

"Okay," I shrugged. Then, holding up the boxing gloves, "You don't really expect me to wear these."

"Yup. But not until I wrap your hands."

"What?"

"A handwrap goes under your glove," Theo explained. "It keeps the joints aligned and protects you from the most common boxing injuries."

I reminded him that I was not a boxer.

"Not *yet*," he said.

"I can't believe I'm doing this," I muttered, feeling a weird flurry in my stomach as his fingers gripped mine.

"Okay," he said, flipping my hand over and patting the

palm. "I'm going to teach you how to do this so next time you can do it yourself."

Next time?

"Are you paying attention?"

I nodded. "Yes."

"Okay, see this little strip of cloth? This is what you use. First, you wrap it around your wrist a couple of times like so . . . wrap, wrap . . . then, you do the palm . . . wrap, wrap, wrap . . . then, the base of your thumb . . . wrap, wrap . . . and at the end, there's this little Velcro tab thingy that you just press here . . . and . . . voilà!. . . . How does it feel?"

"Tight," I said.

"That's by design. The compression lends strength to your hand when you punch and secures your thumb so you don't sprain it. Most important, it keeps you from fracturing one of your metacarpals—these bones here. . . ." He squeezed my hand between his forefinger and thumb. "We want to protect them, especially the fifth metacarpal. *This* little guy."

"Oh," I murmured. "Uh-huh."

His touch was gentle, warm, but all this talk of bones made me think of the hospital. *This is the zygomatic bone. This is the malar. The lachrymal. The maxilla.* Suddenly, I felt dizzy.

"We use the nonelastic handwraps," Theo continued, taking my other hand and starting the process again. "My dad's pretty old school. Some boxers like the Mexican-style handwrap, which has a little give to it. . . . And then there are these gel insert things you can use, too. . . . Personal preference, really . . . Hey," he said, looking up, "you okay?"

I nodded quickly. Even though I was still picturing my face, puffed up like the Goodyear blimp.

"Don't worry," Theo said. "No one's taking shots at you today. You'll just be working on technique. Okay?"

I nodded again.

"Good," he said. "Because we're ready for gloves."

While he slipped them on—two ridiculously bulbous red mittens—and tied them at my wrists, I forced my face out of my mind. *I'm wearing a hood, and no one is going to hit me. I'm wearing a hood, and no one is going to hit me.*

"Okay," Theo said. "You're good to go."

I clapped my gloves together. "Let's do it, Coach."

"Oh, I'm not your coach . . . I'm on laundry duty." I felt a twinge of panic as Theo gestured to a pile of towels in the corner of the room, then looked back at me and shrugged an apology. "Tiny is your coach."

Tiny? Who the hell is Tiny?

Theo must have read my mind because he said, "Go on out there. You'll know Tiny when you see him."

"Tiny," I repeated, ordering myself not to be a wimp. "Okay. I am going out there. Going to find Tiny."

As Theo reached out to squeeze my shoulder, psyching me up, I felt that weird flutter in my stomach again. It wasn't like I'd never been touched by a boy before. There was Ryan and Jarrod. . . . Before that, there were junior high kissing games, boys who felt me up in closets. . . . Not that Theo was feeling me up . . . not that I was even *thinking* about him feeling me up . . . Probably it didn't even have anything to *do* with

Theo. Probably I was just nervous walking into this place where I knew no one. Where it was so glaringly obvious I had no boxing experience. I suddenly realized what an idiot I was for agreeing to this. I wasn't a guy. I couldn't even call myself an athlete anymore. I was completely out of shape. But before I could turn around to tell Theo I'd changed my mind, a voice boomed in my ear.

"Alexa?"

I found myself staring up at a mountain of a man, with skin the color of coffee beans and a completely hairless head.

"I'm Tiny," he said, extending a glove so large mine looked like a baby's mitten beside it.

"Nice to meet you," I murmured.

Tiny smiled. His teeth were eggshell white, with gaps all over the place. "Let's go hit something."

As I followed Tiny across the gym, I marveled at the size of his calves. They looked as thick around as my thighs, making me wonder how he ever found socks to fit them.

When we reached the far corner of the room, Tiny stopped beside a big, blue, cylinder-shaped bag, suspended from the ceiling by chains. "Know much about the fight game?"

I shook my head. "No."

"Ever watch a fight on TV?"

"No."

"Ever want to knock someone's block off?"

I hesitated, then nodded. "Sometimes."

"That'll do," Tiny said. "Now get your hands up . . . like this." He modeled the correct position.

I raised both gloves in front of my face.

"Know why you're doing that?"

"Yeah."

"Why?"

"To protect myself."

"That's right. To protect yourself. *Never drop your gloves.* When you throw a punch with one hand, the other hand stays right here in front of your face. After you throw a punch, the hand you threw with always comes back to join the other one. . . . Got it?"

"Yeah."

"Now watch my feet."

I looked down.

"Why'd you drop your gloves?"

"Sorry," I said.

"Don't be sorry. Just keep 'em up. *Never drop your gloves. . . .* Now, watch my feet."

I looked down again, this time keeping my gloves up.

"What are my feet doing?"

"Moving."

"That's right," Tiny said. "I'm always on my toes. If you're back on your heels, you lose balance and give your opponent the chance to set up. You never want to let 'em get off a good shot."

Tiny shuffled around me—first to the right, then to the left—with a surprising amount of grace. "Get the idea?"

"I think so," I said.

"Show me."

I was pretty sure I looked like a jackass, bouncing up and down on the balls of my feet, gloves in front of my face like someone was actually going to hit me. But I could have looked worse. I imagined untying my hood and yanking it down, baring my graft for the whole gym. I wondered what Tiny would say.

Now he was nodding, telling me my form was good. "Ready to learn some punches?"

"Yeah," I said.

I was drenched in sweat—literally drenched—and so thirsty I thought I might die, when Theo appeared with a bottle of water and an expression of faint amusement on his face.

"Please say that's for me," I said.

"I don't know. . . . I have to ask your coach first. . . . Hey, Coach, has she earned some water?"

"She earned it." Tiny clomped my shoulder with one of his massive gloves. "You did good, kid."

My own gloves, still hovering in front of my face, felt as heavy as bowling balls. "Can I drop them now?"

"Yeah." Tiny smiled like a jack-o'-lantern. "You can drop them."

The water—which I let Theo open because my arms were shaking too bad to turn the cap—was so cold and so wet I don't think I've ever tasted something so delicious in my life.

When I finished chugging, Theo gave an impressed whistle.

"Still . . . thirsty," I panted.

"Well then," he said, "let's get you another."

✦ ✦ ✦

By the time we walked outside to the parking lot, I'd had three bottles of water and a PowerBar. When Theo offered me a second one, I took it.

"I like a girl who's not afraid to eat," he said as I tore open the wrapper.

"What are you saying? I'm fat?"

"No."

"A moment on the lips, forever on the hips," I singsonged, taking a bite. "Nothing tastes as good as looking good feels."

Theo gave me a funny look.

"That's what my mother always says, to get me to stop eating."

"Why would she want you to stop eating?"

I shrugged. "So I don't get fat."

"Well, you're *not*." He said this with such intensity that I almost choked. "You have, like, the ideal balance of fat and muscle. If I were a cannibal, I'd eat you."

Now, I really did choke. The piece of PowerBar I was chewing flew out of my mouth and landed on the pavement.

"That's by far the weirdest thing anyone has ever said to me."

Theo didn't look offended. "I meant it as a compliment."

I thanked him.

"You're welcome. You have a great body."

We were standing on the passenger side of his truck and he was looking down at me and I felt the odd, sudden sensation of shyness.

"What kind of hat is that?" I blurted. Which is what I do when I'm feeling shy. I blurt.

"This?" Theo reached up to touch the short, black brim. "It's a newsboy cap. My mom gave it to me. . . . Whenever I wear it, she calls me Brian, after Brian Williams . . . you know, on NBC? He's her favorite reporter. I tell her she's mixing her media, not to mention her millennia, but—"

"How many names do you *have*?"

Theo gave me a quizzical look.

"My sister calls you Clark Kent. Your dad calls you Taddeo. Your mom calls you Brian. . . . Are there any other aliases I should know about?"

"Right." Theo nodded. "Taddeo is actually my name. My dad's Italian, obviously, and my mom's Irish. Taddeo McConnell Barbuto."

"Wow."

"I know. . . . I think that's why my sister started calling me Theo. She didn't want me getting tortured on the playground."

"I didn't know you had a sister."

Theo nodded. "Becks . . . Rebecca."

"Older or younger?"

"Older."

"High school or college?"

He hesitated.

"Are these questions too hard?" I teased.

"Nope," he said, reaching past me to unlock the passenger door. "But the quiz is over."

I waited for the punch line. When it didn't come, I looked to see if he was kidding, but his face was unreadable. He wasn't even looking at me anymore.

Confused, I climbed (as well as a person can climb on Jell-O legs) into the passenger seat, and Theo shut the door behind me.

I didn't understand what just happened, but the mood had clearly shifted. When he got into the driver's side he was frowning.

"Can you put on the AC?" I blurted. "I'm dying here."

"Why don't you take off your sweatshirt?"

It wasn't an illogical suggestion—if you're hot, remove a layer—but I immediately felt my body tense.

"At least take off your hood," Theo said. "It's trapping all your body heat."

Obviously, I would do no such thing.

"What are you going to do—wear a hood for the rest of your life?"

The question was so shocking, I literally gasped. "I can't believe you just said that."

"Why?"

"*Why?* . . . Because it's a really insensitive thing to say!"

Theo didn't look the least bit apologetic. "Listen," he said, resting his hand on the stick shift, "I know what happened to you."

I turned away from him, stared out at the parking lot.

"Our school's not that big. Things get around."

When I didn't respond he said, "I've seen your face, Lexi. In the darkroom that day and on your friend Taylor's porch. . . . I know what you look like, and I just want you to know . . . you have no reason to feel self-conscious in front of me."

I turned to the window.

"I mean that."

"Right," I muttered.

"You don't believe me?"

I shook my head. "Never mind. Forget it."

"No."

Abruptly, I turned to look at him. "What?"

"I won't forget it."

My mouth opened, but nothing came out.

"You think you're the only one?" Theo said. "Everyone has scars. We just don't all wear them on the outside."

I didn't mean to, but I smirked.

Theo's eyes locked with mine just long enough for me to register his disappointment.

"Sorry," I said. "That just sounds a little . . . I don't know . . . Lifetime Television for Women."

"Right." Theo nodded, turning the key in the ignition. "I thought you and I were going to have a real conversation, but I guess we're not."

I had no idea how to respond to that, so I said nothing. We drove to my house in silence, my mind tracing back over the weirdness of this exchange—the weirdness of Theo in general. The fact that I was sitting in his truck suddenly seemed absurd. We barely knew each other! Still, when he pulled into my driveway, I heard myself chirp like a cheerleader, "Well, thanks for the ride!"

"You're welcome." His eyes were dark and serious, looking straight at me.

"And thanks for the boxing lesson and everything—well,

Tiny's boxing lesson." I was babbling, I realized. I just needed to shut up and open the door, but somehow my lips wouldn't stop flapping. "Oh my God, I just realized I'm still wearing the clothes you gave me! Do you want me to—"

"Don't worry about it," he said. "You can give them back another time."

"Okay . . . I'll wash them . . . you know, so you won't have to."

Theo nodded.

"Well . . . thanks again."

"You're welcome."

"Okay, bye!" I said, flinging open the door and leaping out onto the lawn. *What's wrong with me?* I thought as I ran up the front path. Followed by, *What's wrong with* him?

I hadn't planned on lying to my mother. But in the heat of the moment, when I came bursting through the front door all sweaty and disheveled and she proceeded to flip out because Ruthie was already home and no one knew where I was, and didn't I realize that she had been worried sick? I knew I couldn't tell her the truth. The words just popped out of my mouth: "Dance class."

"Dance class?" My mother raised her golden eyebrows. This was all she had to do to show me how delighted she was. I think it was a mixture of her devastation that I'd quit ballet in second grade and her relief that I hadn't spent the afternoon drinking vodka and stripping down to my underwear.

"Uh-huh," I said. "One of my friends from school—you

don't know her, but her mom owns a dance studio—she wanted me to try out this class. It all just kind of happened. Sorry I didn't call first. My cell was dead."

So many lies, but my mother was too happy to be suspicious. "These things happen," she said, smiling benevolently. "I'm just glad you're dancing again, sweetheart. It's wonderful."

"Uh-huh . . . Well, I should go change. I'm pretty sweaty."

Only then, when she considered my outfit, did she hesitate. "Is that what you wore to dance in?"

"Yeah . . . I didn't know I was going until after school. I wasn't exactly prepared."

This part was true.

"Well, we should buy you some proper attire. Leotards, tights, ballet slippers . . . some of those pretty elastic headbands to keep the hair out of your eyes. . . ."

"No, it's fine," I said, thinking fast. "It's a really low-key class. Modern dance. We can wear whatever."

"Well, honey, surely a bulky sweatshirt like that can't be easy to move around in. At least let me pick you up a few leotards."

"Fine, Mom."

Because—really, did it matter what I said? She would buy leotards, anyway. Just like she kept buying me new clothes for school—cardigan sweaters, corduroy skirts—even though I told her not to, I would never wear them, I was happy in sweatshirts and jeans. She couldn't help herself.

"Great!" My mother clapped her hands like she'd just won big money on *The Price Is Right*.

"Great," I repeated. Then, "Okay, Mom. I'm going up now."

As I walked out of the kitchen, I felt bad about lying, but not horrible. This was a lie that made my mother happy. She had a dancer for a daughter! Someone to buy leotards and headbands for! Maybe I should have told her the truth, but what good would that do? She would be appalled—horrified, really—at the image of me one-two punching the hands of a gap-toothed, three-hundred-pound bald man named Tiny. What if I forgot how to be feminine? What if my face got hit?

Honestly, she wouldn't be able to handle it.

Kissing the Canvas

LATER, WHEN I walked down the hall to Ruthie's room—it took a lot of pride-swallowing to get me there because I'd basically been ignoring her since the night of the dance—I heard giggling. Not laughter; giggling. The last time I'd heard my sister giggle, she was eight.

Curiosity surged through me, but the minute I knocked, she stopped. "I'm on the phone!"

I poked my head through the door. "Can I come in?"

Ruthie was flopped on her bed, cell clutched between her ear and her shoulder, cheeks flushed. "Hold on a sec," she murmured. Then, cupping one hand over the receiver, "What do you want?"

"I need to talk to you," I told her.

"Can it wait? I'm on the phone."

"With who?"

"That's not relevant."

"Why isn't it relevant?"

Ruthie sighed heavily. She lifted the phone and said, "Can I call you back? My sister's here. . . . Yeah . . . I know, me too—" She paused, smiling. "Okay. Give me five minutes. . . . Bye."

When Ruthie looked at me, I could tell she was annoyed, but she arranged her features into a neutral expression. "What's up?"

"Who was that?" I asked.

"Don't worry about it."

"I'm not *worried*. I'm curious. . . ." Staring at my sister, I noticed something. Her eyes looked different—brighter than usual. "Wait—" I said. "Are you wearing *makeup*?"

"Lex."

"Oh my God. You *are*."

Ruthie sighed. "Look, I've got a lot to do tonight. Can we just get to the point of why you're here?"

"Okay fine," I said. "How well do you know Theo?"

"Barbuto?"

"Yeah."

She hesitated then said, "Pretty well . . . We're friends with some of the same people. . . . Why?"

"I don't know. . . . I was hanging out with him today after school, and it was cool for a while and then it was like . . . I don't know what happened. . . . Out of nowhere he got all weird."

"Weird how?" Ruthie said. "Give me some context."

I wasn't sure how much context she needed; I just gave her the basics. "So what's the deal with his sister?" I said. "Is she a dropout or something?"

Ruthie shook her head.

"Teen mom? Drug dealer?"

"No."

"Well, what then?"

"Okay, remember that article that came out last year, about eating disorders? After that girl in the senior class died?"

"Yeah," I said. As soon as it happened, our ninth-grade health teacher, Mrs. Meechan, had led an all-school assembly about the dangers and warning signs of anorexia and bulimia, and then everyone had to fill out some eating-disorder questionnaire.

"Well," Ruthie said, "that was Theo's sister. Rebecca Barbuto. She was the whole reason they wrote the article. Remember the picture on the front page? She was really pretty . . . long, dark hair. She looked a lot like Theo."

"Oh my God," I said.

"I know."

"He didn't say anything. . . . I mean, he made some comment about everyone having scars, but I thought he was just trying to make me feel better. . . . I had no idea."

Ruthie nodded. "He has a hard time talking about it. We were cooking partners in home ec last year. He barely said a word after it happened. . . . Not to me, anyway. But this one day he looked upset, so I asked him how he was holding up, and he told me his mom had to go into the hospital . . . you know . . . for depression. She took a bunch of pills. It was pretty bad."

"Oh my God," I said again, thinking about Theo's face in the truck. My stupid dying-of-heat comment.

"Apparently, he and his sister were really close," Ruthie was saying. "Which is why he feels so guilty."

"Why would he feel guilty?"

"For not knowing she was sick. For not seeing the signs

and getting her the help she needed. . . . I'm not saying he *could* have. It sounds like she was really good at hiding it."

"But he shouldn't feel *guilty*. It wasn't his fault!"

Ruthie rolled her eyes. "Of course it wasn't his fault. Guilt isn't a rational thing."

I frowned down at my hands; half my cuticles were ragged. Then I looked back at my sister. "What do I say to him?"

Ruthie shook her head. "I don't know. There aren't any magical words."

"What did *you* say?"

"I said I was sorry. That I couldn't imagine losing my sister . . . which is true. I can't."

Neither of us spoke. I don't know what Ruthie's throat was doing, but mine was lumping up.

"Will you do me a favor?" she asked finally.

I nodded.

"Don't hurt him. He's been through enough."

Immediately, I got defensive. "What are you talking about?"

Ruthie raised an eyebrow.

"He doesn't *like* me," I said. "He feels *sorry* for me. There's a big difference."

"And what led you to this conclusion?"

"Hello," I said, pointing to my face.

Ruthie snorted. "Seriously, Lex? You think the only reason anyone likes anyone is perfect skin?"

"Well, not the *only* reason, but—"

"Are you really that deluded?"

"I'm not deluded," I snapped.

"You want to know what I think?"

No.

"I think you dated Ken doll for so long he warped your brain."

I shook my head. "This has nothing to do with Ryan."

"Maybe not," she said, "but you can't seem to get anything I say through that thick skull of yours."

I gave her my blankest stare.

"What you look like is not who you are!" Ruthie was practically yelling. "Why do you think Theo asked you to hang out?"

"I don't know. Maybe he has no friends."

"He has friends."

"Who?"

"Guys from the paper, drama club . . . That's not the point!"

"Maybe he's writing an article. 'Butt-Faced Girl Goes Incognito at School Dance.'"

"Oh my God!" Ruthie practically blew my ear off. "He likes you, freak show! It's not about your face!"

I blinked. "You just called me a freak show."

"Because you're acting like one!"

"Wow," I said.

Ruthie's expression softened. "And because I love you and I want you to snap out of it." She reached out a hand as though to pat me on the leg, then pinched me instead.

"Hey!"

"Snap out of it. He likes you."

✦ ✦ ✦

In bed, I cocooned myself under the covers and closed my eyes. For the first time in hours, Taylor popped into my head. I pictured her face in the girls' room—how miserable she'd looked when Heidi accused me of taking those photos. I got mad all over again, just thinking about it.

Which made me think about my bike tires.

Which made me think about having to walk home.

Which made me think about Theo.

Theo and his weird hat and pale skin and green, green eyes, how when they looked at you they seemed to see something no one else saw.

This was the thought that finally got me to sleep—or it was the muscle atrophy I was experiencing after the five million punches Tiny made me throw. Either way, for the first time since the accident, I slept like a rock.

In the morning, parked outside on the front walk, what did I find waiting for me? My bike. When Theo drove me home, my departure had been so spastic that I'd forgotten to take my bike out of the back of his truck.

Now, here it was.

I quickly unzipped the leather pouch under the seat, hoping to find a note. But nothing was there. Only a handful of pennies and an old gum wrapper.

I tried not to feel disappointed. But I was, a little. Because I knew what I would have done if I liked someone and that person left their bike in my truck: I'd leave a note. The lack of note seemed to speak volumes; it proved that Ruthie was wrong. Theo didn't like me. He was just doing the right thing: returning a bike to its rightful owner.

I was surprised how much this bothered me, and I wondered why I cared if Theo liked me or not.

Annoyed, I yanked open the garage door. As I walked my bike in, it took me a second to realize how smoothly it was rolling. I stopped and looked down at the tires. They were full.

I looked for Theo in the parking lot—then in the hall before first bell—but I couldn't find him.

Taylor wasn't in homeroom, either. When Mr. Ziff took attendance and she didn't answer, I overheard Jenna Morelli whisper to Elodie Love that the photos had been deleted from MyPage, and Elodie whisper to Jenna that they were still circulating around school.

As soon as Mr. Ziff finished announcements, I leaned toward Jenna's desk. "Who has them?"

Clearly, she was surprised to hear me speak. When she looked up and saw it was me, her tweezed eyebrows lifted and her shiny, pink mouth puckered into a circle.

"The photos . . . who's showing them around?"

Elodie turned in her seat. "Why, have you seen them?"

"Only on MyPage," I said.

"Me too. But some guys on the football team have them on their cells. I didn't see because they always sit in the back, but my brother said everyone was texting them to each other on the bus this morning."

I thought about Taylor. Then I thought about Ryan, who

lived on the same street as Elodie and her brother and rode their bus. Even though I was afraid to ask, I had to. "Which guys?"

Elodie shook her head. "I didn't see. I don't even know all their names."

This didn't exactly surprise me. Elodie—who always got straight As and had starred in every school play since kindergarten—wasn't the type to memorize the football roster.

"I can't believe Taylor did that," Jenna sniffed. "I mean, it's one thing to take off your clothes for your boyfriend. But stripping for the entire football team and letting them take *pictures*? That's just gross."

Hearing this, I felt like I'd been slapped in the face, even though Jenna wasn't talking about me. It was the same way I felt in sixth grade, when she told everyone I was so stuck-up she hoped I got run over.

"That's not what happened," I said.

"How do you know?"

"I just know. It wasn't the whole team, and she didn't *let* them do anything. They did it without her consent."

Jenna eyed me suspiciously. For one nauseating second, I thought she might have caught wind of Heidi's story that I was to blame for the photos. But then, with a wave of her hand, Jenna dismissed me. "You and Taylor aren't even friends anymore."

Again, I felt the sting. Jenna wasn't close with Taylor. She may have thought she was, but she wasn't. They were homeroom acquaintances—which is to say, they discussed homework and extracurricular activities—but this hardly qualified

Jenna as an expert on the status of Taylor's and my relationship. It wasn't even logical, what Jenna said. I could know the truth about what happened to Taylor at the dance whether or not we were friends. I was *there.*

All morning, a vision kept popping into my head. Taylor, sprawled on the brown leather couch in her living room, stuffing her face with Pop-Tarts. *My life is over,* she is thinking. *The whole world has seen me naked.*

Well. That's what you get for making stupid choices.

In trig, I stared across the room at Ryan, willing him to look at me. *Were you one of them? Were you?*

I tried to picture him in a mask, which made me remember, suddenly, this movie we saw together once. *The Princess Bride.* I teased Ryan the whole time we were watching it because he looked exactly like the farm boy, Westley, who breaks the beautiful Princess Buttercup's heart by faking his own death and running off to become a pirate. For the longest time afterward, Ryan would say to me, "As you wish," which was Westley's secret way of telling Buttercup that he loved her—the only way she knew who he was in his pirate costume.

I stared across the room at Ryan. *Who are you? Westley the farm boy or the Dread Pirate Roberts?*

But his head was down the whole time. He never looked up.

Fifth period, instead of going to the cafeteria, I walked straight to the darkroom. The red light was on, so I leaned my head against the door. "I'd knock," I said, "but my arms hurt too much to move. I could barely get out of bed this morning."

"Bummer," Theo said, and his voice was flat.

"I'm really out of shape. . . . Tiny says I need to start running."

"Uh-huh."

"If you open the door I could limp in and ruin your roll of film . . ."

"No, thanks," he said. Which wasn't exactly the response I'd been hoping for.

"Okay," I said, starting to turn away, "if that's how you feel."

Which is when the door opened. Theo was wearing a green crewneck sweater that made his eyes look like emeralds.

"Hey," I said.

"Hey."

"How are you?"

He shrugged. "Okay . . . you?"

I shrugged, too, wracking my brain for what to say next. "Does anyone else ever use this room?"

"Nope."

"Do you have special permission or something . . . for the paper?"

"Yup."

"Do you think you'll ever go digital?"

Theo snorted. "Digital cameras are for hacks."

"Right," I said, nodding.

Theo was silent.

Finally, I couldn't stand it a second longer. "Ruthie told me about your sister," I blurted. "I'm really sorry. I didn't know."

Theo didn't respond right away. When he did, he looked

me straight in the eye. "It's pretty much the worst thing that's ever happened to me."

I nodded.

"It's left me incapable of bullshit."

I nodded again, though I wasn't sure what he meant.

"Before Becks got sick, I could have superficial conversations, and now . . ." He hesitated. "A lot of stuff I used to care about just doesn't seem that important."

"I know what you mean," I said.

He raised an eyebrow.

"No," I said, "I do. Before my accident . . . I know it's not the same as someone dying, but . . . I used to be different."

"How?" Theo said.

"I don't know. . . . I was just . . . normal, I guess. Just a normal, happy girl who wore . . . you know . . . cute clothes and got along with her mother and played field hockey and went to the mall with her friends."

"And now?"

"Now . . ." My voice was so low even I could barely hear it. "I don't do any of those things."

Theo didn't react. He just kept looking at me.

"I know this sounds stupid," I said, glancing away, "but I feel like I've lost everything. . . . Like, Taylor used to be my best friend and Ryan used to be my boyfriend, and now they're not . . . and I used to be beautiful." I wanted to disappear after I said that. "I mean—not that I went around *thinking* that or anything, it's just how other people defined me, my whole life. *Alexa Mayer is beautiful*. And now . . ." I forced myself to finish.

"I don't know how to act. I don't know how to dress. I don't know . . . who to be."

Theo nodded slowly.

"Sorry," I said. "I'm rambling. We were supposed to be talking about your sister."

"It's okay."

"No. I'm an idiot."

"You're not an idiot."

"How do you know?"

He looked amused.

"Forget it," I muttered.

"Why do you do that?"

"What?"

"Dismiss yourself like that. You say 'forget it' like what you think doesn't matter. It does."

Before I could respond, Theo said, "You want to know how I know you're not an idiot? . . . For starters, Ruth told me how much she admires you. And she wouldn't admire an idiot."

This, more than anything else, came as a shock. My sister—my straight-A honor student, trombone virtuoso, bound for the Ivy League sister—told Theo she admires me? *Me?*

Theo must have read my expression, because he said, "It's true. Last year in home ec, when she was telling me about you, she said, and I quote, 'My sister is the most socially competent person I know.' She said you were amazing."

I shook my head.

"You think I'm making this up?"

"No." I frowned down at his shoes—navy blue Converse. "Just, I'm not that girl anymore."

"I think you are."

"That's nice of you to say—"

"I'm not saying it to be nice," he insisted. "I've seen it. For the past month, I've watched you walking around school with your head held high. . . . Okay, so you're always wearing a hood and you don't really talk to anyone, but still, here you are, going to class, hitting badminton birdies. . . ."

I stared at him. "You were watching me . . . that day in gym?"

Theo smiled a little. "I'm not a stalker, if that's what you're asking. I'm a reporter. It's my job to notice things."

I shook my head, stunned.

"My point is . . . okay, there's this term in boxing, *kissing the canvas*. It's when someone gets knocked down face-first. After Becks died, that was me. I could barely get out of bed, let alone put on a costume and show my face at a school dance. But you . . . you kissed the canvas and got *up*." He shrugged, looking embarrassed. "That sounded way cheesier than I meant it."

"No," I said. "I mean—I like cheese."

Theo got quiet for a moment. Then he said, "She was my best friend."

At first, I didn't understand what he meant, but then I realized he was talking about his sister. "I know what it's like," I said, "to lose your best friend."

"Lexi . . . Taylor's still alive."

I felt like a heel, and I started to apologize, but Theo said,

"No . . . that's what I'm saying. Life is too short for bullshit. If Taylor's your best friend and she means that much to you, fight for her."

"Even if she stabbed me in the back?" I said. "Even if she screwed me over in the worst possible way a girl could screw over her best friend, I should just forgive her?"

Theo shrugged. "Is she worth it?"

From a far corner of the room, the bell rang.

"It's sixth period," I said.

"Yup."

"We should probably go."

"We probably should."

But we just stood there, looking at each other. It was like one of the staring contests Ruthie and I used to have when we were younger. I'd never stared at anyone else for this long, not even Ryan. In a way, it felt more intimate than kissing.

"I can't believe you fixed my tires," I said finally.

Theo smiled. "Stick around. I'm full of surprises."

It Doesn't Take Nancy Drew to Figure It Out

THE NEXT MORNING, I did the unthinkable. I woke at 5:00 a.m., wriggled into my jog bra, laced up my running shoes, and pedaled my flabby self to the high school track—the same track Taylor and I had run on all summer. When I got there, the sky was just beginning to get light, but already someone was there. A stocky figure in a cotton-candy-pink sweat suit at the far end of the track.

I wasn't going very fast—Tiny had said to start off easy—but Cotton Candy was jogging so slowly she might as well have been walking, and I caught up to her within seconds. That's when I saw the two bunches of frizzy brown hair sticking out on either side of her head and the charm bracelet clinking on her wrist.

Crap. Crapcrappitycrappitycrap.

"On your right," I murmured. Because that is running etiquette, no matter who you're about to pass.

Heidi came to a screeching halt. "What are you doing here?"

"What are *you* doing here?" I threw back over my shoulder.

"Right," she muttered. "Of course."

I turned around, jogging in place. "What's that supposed to mean?"

"Why is Heidi at the track?" she said, her voice mocking. "She shouldn't be running. She should be sumo wrestling."

I stared at her. "What are you talking about?"

"Please," Heidi snorted. "I've heard it my whole life. From you and everyone else."

"I'm sorry, but if you can't be more specific, then maybe you shouldn't go accusing people of things they didn't do . . . *again*."

"Okay, Miss I-Can-Do-No-Wrong," Heidi said. "How about the time I put on my Brownie uniform and you and Taylor said I looked like a Thanksgiving turkey?"

"When was that?" I said, genuinely baffled. "Third grade?"

"Second."

I stopped jogging in place. "You remember what I said to you in *second grade*?"

"I remember everything. I remember when we went to sell cookies, every time it was your turn to ring the bell, people would open their door, take one look at you, and say, 'Ohhh, aren't you adorable! I'll take ten boxes!' But when it was my turn they said, 'Looks like *someone's* been doing more eating than selling.'"

"I don't remember that."

"Of course you don't," Heidi said. "You probably don't remember Jason Saccovitch calling me 'Lard Ass Engle' on the playground, either, and everyone laughing. Or how I was always the last girl picked for kickball in gym and you were always first. 'We want Lexi!'" she cried. "'Lexi's so pretty!

Lexi's so awesome! Lexi gets whatever she wants!'"

I shook my head. "That's not true."

Heidi smirked. "It must be nice to lead such a charmed life."

"Are you serious?" I said. I pulled back the right side of my hood. "You call this charmed?"

"So what? You think anyone cares about your cheek? Everyone still loves you."

"Right." I really turned on the sarcasm.

"Taylor won't shut up about how much she misses you. It's so annoying."

"Is that why you told her I took those photos?"

"I didn't tell her. She told me."

"What?" I said sharply.

"She," Heidi repeated, "told *me.* I left the dance at nine o'clock. I didn't know anything until yesterday."

"And what . . . exactly . . . did Taylor tell you?" I was struggling to stay calm.

"That she fell asleep on a wrestling mat in the weight room, and when she woke up, you were there."

"That's it? That's all she said?"

"Come on, Lexi. It doesn't take Nancy Drew to figure it out. Taylor was drunk, and you saw it as your opportunity to get back at her—"

"By what? Taking naked pictures of her and spreading them all over school? Do you think I'm a psychopath?"

Heidi shrugged.

"Oh my God!" I cried. "You are so unbelievable! First, you

guard the door so Taylor can hook up with Ryan and now—"

"Wait a second," Heidi said, cutting me off. "Taylor didn't just *hook up with Ryan*. She was trying to get him in good with the team. It was an initiation thing. She was helping."

"Helping." I nodded. "Right. Since you know so much . . . Whose brilliant idea was it that Taylor 'help'—hers or Ryan's?"

Heidi lifted her chin slightly. "Neither."

It took me a second to realize what she meant. "It was *your* idea?"

"You weren't supposed to find out," Heidi said defensively. "If you hadn't barged into the room, it would have been fine."

"Fine?" I repeated. *"Fine?"*

"I tried to warn you."

"Yeah. You're such a good friend."

"Come on, Lexi," Heidi said. "We were never friends. Not really. Taylor and I were friends . . . and then you came along."

I *knew* it. I *knew* she resented me moving here.

"Ryan and I were friends, too. Way before you."

"When?" I scoffed. "Nursery school? He didn't even *re-member* you that day at the frog pond."

Heidi blinked. And suddenly, her face crinkled up like a raisin.

I wasn't expecting this. I realized, watching a fat tear roll down her cheek, that in all the years I'd known her I'd never seen her cry.

"Oh my God. Are you—"

"No."

"Yes, you are. You're—"

"Go," she said, waving her hand fiercely, shooing me away. "Just go. Run a hundred miles."

I stared at her.

"Go!"

"Fine," I shot back. "I *will* run a hundred miles. But not because you told me to. Because that's what I came here to do!"

My first lap, I ran hard. I was so pissed I didn't even care that my legs hurt. A debate raged inside my head: who was the most deserving of my hatred right now? Taylor, Ryan, or Heidi?

I noticed—as I rounded the bend for lap number two—that Heidi wasn't standing anymore. She was sitting, slumped over, on the players' bench. Like a miserable, pink hunchback.

I *so* didn't care that she was miserable.

I kept running as if I were in shape. As if I were still captain of the field hockey team.

My thighs screamed in protest.

Shut up, thighs.

Lap number three. Heidi was still slumping. And I was still fuming.

Only now I was having trouble concentrating on my anger. I was distracted by my lungs (two blazing infernos) and my legs (two lead pipes).

I made myself sprint the final stretch to the bleachers, but after that, I had no choice.

I had to stop.

"You're . . . still . . . here?" I huffed, marching in place behind the players' bench.

When Heidi turned around, her eyes were as pink as her sweat suit. "What do *you* care?"

I shrugged, trying to catch my breath.

"You think I'm pathetic, just like everyone else does."

"And *you* . . ." I huffed, ". . . accused *me*—"

But Heidi cut me off. "You have no idea what it's like . . . being the third wheel all the time. The girl everyone just . . . tolerates. The girl no boy would ever want to go out with. Of course Ryan didn't remember me. Why would he?"

"Heidi—"

"No. It's true. You think I don't know? You think I don't hear when you guys make fat jokes at the lunch table, right in front of me? You think I don't know who you're talking about? I wouldn't like me, either."

I shook my head, "I have never . . . made a fat joke . . . at the lunch table."

"Don't you get it? It doesn't matter if it's Kendall or Piper or someone else. You and Taylor are *there*. You don't try to *stop* them."

I opened my mouth to protest, then shut it. Heidi was right. When had I ever stood up for her?

"It's like, by not saying anything, you're *agreeing*."

I shrugged. "I never knew it bothered you."

"Sure you didn't," she muttered.

"Heidi," I said, finally having enough oxygen to speak. "I'm serious. I didn't know. You always seemed . . . well . . . impervious."

"Don't you mean *oblivious*?" she asked, narrowing her eyes.

"Maybe," I admitted.

There was silence for a moment as Heidi turned away, gazing out at the football field. Then she sighed. "I guess I'm good at faking it."

"You and me both," I said, plopping down on the bench beside her.

She shot me a suspicious look. "What have *you* ever had to fake?"

"Lots of things . . . confidence . . . courage . . . a few weeks ago I had to fake like I didn't care when some guys in the lunch line were talking about how fucked-up my face was, and how they would only hook up with me if there was a bag over my head."

"What?"

Crap. I should not have said that. The last thing Heidi needed was more ammunition.

"That's ridiculous," Heidi said. "Your face is not fucked up."

"Yes, it is."

"No, it's not. It's . . . okay, your cheek *does* look weird when you first see it. I'm not going to lie to you. That patch thing . . . it makes you do a double take."

"It's called a graft," I blurted. "They took skin from . . . well, from another part of my body, and they grafted it onto my cheek."

"Sounds painful."

"It was. . . . It's not anymore."

"That's good," Heidi said. "Anyway, the rest of you is still *you* and it just doesn't matter. . . . Even with that crazy haircut, you're still . . ." She squinted at me. "Ninety-five percent gorgeous. *That's* the fucked-up part."

"Right," I nodded. "I'm so gorgeous that Ryan is chatting up every girl in school *except* me."

"Forget Ryan," Heidi said dismissively. "He's a tool."

"I thought you liked him!"

"I *did*—until I saw how little convincing he needed from me to cheat on you. And then I realized, *Ryan Dano is a tool.*"

I laughed. I couldn't help myself. "Do you have any idea how hypocritical that sounds?"

"Yes. But in my defense, I didn't exactly *plan* on him being a tool when I fell in love with him in nursery school. The fact that he peed in the sandbox should have clued me in, but somehow that only sealed the deal."

"You're funny," I said.

"Yeah," Heidi said with a wry smile. "The fat girl's always funny. She has to be, to make up for being fat."

I took a deep breath. "You've got to stop talking about yourself like that."

"Why? It won't change anything."

"You want to change?" I demanded. "Do you?"

Heidi shrugged. "Of course, but—"

"No buts. Do you want to *change*?"

"Yes."

"Then stop insulting yourself," I said. "And stop being such a bitch."

Heidi's eyes widened.

"You heard me. It's bad enough that you pushed Taylor

and Ryan together. But accusing me of taking those photos? That's just . . ." I shook my head, disgusted. "I would *never* do something like that. To *anyone*."

"You really didn't do it?" Heidi said.

I shot her a look.

"Fine," she said. "I believe you."

"Good."

"So, if you didn't . . . who did?"

I hesitated for a second. "I'll tell you what I know, but we don't have much time before school and I have to run another mile."

"Why?"

"I just do," I said. I wasn't about to tell Heidi about boxing, or Tiny, or Theo. "Come on," I said, forcing myself up from the bench.

Heidi shook her head. "I can't run a mile."

"Sure you can. . . . Remember seventh-grade gym? We all had to do it."

"Not me. I faked my period."

"Well," I said, "now's your chance to un-fake it. Come on."

"I can't."

"Do you want to hear what happened to Taylor or not?"

"Yeah, but—"

"No buts. You're running with me. . . . Come on. We'll go slow."

"Promise?"

"Yes."

And then, I swear to God, Heidi Engle and I ran a mile together.

✦ ✦ ✦

"Why do girls *do* that?" Theo asked when I'd finished telling the story.

"Do what?" I threw a jab with my right hand. The blue bag swayed slightly, and Theo steadied it.

"Hate themselves. Hate each other."

"Because," I grunted, throwing a left cross. My shoulders were on fire, but I wasn't stopping. "We're gluttons"—*grunt*—"for punishment"—*grunt*—"and we're"—*grunt*—"highly"—*grunt*—"competitive"—*grunt*.

"Nice," Theo said. "Let me see some hook uppercuts."

"Hook," I grunted, throwing with my right. "Uppercut—" *grunt*. "Hook—" *grunt*. "Uppercut—" *grunt*.

"Good . . . Remember to twist and snap on the hook. . . . My sister used to do that."

"What?" *Grunt*.

"Beat herself up all the time. Worry what other people thought about her."

"Oh." I stopped punching and looked at him. "I thought you meant the way she boxed."

Theo shook his head. "She never boxed."

"Isn't it a family business? Weren't you given, like, teeny little boxing gloves as babies?"

"No. My dad's been an insurance adjuster all his life. He opened the gym after Becks died as . . . you know . . . something positive to focus on. . . . His therapist suggested it."

"Is it working?"

"The gym or the therapy?"

"Both."

Theo shrugged. "He has his days. Mostly he holds it together. My mom, though . . . she's still a mess. . . . She was hospitalized last year, after it happened. . . . She couldn't handle it."

I nodded. "Ruthie told me. . . . I hope that's okay."

"No, it's fine. I'm not ashamed of it. I just wish it helped. Mostly she lies in bed all day, staring at the ceiling."

"I'm familiar with that technique," I said.

From the way Theo was looking at me, I could tell he was waiting for me to say more—to reveal something deep about myself. But I couldn't. I couldn't explain about Johnny Depp without sounding pathetic.

So instead, I blurted, "Are you worried about her?"

Theo hesitated. "Yeah."

"Is that why you don't want to go to college?" I asked, instantly regretting the question, knowing it was too personal.

Sure enough, Theo frowned.

"Sorry. It's none of my business."

"No," he said. "It's just . . . that's what my dad keeps saying. 'You can't put your life on hold because of your mother. You have to think about your future.' . . . Like it's that easy. I can't even leave for school in the morning without her crying. Imagine what would happen if I left home for good? She's already lost one kid."

I shook my head, not knowing what to say.

"Anyway," Theo said, raising both hands to his chin and throwing a hard jab at the bag, "my dad went ahead and did it . . . without even asking. . . . He filled out the common application and sent it to fifteen schools."

"Oh my God," I said softly.

"He told me today. After they were already in the mail."

"Is that even legal?"

Theo shrugged, throwing another jab. "Who the fuck knows?"

"How are you dealing?"

"Dealing?" Theo laughed, but not like he thought it was funny. "Like *this*," he said, throwing an even harder jab, then a cross. "I know it sounds whacked, but sometimes I picture anorexia as, you know, an animate object, and I just pound the shit out of it for an hour."

"It doesn't sound whacked."

"No?"

I shook my head.

"Right now," Theo grunted, throwing a hook uppercut, "I'm picturing my dad."

I steadied the bag for him. "When I was in the hospital, I used to picture Taylor, Ryan, and Jarrod lined up against the wall while I threw darts at their faces. Now, when I'm boxing, I picture football players."

"Good thing," Theo grunted, "to picture."

"I can't believe those guys are blatantly texting around Taylor's photo and laughing about what happened. That's just . . . sick."

Theo bounced on his toes, nodding. "It is."

"Assholes," I muttered.

"Yup."

Theo dropped his hands and—out of nowhere—asked whether I'd forgiven Taylor yet. I told him she still wasn't back in school and, because she was grounded, I couldn't just show up at her house.

"Your point being . . ."

"My point being I want it to be face-to-face."

Theo nodded. "Gotcha."

"What—you don't think I'll do it? You don't think I'm capable of forgiving her?"

"No," Theo said, "I *know* you're capable of forgiving her. You're capable of anything."

I lifted an eyebrow. "Anything?"

"Well . . ." he said, rubbing his chin slowly, like he was giving the matter thought. "You *are* Catwoman. . . ."

"Yes, I am."

"You *do* have some amazing powers. . . ."

"Yes, I do," I said, realizing as I said it that this conversation was taking a detour from the serious to the flirtatious.

And I didn't exactly mind.

For the first time in weeks, my father was home for dinner. You could tell it was a big deal because my mother spritzed on the Shalimar, set the table in the dining room instead of the kitchen, and served up steak au poivre.

"Honey, this is fantastic," my dad said.

My mother smiled, spooning mashed potatoes onto his plate. "I'm glad you like it. It's a new recipe."

Because Ruthie wasn't home for dinner—she was tied up in yet another band rehearsal—my father had no one to trade intellectual jousts with. As a result, the conversation ranged from such scintillating topics as grass-fed vs. corn-fed beef (grass-fed was better), the children's choir at church (darling), and the weather (unseasonably warm).

Then, my father wiped his mouth on his napkin and turned to me. "Your mom told me about Taylor and the photographs that were posted on the Internet without her knowledge."

"*What?*" I stared at my mother.

Before she could open her mouth, my father was off and running. "Do her parents know . . . ? Because if they don't, somebody needs to inform them. . . . Voyeurism is a class D felony. Taylor may have a case."

"Voyeurism?"

"Was she under the influence of alcohol?"

I nodded.

"Then she couldn't give consent. If these boys knowingly, maliciously, removed her clothing and photographed her, they can be brought up on felony charges . . . assuming the photos are brought into evidence. . . . Do you know who they are?"

"The boys?" I asked.

"Yes."

"Not exactly . . . I mean, I know the guy who posted the pictures on MyPage, but that doesn't mean he took them. . . . Everyone's saying it was football players, but nobody knows who.

"Well," my father said dryly, "*somebody* knows. It's just a matter of finding out . . . asking around."

"Jeff." My mother was shaking her head.

"What?"

"Alexa doesn't need to be dragged into this—"

"I'm not *dragging her* into anything."

"You're not a private investigator."

"I know that, Laine. I'm merely a concerned parent who happens to possess a certain amount of legal expertise. Expertise that might prove seminal in this particular case. All I would need to do to get the ball rolling is put in a call to Frank at the station and—"

"Jeff."

"What?"

"You will do no such thing! Unless Taylor's parents specifically ask you for legal counsel—"

"Hey," I said, pushing my chair back from the table and springing to a stand. "Is that a car door I hear? I think Ruthie's home!" Before my parents could launch back in, I made my escape.

I had not, in fact, heard a car door, but when I stepped out on the porch I *did* see a green Honda parked in the driveway. It wasn't Ruthie's car. It wasn't a car I'd ever seen before. However, my sister *was* in the passenger seat and—as far as I could tell from my particular vantage point—she was making out like crazy with the driver.

Whaaat???

I pinched myself—not just once, but twice—to make sure I was really seeing this. It didn't occur to me to look away and give them some privacy. I was too shocked. *How could this have happened? How could I not have known that my sister was macking with some strange boy?*

What I did know—when Ruthie finally stepped out of the car and started loping toward the house with her trombone—

was that she looked happy. She didn't even seem annoyed that I'd been spying. She just smiled and said—casual as can be—"Hey."

My jaw dropped a foot. "That's all you have to say?"

"What?"

I gestured to the spot where the car had been. "*What* was *that*?"

"That was Carter Benson."

"Carter Benson . . ." I repeated. "Carter Benson . . ." The name sounded familiar. "Wait—Carter Benson the *soccer player*?"

"Well, I wouldn't define him that way, but yes, he plays soccer. He also plays the French horn."

"He doesn't just *play* soccer, Ruthie. He's, like, *phenomenal*." I knew this because Kendall and Rae had gone to soccer camp last summer and Carter Benson had been there. They hadn't shut up about him for weeks. "Carter Benson is your *boyfriend*?"

Ruthie shook her head slightly. "I'm not a fan of labeling relationships . . . but Carter is a *boy* and he's my *friend* and we've been hanging out for the past couple of weeks, so . . ." She smiled. "Call it whatever you want."

The past couple of weeks? *Weeks?*

I stared at my sister in disbelief. "How could you not tell me?"

She shrugged. "You never asked."

I pressed the palm of my hand to my forehead, still trying to process this information.

"Anyway, it's not like he's the first guy I've ever been with."

"*What?*"

"Please," Ruthie said, rolling her eyes slightly. "Why do you think I keep going back to music camp? The institutional cooking?"

I opened my mouth, but no words came out.

"Speaking of which," Ruthie said, "what's for dinner? I'm starving." Then, "Hellooo?"

"Huh?" I snapped back to reality.

"What did Mom make for dinner?"

"Oh. Steak . . . But I wouldn't go in there yet. She and Dad are having one of their arguments."

"What about?"

"Taylor and the photos. Dad's going off . . . something about voyeurism and malicious intent and how Taylor has a case . . . and Mom's trying to talk him down from the ledge."

"Oh, those two." Ruthie shook her head.

"I know. They're so annoying."

"No—they're perfect for each other."

"Please," I said.

"Dad's the fiery, passionate one, and Mom's the voice of reason."

"*Mom's* the voice of reason? . . . No way."

"Oh, yes, she is," Ruthie insisted. "Dad gets heated up, and she cools his fevered brow."

"Oh my God," I moaned.

"What?"

"Have you gone completely mental?"

All she did was smile. "Opposites attract, you know. It's a tale as old as time."

A scene from *Invasion of the Body Snatchers* popped into my head. My father made me watch it once, and it was a terrible movie, but it seemed as good an explanation as any for Ruthie's bizarre behavior.

"Who are you," I demanded, "and what have you done with my sister?"

So Unbelievable

I WAS LATE for homeroom because I'd spent the entire ride to school—plus ten minutes in the parking lot—pumping Ruthie for information. How did this Carter thing start? (With a joke about banana chips—you had to be there.) Who kissed who first? (He kissed her.) Where? (The instrument room.) The Q&A went on and on. By the time I got to homeroom second bell had already rung, but only Mr. Ziff seemed to notice I was late. Everyone else was lining up at the door, whispering and jostling each other. I scanned the room for Taylor, but she was MIA.

"What's going on?" I asked J. P. Melillo.

"All-school assembly," he mumbled.

"Why?"

J. P. shrugged.

But as soon as we got to the auditorium, I knew. I knew because Mr. Levitt, the principal, was standing at the lectern in his pin-striped banker's suit, holding a cell phone in the air like a hand grenade. The minute we sat down, he announced that—effective immediately—Millbridge High School would be adopting a "no-phones-on-campus policy," and that the next hour of our day would be dedicated to the "unfortunate incident that occurred at our homecoming dance on Saturday night."

Then Ms. Ash, the school counselor, proceeded to give a two-part lecture on alcohol abuse and inappropriate conduct, and Mr. Donovan, the football coach, stood onstage in his polyester shorts and tube socks to announce a zero-tolerance policy against any form of hazing. "Make no mistake," he declared, poking his whistle in the air for emphasis. "The perpetrators. Of this incident. Are. Being. Held. Accountable."

"Thanks in great part"—Ms. Ash added, leaning toward the microphone so that her hippie hair flopped in front of her eyes—"to a student in this school who had the *fortitude* and *integrity* to do the right thing."

Everyone started talking at once. The buzz in the auditorium grew louder and louder. "Who's the snitch?" someone yelled from the back of the auditorium.

"Simmer down, people." Mr. Levitt banged on the lecturn. "Simmer down!" You could tell he was annoyed from the way his mustache was twitching, but that didn't shut anyone up.

"The identities of those involved," Ms. Ash said, gripping microphone again, "are not important. What *is* important is that we all *learn* something from this experience. That we become a stronger *community* because of it."

"Stronger *community*," I said in the darkroom later, imitating Ms. Ash's yoga teacher voice. "Teachable *moment*."

Theo gave me a half smile.

"They should have led those guys up onstage in shackles and let the whole school throw eggs at them. . . . Better yet, stones. A good, old-fashioned stoning. Now *there's* a teachable moment."

"I think Taylor's brother already took care of that," Theo said mildly.

"What?"

"You didn't hear?"

When I shook my head, Theo told me that after assembly, Jarrod walked straight to the principal's office and waited outside until Kyle Humboldt, Jason Saccovitch, Owen Porte, and Will Faller came out, and then he started throwing punches.

"No," I said. It wasn't the names that shocked me—by third period, everyone in school knew who'd taken the pictures of Taylor—it was Jarrod's reaction.

"Yup," Theo said. "Now *he's* suspended, too."

"Oh my God."

"Yup."

I shook my head. "I can't believe El Capitán actually fought back against the Brotherhood."

"Believe it."

"You know what?" I said. "You should write about this. Some big exposé about the football team . . . the hazing . . . the way they treat girls . . . There must be a gold mine of material—"

Theo frowned.

"What?" I said.

"What's the point?"

"What do you mean 'what's the point?' The point is public humiliation. Make them pay—"

"I'm not talking about that," Theo said, cutting me off. "I mean me . . . writing . . . This morning, I tried to explain to my dad again, why I want to take next year off and get an internship . . . you know, at one of the local papers. I wanted him to know how serious I am about this. And he's like, 'Writing is a hobby, Taddeo. Taking pictures is a hobby. It's not a career.'"

"And what did you say?"

"I said, 'Tell that to Bob Woodward. Tell that to Paul Krugman. Tell that to Christiane Amanpour. . . .' He doesn't get it. He wants me to go into accounting. Or . . . I don't know . . . computer programming. He said he won't pay a dime to support me after graduation unless it's college tuition. Can you believe that shit?"

"No," I said softly.

"My mom gets it. She's an English teacher. . . . At least she was . . . until Becks . . ." There was a moment of silence, and then Theo muttered, "I'm sorry. I don't even know where this is coming from."

"It's okay," I said.

He shook his head, frowning.

"Hey," I said. "You know what would make you feel better?"

"What?"

I held up both hands, threw a jab, then a cross.

"No," Theo said.

"No?"

He shook his head. "*I* know what would make me feel better."

"What?"

"This."

As he reached out to cup my face in his hands, I had two simultaneous and contradictory impulses. First, to back away—and then, to slap him.

For a second, I just stood there, frozen with indecision, and then it happened.

Theo kissed me.

And I didn't pull away.

For a long time that's all we did—kiss and kiss. And it wasn't anything like Ryan. Not that I hadn't enjoyed kissing Ryan; I had. (How can you not when the guy looks like he just stepped out of an Abercrombie & Fitch ad?) But there was always something . . . I don't know . . . *mechanical* about the way we did it. *Tilt head to side; open mouth; stick in tongue; swirl to the left; swirl to the right*. Every time, the same routine. But with Theo . . . with Theo it was nose bumping lip touching tongue twining heart thumping knee weakening body pressing kissing kissing kissing until the bell rang and he took a sudden step back, breathing hard. "Wow."

"Yeah," I said, feeling my cheeks flush, and for once I didn't even think about my graft. My chin, which had been scraping against Theo's, burned slightly.

"I've wanted to do that for a really long time," he said.

"Really?"

"You have no idea."

He reached out to smooth down my hair, which must have been sticking up, and then, very gently, he brushed my cheek with his thumb.

I spent the rest of the day in a kind of a haze. I felt like, even with my hood back on, the whole world could tell what just happened to me—like every cell in my body was flashing neon yellow. I wanted to do a hundred different things at once. Hide. Laugh. Cringe. Sing. I tried to focus in class—to absorb what people were saying—but everyone sounded like Charlie Brown's teacher: *"Wah, wah, woh, wah, wah."*

Between seventh and eighth periods, I was so distracted that I didn't even notice Kendall and Rae barreling down the hall toward me until they suddenly materialized in front of my locker.

"Oh my God, Lexi!"

"We're been looking for you everywhere!"

"We just saw your sister—"

"—and Carter Benson—"

"—totally macking in senior hall!"

"*Totally* macking!"

"How could you not tell us?"

I glanced from Kendall to Rae and then back to Kendall, who was chomping her Juicy Fruit so violently that I was afraid she might hurt herself. "How could I not tell you?" I repeated.

"Yes!" Kendall twirled a lock of shiny, brown hair around her finger. "It's, like, unbelievable!"

"*So* unbelievable," Rae chimed in.

"Why?" I said. Although disbelief had been my primary reaction, too—*Ruthie and Carter Benson? How was this possible?*—I suddenly felt defensive of my sister. "What's so unbelievable about it?"

"Well . . ." Rae hesitated. "It's just that they're so . . ." She glanced at Kendall who, true to form, completed the thought. "Totally different."

"Hey." I shrugged, sliding my biology book into my backpack. "Opposites attract."

"Lex-*i*," Kendall said. "How could you *keep* this from us?" She shook a finger at me in mock disapproval. "Bad girl."

And Rae said, "*Very* bad."

I told them that perhaps they should call me sometime and I would put them on speakerphone; that way they could stay up to speed on all pertinent information. "It's really a great tool," I said. "It's how I find out everything."

Kendall and Rae looked confused. They glanced at each other and then back at me, waiting for an explanation.

"That day you called me? From JB's? You thought you were putting me on mute, but really it was speaker."

"What?" Kendall said.

Rae's brow crinkled. "When was this?"

They weren't faking it; they were genuinely clueless.

Well, what good would it do to rehash it now, when they didn't even know what they'd done wrong? Maybe Ruthie was right. Maybe they weren't necessarily bad friends; they just hadn't known how to act, how to treat me after the accident. Was that all it was? Had I blown everything out of proportion?

First bell rang.

"Never mind." I sighed. "I have bio." I shut my locker and added, "Anyway, shouldn't you guys be a little more concerned with what's going on with Taylor than who's kissing my sister? Why don't you stop gossiping for one second and figure out how to help?"

Kendall and Rae went silent.

I instantly felt queasy, worried that I'd made a fatal mistake—that the two of them would turn on me and make the rest of my high-school experience a living hell. Then I remembered what Ruthie said, about growing a backbone. Translation: *Don't be a wimp. If you speak your mind and people don't like it, well—*

"I thought you hated her," Kendall said.

I blinked. "What?"

"Taylor. You said the friendship was over."

"*Beyond* over," Rae piped in.

"Yeah, well . . . that was then. This is now."

Kendall squinted. "Isn't that a movie?"

"I don't know. . . . Second bell's about to ring."

"No. It is," Rae said as I started to speed-walk down the hall. She scurried after me like a puppy. "We saw it at your house, Lex, remember? It had that guy in it . . . what's his name . . . the hot one who played that coach . . ."

"From *The Mighty Ducks*!" Kendall galloped to catch up.

"Emilio Estevez?" I almost choked. "He's, like, fifty years old."

"So? He's still hot."

"*So* hot," Rae added.

I shook my head. "Whatever. My *point* is that Taylor needs her friends right now. We need to go to her house after school—"

Rae cut me off. "We have soccer after school."

"Let's see . . ." I stopped walking and raised my palms in the air like a set of scales. "Soccer . . . friend in crisis . . . soccer . . . friend in crisis—"

"Okay!" Kendall cried. "We get it!"

"Friend in crisis!"

"Good." I dropped my hands and resumed walking. "So you guys, me, and Heidi—"

Double groan.

"Heidi?"

"Why does she always have to tag along?"

"She's so annoying."

My mind worked overtime, deciding how to respond. Was Heidi annoying? Absolutely. But then I remembered our talk at the track. I thought about how everything got so messed up to begin with: Heidi feeling left out. All the times people made fun of her. Her thinking I lived this charmed life and wanting to punish me by pushing Taylor and Ryan together.

"Listen," I said as we arrived outside the bio lab. "Heidi is Taylor's oldest friend. She's coming. If that means you guys *aren't* . . . well . . . that's a shame. Because Taylor could really use your support." I hesitated, then brought out the big guns. "Jarrod, too. You guys heard, right? He got suspended? He's stuck at home right now, all lonely?"

"Omigod! Right!" The change in Kendall's expression

was so dramatic—so pure, classic, boy-crazy Kendall—it was almost funny. "Of course we're coming!"

Rae's head bobbed. "We're *totally* coming!"

"Good." I didn't care, at that point, what got them to Taylor's house, as long as they came. "Meet me outside after school."

Never Is a Strong Word

AN HOUR AND a half later, Kendall, Rae, Heidi, and I were standing on Taylor's front stoop. All the way here in Theo's truck, I'd told myself the reasons Taylor was worth forgiving. How she was the boldest, funniest, wildest person you could ever meet—the kind of person who made *you* bolder, funnier, and wilder by association. Like the time we snuck out of the LeFevres' house in the middle of the night to rearrange her neighbor's patio furniture. Or how we'd call up companies to complain about their products, just to get them to send us free stuff. I'd always chicken out when customer service answered, but Tay was fearless. She'd put on this crazed housewife tone and demand to speak to the manager. There was the time in fourth grade when I tripped down the LeFevres' back steps, hit a rock, and sliced open my knee; Taylor rode me to the doctor on the back of her bike. And the time Brinley Couette—the meanest girl in ninth grade when we were in seventh—called me the C-word, and Taylor gave her a lecture I will never forget, right in the middle the cafeteria. And the time I got my period straight through my white Lucky jeans, and Tay gave me her new Patagonia fleece to wrap around my waist the whole day, even though it was freezing and all she had on was a tank top.

Before I got out of Theo's truck, I'd rehearsed in my head what I was going to say to her parents. *Mr. and Mrs. LeFevre, I know Taylor's grounded, and I respect that, but this is important.*

"You got this," Theo said as I took a deep breath and opened the passenger door.

"You think?"

"I *know.*" He gave me a hug for luck, making Kendall, Rae, and Heidi, who'd just clambered out of the flatbed, raise their eyebrows.

"What was *that*?" Kendall demanded as we were walking up the front walk.

"Nothing."

"It looked like something," Rae piped in.

"A whole *lot* of something."

"I'll explain later," I said. "Stay focused."

Now, as I stood with my finger in front of the buzzer, I remembered the look on Mr. LeFevre's face the night of the dance and felt a sick sense of déjà vu. But when I finally got up the nerve to press it, Taylor's dad didn't open the door.

Jarrod did.

I don't know who was more startled, him or me.

"Hey," I blurted, my eyes flitting from the gold chain around his neck to the rumpled Patriots jersey to the Coke in his non-sling hand. I realized, suddenly, that however many punches Jarrod tried to throw outside the principal's office, he'd had only one arm.

"Hiiii, Jarrod," Kendall and Rae chorused together.

He squinted into the sunlight. "Welcome to LeFevre House of Corrections. We hope you will enjoy your stay." The tone was spot on—sarcastic irony—but Jarrod wasn't smiling.

"We heard you got suspended," Rae said.

He raised the bottle to take a slug of soda then lowered it. "Two weeks."

"Two weeks?" Kendall cried.

"That's nothing," he said flatly, "compared to how long I'm grounded."

I looked into Jarrod's eyes, which for once looked neither cocky nor flirtatious; they looked bitter. And in that second, I almost felt sorry for him. I still hadn't forgiven him for mauling me on the Merritt Parkway and letting everyone believe we hooked up, but somehow, in that moment, I couldn't help feeling bad. Especially when his mother sauntered into the foyer wearing the tightest leather pants and the highest heels I'd ever seen.

"No visitors," she said, patting Jarrod's cheek with her manicured hand. Then, turning to us, "Sorry, girls. I'm going to have to ask you to leave."

Before anyone could respond, Taylor appeared at the top of the stairs. "Mom," she said. "Come on."

"No, no." Mrs. LeFevre shook her head. "His Majesty's orders . . . and you know what happens when you defy His Majesty—"

"He has a late meeting, remember?" Jarrod said, cutting her off. "He won't be home until tonight."

"Late meeting." She snorted. "Right."

"Dad doesn't have to know," Jarrod said. "Come on." He placed his non-sling hand on his mother's shoulder and steered her firmly away from us. "Let Tay talk to her friends. I'll make us some tea."

Tea? Kendall mouthed to Rae.

Omigod, Rae mouthed back, pretending to faint from ecstasy.

Heidi, at least, was staying focused. "How're you holding up, Tay?"

"Okay," Taylor said, not moving from the top of the stairs.

"Just so you know . . . Levitt is fired up."

"Levitt is *ripshit,*" Kendall said. "You should have heard the assembly this morning. Those guys are so busted for what they did to you."

Rae's head bobbed. "So busted."

"Kyle and Jason I get," Kendall mused. "They've always been assholes. But that kid Owen? . . . I've never heard him say boo. . . . And isn't Will Faller's mom, like, a cop?"

"Assistant deputy sheriff," Heidi corrected her.

"Whatever," Kendall said. "It's still ironical."

Taylor said nothing. She just stood there, gripping the banister, looking pale.

"You guys?" I said softly. "Could you . . . give us a minute?"

Kendall looked at me. "What?" Then, "Ohhh. Right . . . Excuse me, ladies. Me and Rae and Heids are going to have some tea."

Rae nodded. "We love tea."

"Tea is the new coffee!"

Heidi huffed a sigh. "Whatever."

When it was just the two of us, Taylor and I stood in silence—her at the top of the stairs, me at the bottom.

"So," I said.

"So," she said.

We were making eye contact, both nodding politely. It suddenly occurred to me that it was mid-afternoon and Taylor was still wearing pajamas—pale orange bottoms with rust-colored polka dots; rust-colored top with pale orange polka dots—and that they were not pajamas I recognized. This gave me an irrational pang. Taylor and I had been borrowing each other's clothes since kindergarten. We'd always known each other's wardrobes inside and out. So I had to ask, "New pj's?"

"Pretty new," Taylor said.

"I don't remember seeing them," I said.

"You haven't."

"Did your mom buy them for you?"

"No," Taylor said. "I got them at the mall. With Heidi."

I almost said something about seeing Heidi at the track, but then I changed my mind. She might not want me telling anyone. Instead, I nodded and said, "Nice. The orange looks good with your hair."

"Thanks," Taylor said. "I got new highlights."

"I know. I mean—I noticed."

"Yeah?"

"Yeah."

Silence filled the stairs again. I realized there was too much distance between us to have this conversation.

"Look," I said, taking a step forward. "I came here to talk to you. We really . . . need to."

Taylor nodded. "I know." She started walking down the stairs just as I started walking up.

I hesitated, then said, "Do you want to . . . where do you want to do this?"

She shrugged. "Here's good."

"Okay."

We sat side by side in the middle of the stairs for what felt like a long time. Taylor fiddled with the buttons on her pajamas. I yanked on the cord of my sweatshirt, tightening the hood to the left, then to the right. Finally, we turned to look at each at the exact same time.

"I'm sorry," we said simultaneously.

Then, "*You* go."

Then, "Jinx!"

We both laughed, but only for a second.

"Do you think I'm a slut?" Taylor blurted.

"*What?* . . . No."

"I wouldn't blame you if you did. . . . Did you see the pictures?"

I nodded slowly.

"Of course you did," Taylor said bitterly. "Everyone did."

I shook my head. "It's not your fault. What those guys did . . . It was so wrong. And the reason I came here—"

"No," Taylor said, cutting me off. "I know you came here to apologize. I know you think I'm mad at you for turning me in to my dad, but I'm not—I mean I *was*, when I wrote you that note, but I'm not now. . . . I know you were just looking out for me . . . because that's the kind of person you are, and I . . ." She hesitated and then the words came flying out. "I wanted to be mad at you when really I was mad at myself and I don't deserve your friendship after what I did and I know I tried to justify it by saying I was helping Ryan make the team . . . and I *was*. . . . I mean, he really *did* get told to do it and he really *didn't* want to ask you, but now . . . looking back . . . I don't know what I was thinking. . . . I was drunk and Heidi came up with the idea, and it sounded . . . I don't know. . . ." Her voice trailed off.

"Since when do you listen to Heidi?"

"What?"

"Since when do you listen to Heidi? You *never* listen to Heidi. I don't care how drunk you were that night. It doesn't make sense."

Taylor fell silent.

"I mean—I get what *her* motive was. She wanted you to herself. She wanted me to get burned. But you? . . . Ten years you've been my best friend. *Ten years* and you go and throw it all away—"

"You think I don't know how long we've been friends?" Taylor snapped. "I *know* how long we've been friends."

I stared at her.

"I just wanted to know, for ten *minutes*, what it felt like to be you . . . okay? . . . To have a guy look at me like that."

At first, I was too stunned to speak. When I finally did, the words sounded caught in my throat. "How did it feel?"

Taylor didn't answer.

"No, really," I said. "I want to know. Was it as great as you imagined?"

She shook her head. "It was horrible. It was the worst night of my life."

"Same."

"Oh my God." Taylor groaned, covering her face with her hands. "I am so sorry, Lexi. I am such a fuck-up."

"You're not a fuck-up."

"No. I am. I've only gotten drunk two times in my life, and both times I acted like a crazy slut and ruined people's lives."

"Tay," I said firmly. "You are not a crazy slut."

She lowered her hands and grimaced. "Spoken by the girl who's never done anything more than kiss."

"Wait a minute—" I said slowly. "So you *know* I didn't hook up with Jarrod?"

She nodded.

"How?"

"I asked him. He said he had nothing to do with those rumors. Someone must have seen you in his car."

"Huh," I said, processing this.

"So," Taylor said a little sarcastically, "you're still pure as the driven snow."

"Right." I took a deep breath. "Want to hear a funny story? . . . You might get mad, but I think you'll appreciate it."

"Well, when you put it *that* way . . ."

So I told her about my plan to seduce Rob at the dance. Right down to the part where I pictured his penis as a hotdog and ran away sniggering like a little kid.

Taylor stared at me. "Nuh-uh."

"Yes."

"That was your big revenge plot?"

"Sadly, it was." I shrugged, feeling foolish all over again. "Are you mad?"

"I *might* be if it weren't so ridiculous." Taylor smirked a little. "Or if you'd really done it."

"I didn't. I would never."

She rolled her eyes. "You're making my point."

We sat in silence for a minute—not quite as awkward as before. We stayed that way until I finally said, "I'm sorry about what happened at the dance. I wish I could have stopped it."

Taylor stared at me. "It's not *your* fault."

"Yeah, well . . . I'm still sorry."

"I'm sorry about Ryan," she said, her voice cracking a little, "I'm sorrier than you will ever know."

"Okay," I said. "Are we done apologizing now?"

"I don't know. Are you done hating me?"

"Yes . . . but if you ever do anything like that to me again—"

"I won't," she said quickly. She raised three fingers—the old Girl Scout salute. "Taylor LeFevre is never drinking again."

"Never?"

"Never."

I suddenly remembered what Ruthie called me during our last conversation, after I'd expressed my amazement that she, the anti-jock, was getting it on with Carter Benson, the über-jock. *"My little extremist."* That's what she said. *"Always painting the world in black and white."* It was with affection, but still. Those words stuck with me.

"*Never* is a strong word," I said.

"Well." Taylor shrugged. "It applies."

"Not even when you're twenty-one?"

"Nope."

"Not even champagne at your own wedding?"

"Well . . ." She smiled a little. "Maybe at my own wedding."

I smiled, too. "Good."

"Are you still going to be my maid of honor?"

"Do you still want me to?"

"Are you kidding?" Taylor started to choke up again. "You're my best friend."

There was so much more I wanted to say. *I've missed you. . . . I kissed Theo. . . . Ruthie has a boyfriend. . . .* But I couldn't talk now because Taylor was hugging me so tight I could barely breathe. Hugging me and crying and laughing and telling me to *take off that stupid hood, damn it*, she wanted to see my face.

Peace Offerings

I SPENT EVERY afternoon of the next week at the boxing gym. This was partly to spend time with Theo and partly to channel the anger I was feeling on Taylor's behalf. Kyle Humboldt, Jason Saccovitch, Owen Porte, and Will Faller had been suspended indefinitely. Their cell phones—which, according to the rumor mill, contained not only photos of Taylor but also text messages bragging about that night—had been turned over to the police. You would think this would mean something, but as soon as Taylor returned to school she'd been getting it from all angles. Dirty looks. Choice words muttered in the hallways and scrawled across her locker. It was mostly guys—football players or friends of football players—but there were girls doing it, too.

"And you know what her mom said?" I cried, throwing a hard jab. "When Taylor told her what's been happening at school?"

"No, what?" Theo steadied the blue bag in front of me.

"'Maybe you should have thought about that before you let those boys take your clothes off.'"

Theo shook his head. "Wow."

"I mean"—jab—"what kind of mother says that to her daughter?" Cross.

I bounced up and down, thinking of my own mom, who would be in the kitchen right now, fixing an after-school snack and waiting for me and Ruthie to burst through the front door and tell her all about our day. I remember Taylor oncc teasing me, saying, "Your mother is like Barbie, Betty Crocker, and Mary Poppins rolled into one." And then, dissing her own mom, "*Mine's* never baked a cookie in her life." At the time, I'd told Taylor how cool I thought Bree was—how I loved everything from her spiky red hair to her outrageous clothes to her every-day's-a-party attitude.

"What about her dad?" Theo said.

"Her dad is so pissed"—jab—"that Jarrod got suspended"—cross—"he grounded both of them"—jab—"until the end of the school year."—cross—"He wouldn't even listen"—jab—"to their side of the story!"

I hesitated, then threw the hardest punch I could. "How can you not listen to your own kids?"

"Good question," Theo muttered.

"There should be a license"—hook—"for parenting"—uppercut—"and you can't be one"—hook—"if you don't pass"—uppercut—"a test."

"There should be."

"I feel so bad for her. . . . What do I do?"

"I don't know," Theo said. "Maybe you should just be glad you don't have her parents."

✦ ✦ ✦

It was this sentiment that sent me straight to the kitchen after Theo dropped me off, fully expecting to find my mother waiting for me.

Only she wasn't.

Nothing was waiting for me. No after-school snacks, no pitcher of ice water. No Post-it Note stuck to the counter, explaining that she'd run out for milk.

It was 5:30, and the table wasn't even set. My mother *always* set the table for dinner. Four places, every time. Regardless of whether my dad would be home to eat with us, regardless of my field hockey games or Ruthie's band rehearsals.

"Mom?" I called out. "I'm home!"

When there was no answer, I walked through the house looking for her, my mind starting to spin. *She left. She left her rotten, ungrateful daughter to run off and be someone else's mother. And on the way, she crashed the car.* . . . But when I pushed open the door to my parents' room, there she was, sitting on the bed, surrounded by photo albums.

"What are you *doing*?" I asked, overcome with relief, but it came out like annoyance.

"Looking at old photographs," she said in a voice I didn't recognize. Her nose sounded stuffed. Her eyes, I realized, were rimmed with red. There was a box of tissues on the pillow beside her—a few crumpled ones on the floor.

"*Why?*" I said, eyeing the albums, which my mother had spent a lifetime assembling. Documenting every moment of our lives in color-code. Green for Ruthie. Purple for me. Blue for family. Red for holidays. "You know you can do all this on the computer," I said. "It's way easier."

"I like albums," she said.

She lifted the one on her lap and placed it, still open, on the bed beside her. My eyes darted to the pictures. Me at the age of seven or eight, wearing some fancy white dress and a veil, mugging for the camera.

"What's that?" I said.

My mother smiled. "Your first communion."

"I had a first communion?"

"You did."

I shook my head. "I don't remember that."

"You don't?" She looked surprised.

"No. I remember going to church when I was little, but . . . Did Ruthie have a first communion?"

My mother smiled. "Ruthie refused to put on the dress. She said white was a sign of—I'll never forget this—*patriarchal oppression.*"

"Yeah, well, she might be changing her tune," I muttered, thinking that at the rate Ruthie and Carter Benson were going, they'd be dropping out of high school to get married and raise their love child.

"What's that?" My mother raised her eyebrows.

"Talk to Ruthie," I told her. "Anyway, I thought first communion was for Catholics."

"It is."

"But Dad's Jewish and you're . . . what? Congregational?"

She nodded. "I attend a Congregational church now, but that's not how I grew up." She went on to explain that her mother, my grandmother Julia, had been Catholic, and that her father, my grandfather James, had been Baptist. "I was raised with both faiths and I wanted you and Ruth to grow up the same way . . . understanding where you came from . . . and knowing that someday you could make your own decision. Just like I did."

I knew I should say something deep and meaningful—about faith, or about my mother's parents, who died before I was born and who I'd only seen in pictures—but I couldn't think of anything. Except for the Landry McCoy story, I'd never heard my mom say this much about herself in one sitting.

"God," she murmured, glancing down at the album. "You were so beautiful. So, so beautiful."

I stared at her, feeling a surge of shock and anger. I couldn't believe what I was hearing. I could barely choke out the words. "Thanks a *lot*."

"What?" My mother looked up, startled.

"You're up here crying because I'm not that girl anymore. That beautiful girl in the white dress with the perfect face that you lost and you can't ever have back. Ever. Because she no longer exists!"

"You're wrong."

"I *see* the tissues, Mother. I'm not *stupid*."

"I know you're not stupid," she said quietly. "I *have* been crying, but it's not for the reason you think. I've been crying for the girl who used to jump out of bed in the morning and come running in here." My mother patted the space beside her. "That's what I want back. . . . Ruth always needed her space, her independence, even as a little girl. But you—you were my koala baby." She shrugged, giving me a sad smile. "I guess I just miss being your mom."

I shook my head, my throat filling with something—relief or sorrow, I didn't know which. "You're still my mom."

"In title, maybe. Not in practice."

"That's not true—"

"Alexa." She gave me a look. "You barely talk to me anymore if you can avoid it, let alone tell me anything about your life. It's like pulling teeth just to get the most basic information out of you."

She was right, of course. She was spot on, and there was no point in denying it. "Well . . ." I said, swallowing hard. "I'm talking now, aren't I?" I picked up the first communion album and placed it on her bedside table so I could sit on the bed. "I'm sitting, aren't I?"

She nodded, tearing up a little.

We stayed that way for a long time, both of us quiet, until I finally blurted, "I haven't really been taking a dance class."

"You haven't?"

I shook my head.

My mother sighed. "I guess that explains why those leotards I bought you are still sitting on the end of your bed." She hesitated. "Do you want to tell me what you *have* been doing?"

"It's kind of a long story."

"Well," my mom said. "I've got time."

On Sunday afternoon, I went to New Haven to volunteer at the community soup kitchen. My mother's church did this once a month. Every time she asked me to join her before, I'd made up some excuse. Now—as a peace offering—I was coming. I'd discovered over the past two days that it doesn't take much to make my mother happy. Just getting in a car with her, talking about boys for an hour, can make her day.

I told her everything about Theo, but of course, she still brought up Ryan. "Have you tried talking to him, honey?" she asked. "Have you given him a chance to make things right?"

I sighed. "There's nothing to make *right*, Mom. He's moved on. *I've* moved on."

"You could turn the other cheek," she suggested. "Try being friends."

"I don't want to be friends with Ryan."

"Why not?"

I threw up my hands. "Besides the fact that he cheated on me? . . . Why do you care if we're friends? . . . 'Turn the other cheek,'" I muttered. "What is this, some kind of Bible lesson?"

"No," my mother said, smiling a little. "It's not a Bible lesson. I just thought you were sweet together."

"Yeah, well. We're not together anymore," I said. "And I think it's pretty ironic that you want me to 'turn the other cheek' with Ryan, when just the other day, when I told you I made up with Taylor, you acted all miffed."

"I wasn't *miffed*," my mother said.

"You were miffed."

"No—I suggested that you proceed with caution."

"What does that even *mean*?"

She sighed. "Oh, honey. Female friendships are complicated. . . . There's jealousy . . . competition. . . ."

"Here we go," I said, rolling my eyes.

"I just don't want to see you get hurt again."

"I'm not going to get hurt," I said. "Anyway, Taylor's still grounded. We barely get to see each other. . . . Can we please just drop the subject?"

"Of course," my mother said. "We're here, anyway."

She pulled into a spot in the parking lot and cut the engine. Then suddenly, as if stung by a bee, she yelped, "Oh!"

"What?"

My mother squinted into the rearview mirror. "Sharon Dano. She's on the soup kitchen committee."

"So?"

"So . . ." Her voice trailed off, and she motioned for me to look.

I peered into the mirror. There, across the parking lot, getting out of their black SUV, were Ryan and his mom.

"Mo-*ther*," I said, my voice rising.

She held up both palms. "I didn't know. Honestly . . . Do you want to go home? I can just run this food in and—"

"No," I said firmly. "I came here to serve soup. And that is what I am going to do. Serve soup."

I didn't have to talk to Ryan. I'd successfully ignored him for the past eight weeks. I'd successfully ignored him for the past half hour, both while greeting his mother and while peeling potatoes in the church kitchen. Why start talking now?

But here he was, standing at the bread station—with his gelled-down hair and his look-at-me, I'm-such-a-good-citizen blazer—and something just compelled me to choose the butter station.

I went to stand next to him. I watched his body stiffen as

though he sensed that I was there and wasn't sure what to do.

"Hello, Ryan," I said. Cool. Polite.

"Oh . . . hey, Lexi." As if he was surprised to see me. As if he hadn't noticed I was in the same room with him this whole time.

"Don't worry," I said. "I'm not going to throw any plates."

He shot me the old crooked grin—the one that used to make me weak in the knees—but this time I felt nothing.

"You look nice," he said.

"Thanks." Out of habit, I reached up to straighten my hood, but then I remembered it wasn't there. I was wearing a cardigan, for my mom. So I swung my hair in front of my face instead.

"Would you like some bread?" Ryan asked our first customer, a wispy-haired lady with earmuffs, shuffling along with her tray.

"Well," she said, blinking up at him, "aren't you handsome."

"Butter with that?" I asked, holding out two foil-wrapped packets.

"Bread?" Ryan said to a man in a stained, orange hunting jacket.

"Butter?"

It was all very civilized. Two exes, dressed in their Sunday best, putting aside their differences to serve the greater good.

Ryan was blissfully unaware of what was coming.

"Bread?" he said to a man with stubbly cheeks and a big, red nose.

"Butter?" I asked. Then, casual as can be, as though I were

inquiring about the weather, I turned to Ryan and said, "How can you live with yourself? How can you defend those assholes?"

"What?"

"You heard me."

"I'm not going to dignify that with an answer," he muttered, dropping a slice of bread onto the next plate.

"Why? Loyalty to the Brotherhood?"

"No," he said low. He sounded mad, but he kept his composure. "Because you don't know what you're talking about."

"I know exactly what I'm talking about," I hissed back. "Everyone on your team is calling her names. . . . She got tripped in the hall today. You think it's cool, what they did? You think they're big studs?"

"Yeah," Ryan said sarcastically. "That's what I think."

"It's a class D felony, you know. Voyeurism. This could go to court."

"Well, it's not really any of your business," Ryan muttered.

"But see . . ." I dropped two pats of butter onto the next plate. "That's where you're wrong. It *is* my business because Taylor's my friend."

"You're friends again?"

"Yes."

"Good," he said.

For a second I was speechless. "*Good*?"

"Why wouldn't I want you to be friends again?"

"Why wouldn't you want us to be *friends again*?"

"Is there an echo in here?"

I shot Ryan a look. "If you cared about our friendship,

even a little bit, you never would have hooked up with her."

"Come on, Lex," he muttered. "I already apologized. We really don't need to rehash it."

I felt stung.

We really don't need to rehash it. . . . We really don't need to rehash *it?* That night put me in the hospital! That night changed my *life*! How could he be so offhand about it, like what happened was just some annoying incident that we should put behind us?

"Bread?" Ryan said, smiling at a tired-looking woman in a turquoise tracksuit.

"You have beautiful eyes, sweetheart," she said.

He shrugged modestly. "Thanks."

I took a deep breath as I held out two packets of butter. I decided to concede the point, even though it hurt. It wasn't what mattered now.

"I thought you were different," I said softly.

"Yeah," he said. "I thought you were, too."

There were four packets of butter in my hand, warm now from the heat. I didn't have to squeeze very hard to make those shiny yellow bombs explode.

"What are you *doing*?" he said, jumping back, staring down at his blazer.

"Oops. Sorry."

"Are you *crazy*?"

"I already apologized, Ryan," I said. "We really don't need to rehash it." Then I turned to the man in front of me, whose beard was as white and fluffy as new snow. I smiled and said, "Would you like some bread and butter?"

✦ ✦ ✦

"I know," I told my mom on our way to the car. "I know it was rude. I know it was immature. I know it was not proper soup kitchen etiquette."

I could feel her eyes boring into me.

"Although believe me," I added, "Ryan deserves a lot worse than he got."

I opened the passenger door, getting ready to explain everything, when I heard my name.

"Lexi!"

Crap.

"Wait!"

He's going to squirt me with butter.

I turned around and sure enough, there was Ryan, still wearing his blazer and sprinting straight toward me.

Double crap. He's going to beat me up.

"What in the world?" my mother murmured.

"Hey," Ryan said, screeching to a halt in front of me. "Don't you wonder who it was?"

"Huh?" I said.

"Principal Levitt," he said. "Coach Donovan . . . Who do you think gave them those names?"

"How should I know?"

"Think about it," he said. Then, "I've done some fucked-up things in my life, Lexi . . . I probably deserved this"—he paused, pointing to the grease spot on his lapel—"but I'm not a complete asshole."

While Ryan turned to my mother—"Sorry, Mrs. Mayer"—my mind worked overtime to understand what he was saying.

"Oh my God," I murmured. "You're the snitch?"

He looked me in the eye, holding my gaze. "I don't know what you're talking about."

"Ryan," I said softly.

He shrugged. "I don't know what you're talking about."

I understood then, it was like *The Princess Bride*—like Westley and Buttercup. Ryan was saying one thing while telling me something else entirely.

"Oh my God," I repeated.

He held my gaze a moment longer. Then he said, "See you in trig," turned, and walked away.

It took a long time to explain everything to my mother.

At first, she didn't react. When she finally did, it was like she hadn't heard a word I said. "Squirting people with butter, Alexa, is not how I raised you to behave. There are other ways to express your frustration. More socially acceptable ways."

"Yes," I said, "I *know* that." I felt myself getting mad at her again, but I willed my voice to stay calm. "I've spent my whole life trying to be the girl you raised me to be. Kind, sweet, polite . . . all those good qualities. But sometimes . . ." I hesitated, choosing my words. "Sometimes a girl needs to squirt butter on people . . . or throw ice cream at the wall or a plate across the room . . . and it's not that she's *proud* of this behavior . . . it's just . . . well, she needs to flip out once in a while. To relieve the pressure."

My mother shook her head, trying to make sense of this.

"I'm sorry," I said, and meant it.

She nodded slowly.

"You should try flipping out some time," I said. "It's kind of fun."

For the first time since we got in the car, she smiled, and I could tell that her disapproval was lifting. When she reached out to pat my knee, I thought how weird it was that we could go from fighting to making up in the same conversation. I wondered if it was like that for all mothers and daughters.

Turning the key in the ignition, my mom asked if I wanted to pick something up to bring home for dinner. We could swing by Illiano's on our way. Salads? Sandwiches? Pizza?

I looked at her, surprised. "Pizza?" The last time my mother let me eat pizza I was twelve. Since then, I only got to eat it at other people's houses, when she wasn't watching.

She shrugged. "Why not?"

"Okay," I said. "Pizza then."

As we pulled out of the parking lot, it occurred to me. The whole time I was talking and my mother wasn't listening, she might have heard more than I thought.

Just Happy Not to Be Barfing My Guts Out

"LOOK AT YOU with your bad self," Heidi said a few mornings later. "Showing up without a hood."

"Uh-huh." I kept jogging, my eyes on the track. "I needed some peripheral vision so I could see your technique. Which *rots*, by the way. Get your elbows in. You want to move forward, not sideways. . . . And lower your shoulders. You're hunching."

"Sir, yes sir!"

I rolled my eyes. "Do you want my help or not?"

"Yes," she said, adjusting her form.

"Better." This time I gave her the thumbs-up, reminding myself that a little praise goes a long way with Heidi. She likes to act all tough and cynical, but really, underneath that crusty exterior, she's as soft as they come.

"We're going for two today," I said.

"*Two?*" Heidi stared at me. "Are you insane?"

"A little bit . . . yeah."

"I can't run two miles!"

"That's what you said about *one,* remember? And you did that."

"Barely," she muttered. "And it was torture."

"But you felt great after, right?"

"Sure. Like you feel great after the stomach bug, when you're just happy not to be barfing your guts out."

I shook my head and sighed. "Keep moving, Sunshine."

As we ran, I marveled once again that the two of us were here together. Me and Heidi Engle, running. Cracking jokes. We never planned for it to happen; we just both kept showing up at the track in the mornings, and now . . . well . . . I guess you could say we're workout partners.

It's funny how your whole life can shift. How friends can become enemies and enemies can become friends. How the guy you thought you loved turns out to be a jerk—and then, against all odds, tries to redeem himself. And the guy you thought was a jerk turns out to be someone you can't stop kissing.

Yesterday at the boxing gym, Theo did the weirdest thing. After we hit the bag, he led me around the whole building, introducing me to people and telling me about their injuries. There was Carl, a plumber, and his friend Tyrone, a hospital orderly, who had both broken their noses so many times they barely had any cartilage left. Lyle, who lost half an ear in a street fight. Steve, a baseball player for Fairfield U, who got hit in the eye with a line drive last season and has the glass eyeball to prove it. Did that make him quit baseball? Hell no. He still plays second base—*and* he boxes middleweight.

"I know what you're trying to do," I murmured as Theo grabbed my hand, leading me over to three guys jumping rope.

"What?" he said innocently.

"Don't play dumb with me."

"I'm not playing dumb. I'm making introductions."

"No, you're not."

"I'm not making introductions?"

I shook my head. I couldn't put into words what I was feeling. I wanted Theo to know what this meant to me, how touched I was that he would even think to do what he was doing. After a long pause, I said, "You're unbelievable, you know that?"

Theo leaned over and, gently pushing back my hood, he kissed my hairline. "I know you are," he whispered. "But what am I?"

I could feel myself smiling, just thinking about it, as Heidi and I stood on the fifty-yard line doing our cooldown.

"What's so funny?" she demanded.

"Nothing's funny."

"You're smiling."

"So?"

"So . . ."

"Maybe I'm just happy not to be barfing my guts out."

"Uh-huh." She narrowed her eyes at me.

"What?" I said. "Stop staring."

"You know," she said musingly, "I actually like your face better now than I did before."

I snorted. "Of course you do."

"No, it's not an insult." She pulled on her foot for a quad stretch. "You've always been beautiful and you still are. But before, you were kind of . . . *bland* beautiful. *Vanilla* beautiful."

I opened my mouth, full of defensiveness, ready to lash out, but then I changed my mind. "What am I now?"

"Now," Heidi said, "you're interesting."

"Uh-huh." I nodded. "I'm interesting, all right."

I thought about my graft, how it wasn't as hideous as it used to be, but it was still bad. Instead of purplish red, it was pink. Instead of two millimeters higher than the rest of my face, it was one.

"Look at it this way," Heidi said. "You'll always have a story to tell at cocktail parties."

I gave her a funny look.

"What? Everyone needs a good cocktail-party story. Taylor's mom taught me that."

We both got quiet for a moment, thinking about Taylor.

"She won't be grounded forever, you know," Heidi said.

"You sure about that?"

"It's not until summer anymore. Her dad said Christmas."

"I know what he *said*. I just don't trust him."

Heidi shrugged. She bent down for a hamstring stretch, then popped right up again. "Did you see what those guys wrote on her locker today?"

"No, what?"

"*Open 24 Hours.*"

"Imbeciles," I muttered.

"Will they *ever* run out of insults?"

"Probably not."

Heidi shook her head. "I feel so bad for her."

"I know."

"She won't even talk about it. She won't even *try* to clean off her locker."

"I know."

"So what do we do?"

"We wait," I said. "Until she's ready to deal. And when she is, we'll be there."

Heidi nodded. "Yes we will."

I handed her a bottle of water. "In the meantime, we hydrate."

Heidi took a few sips. Then she handed the bottle back to me. I tipped back my head and drank, long and deep, feeling the cool wetness on my throat and sting of the November air on my cheeks.

Epilogue

HERE IS A picture. I am standing in a boxing ring in Quincy, Massachusetts. It was Theo's brilliant idea, entering me in the New England Girls' Boxing Competition. I told him no, but the entrance form kept magically appearing in my locker. And my backpack. And my sweatshirt pocket. It was so annoying I finally caved, filled the thing out, and mailed it in.

So now, here I am, wearing the ridiculous boxing shorts Ruthie gave me for my sixteenth birthday—shiny gold with red stripes. My hair is in a ponytail, long pieces and stumpy pieces all mixed in together. It is a warm spring day, and the gym is a sauna. Everybody's sweating.

I am supposed to have on my game face, but I keep sneaking glances at the bleachers. I can't believe they're all here. I knew they were coming, but still—the fact that they drove this far, for me . . . I can't explain how it feels.

I know my mother will watch the whole thing from behind her fingers. She doesn't like boxing, and she's worried about my face. Even though I'm wearing this puffy red helmet thing Theo gave me that makes me look like a Martian and protects every bone in my skull. My mother will never understand my need to do this, just as I will never understand her need to freak out.

I still get annoyed with her sometimes, but she's backed way off on certain things, too. Like food. I no longer have to stuff my mouth in front of her just to make a point. I eat when I'm hungry, and I stop when I'm not.

I didn't realize how much my body had changed until this one day Theo brought his camera to the gym and started clicking away. I was totally self-conscious at first. I wouldn't let him shoot my right side. But pretty soon I forgot he was there, and now, Theo has this photo over his bed, of me throwing a jab. You can see all the muscles in my arm, like mountains on a relief map, and the shadow of my punch reflected on the ground. It's really cool. Theo made a copy for my dad, so now it's hanging on the wall outside his study, too.

My dad is in the bleachers right now . . . and so are Ruthie and Carter, even though the clock is ticking until she leaves for Oberlin and he leaves for Cornell and they want to spend every last millisecond making out. . . . Kendall and Rae are 90 percent texting and flirting with the refs, but every so often they stand up and whoop like maniacs, waving the banner they spent last night painting in Kendall's rec room: LEXI IS SEXY AND SHE CAN HIT! *Heidi keeps jumping up, too, allegedly to cheer, but I think it's to show off her new butt. She's lost twenty-five pounds in five months and looks amazing. Yesterday, when we were running, I reminded her of Theo's sister. "Don't get too obsessed," I warned. "Or too skinny." Heidi rolled her eyes. "You worry too much." And I said, "I'm just looking out for you."*

Heidi is waving now, from the bleachers.

I wave back.

I take a sip of water. Roll my head from side to side.

"Yo, Lex!" a voice rings out.

I know who it is before I even spot her. Meagan O'Hallahan, the only girl in Millbridge, Connecticut, who uses the word yo. It took me three months to call her and apologize for my Labor Day flip-out, but as soon as I did, she forgave me. Just like that. A simple phone call.

Sometimes a problem is so built up in your own mind, you don't realize how easy it is to fix. Swallow your pride; pick up the phone.

Other times, it's harder than you ever imagined.

Watching your best friend's life implode makes you feel powerless. You want to help, and you try in every way you can, but you don't have a magic wand. You can't fix everything.

I look at Taylor now, sandwiched between Meagan and Heidi, and try to catch her eye, but she's staring into space. I hope she's not thinking about those guys or what was written on her locker yesterday. I hope she's thinking something good.

Sometimes that's all you can do. Hope.

That's what I'm doing now, as I stick in my mouth guard: hoping I don't get my ass kicked. Theo says it's all part of the game. When you step in the ring, you never know what they're going to throw at you. You have to be ready for anything.

Theo and I talk a lot about boxing, the technical aspects and the connections to life—cheesy analogies and all. We watch a lot of movies, too. Rocky, Raging Bull, The Champ. And when we get burnt out on boxing, we watch comedies. Theo says I laugh like a horse, which offended me at first, but now, whenever he neighs, I laugh louder.

That's a big thing that's changed for me. I can laugh at myself in a way that I never could before. When Theo suggested I name my graft, I picked Harriet. On a good day, I pretend I'm wearing a *sticker. Or a tattoo. But just last week when I was looking in the mirror, my face reminded me of some crappy kindergarten collage that only a mother could love.*

When I told this to Theo, he said, "Can I tape you on my refrigerator?"

Right now he is squeezing my shoulders, getting me pumped. "She's bigger than you, but you're tougher."

"You think?" I say.

"I know."

It occurs to me that Theo might be selling me a bill of goods. The girl across the ring from me isn't just bigger; she's huge. She has muscles on her muscles. She could eat me for lunch.

When I whisper this to Theo, he smiles. He kisses the top of my head. Then he says, "Give her all you've got."

"I'll give her a knuckle sandwich."

Theo laughs.

I bounce on my toes. Bounce, bounce, bounce. I raise my gloves in the air. Up, up, up. I don't know what will happen in the next year, or even in the next five minutes, but I am in it right now.

Sound the bell.

I'm ready.

Acknowledgments

THIS BOOK WOULD not exist without Joy Peskin, editorial genius and cofounder of the Mutual Admiration Society. Thank you for believing in me, for pushing me to dig deeper, and for cheering every step of the way.

My parents raised me in a house without a TV. Turns out this wasn't child abuse after all; it was the greatest gift of my life. You made me a writer.

To Evan Borg, thank you for the ultimate compliment (see page 213). You may have been drunk, and you may not even remember you said it, but you changed the way I saw myself forever.

To Mar at Mar's Hairy Business in Hamilton, N.Y., thank you for all the transformative haircuts of my youth, especially the bi-level.

Kate Reilly LaPia, thank you for *not* crashing the car on the way to Middlebury.

Kuj, thank you for brewing the coffee and manning the troops when crunch time hit. I couldn't have done it without you.

Jackie, Baya, and Emo: My love knows no bounds.